Flay'd as good as Golf'ry ed
almost as good as 104 and/or ed
Best wishes
Beck

The Sound of

Death

Library of Congress Control Number 2004114289

ISBN: 0-9712189-3-5

Published by Dream Catcher Publishing, Inc.
P.O. Box 14058
Mexico Beach, Florida 32410
Email: dcp@DreamCatcherPublishing.net

This book is dedicated to my wife who spent so much time reviewing the manuscript and for being my partner in life. I couldn't have done this without her.

It's also dedicated to my son Patrick, his wife Lisa and their three children, Katie, Megan and Madeline; and to my daughter Laurie and her husband John and their three children, Jacob, Erin and Samuel.

A very special thanks goes to my sister-in-law, Ingrid from Pennsylvania and good friend Betty from Ohio who contributed so much to this book.

The Sound of Death

Jack Mullen

Dream Catcher Publishing, Inc.

CHAPTER ONE

Sunday, September 4

<u>Columbus, Ohio</u>

It was most likely the last Sunday of the year that Charles Hancock could sit on his back patio deck and enjoy his morning coffee. The weather was starting to turn and next weekend would probably be too chilly to be outside. Charles wasn't really enjoying himself this crisp September morning. His mind was racing with thoughts of how his career might end in disgrace - and possibly prison. His many years of dedication and work in the medical profession mandated the action he would take the next morning. Regardless of what happened, it wouldn't be a total collapse of his life. After all, he was a tenured professor at Ohio State University, and financially very secure. With wise and reliable advice from a life-long friend and investment broker, Charles had accumulated a very profitable portfolio over the years. He was also eligible for a generous pension from the Ohio Teachers Association. He was in very good health and, while time had aged him, he was a good-looking, fifty-three year old man. His reflexes had slowed from when he played basketball for Ohio State and, naturally, his speed was entirely gone. However, his tall lean body, clean-cut jaw and the now-silvered hair that never seemed to be out of place gave him a patrician look. Women still found him very handsome.

When he honestly considered the odds, he concluded that he had very little chance of actually going to prison, but it was a long-shot possibility. In greater peril was his personal reputation built on the years he devoted to medical research, teaching and caring for the sick. It could all be forgotten. He comforted himself with the thought that if everything went as wrong as possible, his children and grandchildren would be able to say that ultimately he had done the right thing when it counted.

Tomorrow would be the first step. He had a ten o'clock meeting with Dr. Randall Brookman, Jr., President of Ohio State University, and the Dean of the College of Medicine, Dr. Sheila Gordon. His relationship was not very friendly with Dr. Gordon for reasons he never could understand. She seemed to consider him somewhat of a rival. Dr. Gordon was an unattractive woman who hadn't aged well and looked more like a chambermaid than a physician. She came from a hardscrabble background in Philadelphia and had to fight for everything she'd accomplished. She was, however, a very fine surgeon and an excellent administrator. Charles had never aspired to be the Dean of the Medical College and had welcomed her several years ago as an accomplished professional who was well suited for the position of Dean. He worked hard to foster harmony, but despite his efforts the two doctors never enjoyed the camaraderie that makes a professional relationship enjoyable.

On the other hand, Dr. Randall Brookman, the towering 6'4" teddy bear and University President, was another story. A gregarious man with a smile for everyone, Dr. Brookman was popular with the faculty, students and alumni. Professionally, he was considered one of the top university presidents in America. The two men had known each other as undergraduates and had remained close friends over the past thirty-plus years. When Randall had waged his battle with cancer three years ago, Dr. Charles Hancock was the only physician he considered to oversee his course of treatment. It was successful and it strengthened an already rock-solid friendship. They often saw each other socially and their wives had developed a close friendship over the years. But Charles never forgot the old General Black Jack Pershing motto: 'When two individuals are in a superior-subordinate relationship, the superior never remembers it and the subordinate never forgets it.' First names were only used in social and private situations - formal and business situations demanded formal terms.

On Monday morning, when Charles made his presentation, he expected that he would initially receive support from the University. But, he expected support to weaken as pressure was brought on the University. Charles understood the politics of it all and would later look back on his predictions and wonder how he could have been so far off the mark.

Roberta 'Bobbie' Hancock was still a very attractive and sensual woman - even after celebrating her fiftieth birthday last month. She

2

described herself as a 'health-nut' and her efforts showed. Her figure was the same as it always had always been and she was the envy of every woman over forty years old. The only concession she had made to age was to cut two inches from her shoulder length brunette hair last year. She always looked like she just walked out of a beauty salon. This morning was no different.

"Good morning, Bobbie," Charles said as he stood up and pecked her on the cheek on his way to the kitchen to get her a cup of coffee.

She took a deep breath of the crisp morning air, "Morning, dear." After getting the coffee he returned to the kitchen to get her raisin bagel he had put in the toaster. It was the only off-diet indulgence that Bobbie ever permitted herself.

As Charles put the bagel on the table next to her, she asked, "Anything in the paper?"

Charles reached for the arts and leisure page and handed it to her. "Yeah, want to go to the Rolling Stones Concert?"

She smiled a warm, genuine smile that slightly crinkled the lines around her eyes. "Of course, I'd like to go again. After all, we're kinda' charter members of the club, aren't we? We saw them when they made their first concert tour in the States - when we were all young." They both chuckled.

She slowly sipped her coffee. "Are you nervous about tomorrow?"

The smile on Charles' face faded and he nodded his head. "Yeah...yeah, I am. Tomorrow I'm going to make an announcement to the University that's going to stir up a lot of powerful people. Those people aren't going to like what I've said. It's not going to be fun for this family for a little while. But, I'm right and that's what's important. Are you ready for all of this?"

"Not really," she replied. But, I'll be alright." Her eyes twinkled and a slight smile crossed her face. "I just hope the photographers take good pictures of me. What do you suppose the headline will say, "Crazy Doctor's wife sticks with him?" They both chuckled again. It was an enjoyable Sunday - one that would be remembered and cherished for its serenity.

Fort Valley, Georgia

Being in the peach business, especially in Peach County, Georgia, seems appropriate and a dream way of life to many people. Tourists always remarked how they would like to leave their cold northern homes and raise peaches in Georgia. Of course, they had no idea how much hard work goes with a peach orchard, or any other agricultural business. Always at the mercy of the weather, trying to find reliable workers and the changing public tastes made growing and selling peaches a tough business. It was especially tough for Vonda Fluellen. George Fluellen was already in the business when he married Vonda and he provided a very good living for her and the children. But, when George acquired the property next to the exit from Interstate 75 the business had a dramatic growth spurt. With some strategically placed advertising and the quick on-and-off the interstate access, the tourists came by the thousands. When George opened the ice cream store featuring peach ice cream, and introduced the little shuttle bus for the packinghouse tour, business skyrocketed. But George's untimely death three years ago had left her in charge of a prosperous peach business she knew almost nothing about. Vonda was a good student and not afraid of hard work. She learned quickly, and, after a slump, the prosperity continued. She smiled occasionally thinking about the fact that she never ate peaches. She was sick of looking at, smelling, touching, talking about and worrying about peaches. She would not increase her misery by eating the fuzzy little things.

When George was alive, she rarely thought of the old days. But since his passing, inexplicably, she found herself thinking of those days more often. Being a beauty queen was every little girl's dream. Her dream was realized when she was ultimately crowned 'Miss Macon.' Her 'reign' was wonderful and she banked a lot of unforgettable memories that she wouldn't trade for anything. She knew, and accepted, the old adage that 'you can't go back.' She still turned heads when she was in public and often thought about what life might be like without the farm and the business.

Los Angeles, California

She was crying and screaming so hard into the telephone that she was very difficult to understand. "Daddy, it's the worst thing that could happen. Why me? Why me?" Her sobbing the words and crying uncontrollably made the conversation very difficult for Richard Stephen 'Steve' Parson.

"I'm so sorry honey, but we can work through it," he replied.

She shouted back. "We can't work through it," and started sobbing again. "Joey has cancer...he's only ten years old. It's not fair! It's not fair! Joey was happy like all kids and now this! I'm not sure I can go on Daddy...I'm a good person. All I ever wanted was for Joey and me to live normal lives. Now this!" She was wailing into the phone.

Steve Parson was a man who existed on logic. He was uncomfortable dealing with emotions and illogical thinking. Although he understood what his daughter was experiencing, he was exasperated and almost crying himself. "What exactly did the doctor say?"

Between her sobs and wails Linda was able to cry out the report. "Joey has a serious type of liver cancer and will have to undergo radiation therapy." When she said "he might die," her voice was a whisper. "It's going to be painful and he's going to suffer...and there's no guarantee." She whispered again. "My son might die!!!"

Steve Parson's eyes were closed. "Please try to calm down, sweetheart. It won't help Joey and we need to remember that Joey's number one. Your mother and I are leaving immediately, and we'll be there as quickly as we can. Your mother will stay until Joey's treatments are finished and everything's OK. I won't be able to stay, but we'll do everything we can to help you. Please try to stop crying, we'll be there soon."

Linda sobbed, "OK," and hung up the phone without saying anything else.

The White House

Harrison Jenkins was comfortably settled into his second term as President after a relatively easy campaign and a big victory last year. He was confident in his performance on the job and satisfied with the staff he had built to run the government on a day-to-day basis. At six foot, five inches tall, the press often referred to him as the tall John Kennedy, and he considered it a compliment. Although he didn't come from a family background like the Kennedy's, he shared the assassinated President's good looks, beguiling wit and some similarities in military service.

He saw the note from his daughter, Laurie, and asked his secretary to return the call and see if she was still in her dormitory room. He settled his lanky frame behind the Oval Office desk and gazed out the window while he waited for the call to be placed.

His eyes wandered to the wall near the window where he saw the Medal for Valor that he had earned when he was the Executive Officer of the Coast Guard Cutter *Vigilance*. He still had fond memories of those days and was still in awe of his medal. Harrison believed most people worried about themselves when in danger and that heroes were those who worried about others. His actions to board a burning schooner and rescuing a trapped family seemed so out of character for him. The Coast Guard thought it was an extraordinary act of bravery and awarded him a medal to recognize his valor. He considered his actions a combination of naiveté and youthfulness. Nevertheless, he was proud of the award, and it was framed and hanging in the Oval Office. The intercom rang to announce that Laurie was on the private line, and he was soon bantering with his daughter in Athens, Georgia. "I told the chief of the Secret Service to make sure he got you good-looking agents this year, and to be sure they were all unmarried," the President chortled.

"Well, thank you daddy," a smiling and giggling Laurie Jenkins responded. "You're so thoughtful, but you don't really have to go to all that trouble. After all, there are a lot of boys here who want to meet a girl whose father has a steady job. They're a little bit cautious when they find we don't own our own home and have to live in government housing. But, after they meet me, they find a way to overlook any concerns they have."

The President chuckled. "Well, I see in the newspaper that the University of Georgia is expecting the best season since Hershel Walker played there. Is there really a chance the 'Dawgs' are a contender for the national championship? Oh, by the way, is there any chance you might get your mother and me a couple of tickets to a game this year? Maybe we could sneak into the student section?"

Laurie laughed. "I think they might figure out that you're not a student. But I think you can probably get a couple of tickets if you really try. In fact, there may even be a professor or two here who remember when mom was a student, and maybe they could exert some extra influence."

The President roared. After another ten minutes of chatter, he could see his hot line ringing. "OK! That's about it from Washington. I've got a hot line call here. Your mother will be back from the West Coast tomorrow, so give her a call if you get a chance."

"OK, Daddy. Do a good job of running the country!"

Talking to his daughter always lifted his spirits. She had a marvelous sense of humor and she brought out the best in him. The American people have rarely seen the side of him that Laurie had always seen. He missed her and wished she had gone to school in the DC area so he could see her more often. If it couldn't be DC, he had hoped she would have gone to his alma mater at Ohio State. But, Laurie preferred her mother's alma mater at the University of Georgia. It was her second year and she was doing well, and almost living the life of a normal college student - normal except for the Secret Service. But Laurie never complained and actually seemed not to mind.

CHAPTER TWO

Monday, September 5

Ohio State University, Columbus, Ohio

It wouldn't surprise anyone that the President of Ohio State University had such a luxurious office. A dark red textured Persian rug and Norwegian furniture complemented the deep, dark paneling. The office was fit for a President and had actually seen several American and foreign presidents when they visited the University. President Randall Brookman was waiting in his office with Medical School Dean, Dr. Sheila Gordon, and Chief Legal Counsel to the University, Mr. Robert Pillars. Since they didn't know the specifics of the meeting with Dr. Charles Hancock, they were speculating about the recent research that Dr. Hancock had been conducting. Nobody liked surprises, but Charles Hancock had enough respect that he could ask for a meeting with the University President without a specific meeting agenda. So, everyone was anticipating something special. Dr. Gordon thought she was going to hear a retirement announcement.

Charles parked the car and enjoyed the walk with Bobbie from the parking area near the President's office. The trees had begun to shed their leaves, and the crisp cool air was refreshing and head-clearing. Bobbie was somewhat nervous, but Charles seemed to be inordinately calm. If he had any apprehensions they were well hidden. Entering the spacious office building, the Hancocks turned and climbed the steps to the second floor suite of offices where they were met by Mrs. Mitchell, executive secretary to the President.

"Good morning, Mrs. Mitchell. I believe Bobbie and I have an appointment with Dr. Brookman this morning."

Mrs. Mitchell looked up from her desk and smiled the genuine smile she had for everyone. "Good morning, Dr. Hancock... Mrs. Hancock. You're correct about the appointment and you're right on time. Dr. Brookman is expecting you. I'll see if he's ready." She stood up and headed toward the closed oak doors. Shortly, she returned followed by a

8

smiling Randall Brookman with an extended hand. Charles shook his hand and then Randall Brookman hugged Bobbie.

"Good morning, Charles… Bobbie. It's always good to see you. Please come in." The three entered the office and pleasantries and handshakes were exchanged all around. Charles had not known that the lawyer would be in attendance, but he wasn't surprised. Randall Brookman had a reputation for caution and often thought the presence of a lawyer was useful. The meeting started with small talk and they spent a few minutes talking about the weather and the most discussed subject on campus - football.

Finally, President Brookman got to the point. "Well, Charles, given the effort and dedication you've put into your research, I hope you have a breakthrough announcement that we can now treat and cure cancer. It would be great for you and for the university."

The Dean of the medical school also spoke up. "It certainly would be a highlight to such a laudable career in medicine." The lawyer remained silent.

Charles didn't smile. "I wish that was the announcement that I'm going to make, Dr. Brookman, but it's not. What I'm going to tell you will be the biggest breakthrough yet in the fight against cancer, but it's also going to be a big controversy in medicine. It will be a wrenching experience for our country; and involve a lot of powerful people before it's all over. I only hope that my good deeds, my reputation and everything I've worked for will be intact. I'm not sure that'll be true." Dr. Hancock's head imperceptibly sagged as he started his announcement. "I know you're all busy, so I'll make a long story short. Seven years ago, my good friend and colleague, Dr. Jerome Wilson, or 'Jerry' as we all call him, performed charity work on the southernmost island in South America - Tierra del Fuego. It's cold, windy, primitive and generally inhospitable, even in the summer. When Jerry returned we spent considerable time together talking about what he had seen, and especially the health conditions of the local inhabitants. He provided some very interesting insight into the health of the people of Tierra del Fuego. Most dramatically, they have a dramatically lower cancer rate than Americans. He indicated that there was some lung cancer and attributed it to the high incident of smoking and some skin cancer which was attributable to being outside often without any protection. But that was it. Jerry wasn't able to explain why, but he remarked often regarding condition of their bodies when he did autopsies. He said their internal organs were very healthy looking, including the old people who died of natural causes. But Jerry found few instances of pancreatic cancer, liver cancer, leukemia, prostate or other internal cancers. He kept extensive notes and pictures to document his findings. After two years in Tierra del Fuego his next assignment was in New York City. He contrasted his findings in Tierra del Fuego with the incredible amount of cancer he found in the city. He wasn't surprised by the amount of lung cancer, which he expected given the quality of air and high number of smokers. But he was stunned with the amount of internal cancers that existed in the local city residents. He was also impressed, or maybe depressed is a better description, with the condition of the bodies during autopsies. The healthy look of pink tissue was noticeably absent in the city patients compared to what he had been seeing for the past two years in South America. In fact, he remarked how the bodies looked deteriorated, including younger people who had died accidentally."

Dr. Hancock paused for a few moments before he continued. "I talked for many hours with Jerry and we considered all the possibilities that might cause the difference between Tierra del Fuego and New York City. We considered everything from simpler diets to more manual work, to less stress. We also talked about the high cancer rates in the United States and other parts of the world." All attention was focused on Dr. Hancock as he sipped some of his coffee. "You might be inclined to snicker at what I'm going to say next...but I would wait until you hear my reasoning and analysis before you do. In my judgment, the increase in cancer can be attributed to the amount of electromagnetic rays in the atmosphere...you know, radio, television, cell phones, satellites, just to name a few..." These electromagnetic rays, or EM's, as they're called, are constantly bombarding us."

Dr.'s Brookman and Gordon were clearly stunned at what they heard. Both sat up noticeably straighter. Mr. Pillars, the lawyer, didn't seem to fully understand the importance of what was said.

"This idea at first seemed absurd to me and I finally decided that it needed some preliminary investigation. I didn't give any public notice of my action because there was no cost to the university and I expected to quickly find I was wrong." Charles continued. "But as I pursued it, I kept looking for that piece of evidence, that stop sign that says, 'you're wrong - stop the investigation.' I never found that stop sign. In fact, the more I looked, the more believable it became. If you'll recall from your high school days, there are large numbers of electromagnetic frequencies in existence. For example, in New York City alone, there are hundreds, if not thousands, of possible frequencies for all kinds of broadcast transmissions. These include all radio and television stations, the airlines, the military, the gigantic cell phone networks, radar, satellites beaming down, and even such low-level sources as garage door openers and TV channel changers. Except for the TV channel changers and garage door openers, the others are all active 24 hours a day... every day. Turn on your radio to one of the over one hundred stations in New York City and you hear music - turn it off and the music stops. But, those electromagnetic rays are still there and still hitting the radio… and your body."

Charles paused briefly. "Those rays produce Joule heat - just like a microwave oven. The amount produced is very, very small, but in the human body those electromagnetic rays produce cancer. You wouldn't put your hand in the microwave would you? Of course not, but you don't have that option with the other electromagnetic rays. Each of us is right now in a kind of microwave oven that we can't get out of."

Nobody moved and every bit of attention in the room was focused on Charles. "So, how did the research proceed? I first started by studying the amount of reported cancer to the amount of rays present in the atmosphere. Tierra del Fuego fit the mold perfectly...low cancer and almost no electromagnetic rays. New York City was the opposite with high cancer and very high EM transmissions every moment of every day."

He paused and looked at his colleagues. Their faces were like that of a teenage boy seeing a naked woman for the first time. There was total attention, almost to the point of not breathing for fear of missing something.

Charles continued. "Of course, that's still not scientific proof...is it? So, I devised a controlled experiment in my lab. I took lab rats that were born within days of each other and separated them. One group lived normal in the lab and the other group lived in a metal box that prevented any exposure to electromagnetic rays. After they grew to adulthood and reproduced, I performed autopsies on both groups. The group that lived in the lab had about the amount of cancer you would expect, and their internal organs had a gray and brown tint instead of being red and healthy looking. These were the same characteristics noted in the autopsies done by Dr. Wilson when he did the autopsies in New York. The other rats that lived in the metal box were also examined. I found no cancer and the internal organs were noticeably healthier looking. My results were the same results that Jerry Wilson reported after autopsies on humans in Tierra del Fuego and New York City."

The mood was somber at this point, and nobody interrupted to ask a question.

Dr. Hancock continued. "I experimented with another generation of lab rats and found the very same results. As a further check, I then contacted colleagues in London, England, Brisbane, Australia and Los Angeles to ask them to privately perform the same experiment. All three results were identical. A physician friend of Dr. Wilson in Tierra del Fuego also performed the same experiment as a sort of a reverse test. What did he find? He found no differences in the rats that were in the metal box and those that weren't. In other words, no electromagnetic rays, no cancer! I've just finished the same experiment on monkeys. Autopsies show the same condition as the lab rats - identical in all respects. There's one other interesting thing I noticed in the autopsies I've reviewed and those I performed. In all the cases the electromagnetic rays seem to do the most damage in the denser internal organs and, for some unexplainable reason, the breasts. Lungs and fatty tissue aren't damaged as much as the pancreas, prostate, liver, and stomach. The rays seem to pass thorough the less dense flesh and do little damage. It's very much like the effects of a microwave on meat and water. The meat heats up much faster than the water. However, there is no doubt as to the general health of the organs. You don't have to be a physician to observe the differences in the animals or the humans; it's so noticeable that a person with no medical training whatsoever can see the difference.

Charles paused again and sipped his coffee. "Now, some will look at the work I've done and say it lacks details. In some respects that's a correct statement. It's much like Isaac Newton getting hit in the head with an apple and discovering the law of gravity. He may not have known all the details of why the apple fell, but he had a knot on his head and there was a clear cause-and-effect relationship. The same applies here. If individuals are exposed to the amounts of electromagnetic rays that are in the atmosphere today, they'll significantly increase their likelihood of getting cancer. Much like Newton, we can learn from the results. Newton would say that based on what he saw regarding gravity, it's not a wise decision to park your car on a hill without putting on the parking brake - same thing here. Based on what I've seen, it's not a wise decision to expose oneself to the EM rays that are in our atmosphere. In fact, it's not just unwise. It's lethal!"

Charles paused again to let his words sink in and allow comments – but there were none.

He continued. "Well, that's it in a nutshell. I believe that I've identified and isolated a very clear cause of cancer. I want to stress that it's not the only cause of cancer, but it's the major cause of the cancers

12

I've discussed and creates a favorable condition for other types of cancers to develop. Stopping it will be something else. If you have any questions, I'll do my best to answer them."

There was a pause and then Dr. Brookman spoke. "Dr. Hancock, your comments are stunning and the most radical announcement I've ever heard. I'm at a loss for words. I frankly don't know what questions to ask or what to say." He looked at Dr. Gordon and Mr. Pillars, "Any questions?" Both were reacting like the University President and had no questions. After a moment Dr. Brookman said, "Charles, I think I'd like to confer with my colleagues for a few minutes. Could we take a break then meet back here in about fifteen minutes?"

"Of course," said Dr. Hancock. He and Bobbie stood up, as did everyone else. They left the office and the three stunned academics looked at each other. As they passed Mrs. Mitchell's desk, Charles said, "We're going to take a walk around campus, Mrs. Mitchell. We'll be back in about fifteen minutes."

Going down the walkway they headed toward the football stadium where both Charles and Bobbie had banked many memories over the years. Charles had met Bobbie when he was in medical school and she was a senior in the business school. Football had been something they both enjoyed. They attended many football games in 'Buckeye Stadium' and enjoyed many more victories than losses. As they strolled down Woody Hayes Drive, Bobbie broke the silence, "Well, what do you think?"

Charles looked away toward the stadium. "I'm not sure. They're smart people and I can only assume they understand all the results and the ramifications of what I just told them. I'm sorry for Randall. He's an old and good friend and this could cause him a lot of problems. I'm certainly not trying to make trouble for him, and I'm sure he knows that. He also knows what he needs to do if he's convinced I'm right." A slight smile crossed his face. "Of course, he wanted to be the President, and he knew it was a tough job. If being Ohio State President was easy, we could outsource it to Disney, couldn't we?" He looked at Bobbie. "We'll have more grief than the University will ever experience. But, we have our eyes open, don't we?"

Back in the President's office, behind closed doors, conversation started immediately with Dr. Gordon talking first. "He said not to laugh before he proposed his electromagnetic ray theory and I still almost snickered when he said it. I'm glad I didn't. The more he talked, the more sense it made. I couldn't discredit any of the theory or possibility that everything he said was valid. We've always known that a small amount of EM rays were generated, but we never believed it was harmful. We need to consult with professionals who understand this technical information and we should probably start with the Physics Department and the Medical School. But still, on the surface it's very rational, very believable and downright frightening. If he's correct, this is a major breakthrough in medicine and a major national debate."

Attorney Pillars chimed in. "We thought the tobacco problem was big: This will dwarf that. This will be the 'full-employment-act' for my law school brethren."

President Brookman still hadn't said anything. He looked out the window and then finally spoke. "I'm not sure how to approach this. It seems to me that we need to make a private assessment of the merits of this claim and the science behind it. If it's accurate, people are being killed and we need to stop it." Randall Brookman looked at his two subordinates. "Do you two agree?"

Dr. Gordon and Attorney Pillars both nodded their heads.

'Then I propose this. I'll ask Dr. Hancock if we can audit all of his research. I think that should be done by a team headed by you, Dr. Gordon, with other forensic doctors, representatives from the Physics department, whatever other experts you deem necessary, and a lawyer familiar with medicine. If we agree with the science that Dr. Hancock has developed, the University and each of us need to stand shoulder to shoulder with him and we should tell him that. If we find any flaw or insupportable part of this work, we take the position that it's a product of Dr. Hancock personal research and not associate the research with the University. Comments?"

"I agree," said Sheila Gordon

"I agree also," said Robert Pillars.

President Brookman looked at both of his colleagues. "Good! Then let's see what Dr. Hancock thinks of all of that."

The follow-on meeting was relatively short. The only real question asked was why this cancer danger was only now being discovered.

Charles offered an opinion. "I'm not sure I can really answer that question completely. However, I think what we've seen is a tremendous growth in the broadcasting industry that changed a benign result of broadcasting into a lethal effect. Back when I was growing up in the fifties, we only had an AM radio and only three television channels. That's a far different time than we have now. I think the relatively little amount of exposure was harmless. But when we expanded the transmissions it became increasingly more dangerous. For example, at last count I found about one hundred and six radio stations in New York City. Add to that the TV stations, the satellites, the cell phone networks and every other source, it reaches lethal proportions. That accumulation is what is causing the problems and the cancer."

After the discussion was complete, Dr. Brookman explained the plan he and his advisors had discussed. Charles agreed with a few comments and reservations. "I understand your concerns for the reputation of the University, and I would do the same thing if I were in each of your places. However, while you are doing your review, I plan to send my findings to the Journal of the American Medical Association and other places for publication. I don't know if JAMA or anyone else will publish my work, but I believe the information needs to be made available. It will probably take me a few weeks to get something ready for publication, but I'm going to start working on it immediately. If anything is published, the University will undoubtedly be asked for comment. I think your review should be well on its way to completion and you could possibly comment. You will, of course, take whatever position you believe is right and I fully understand. Any objection to that?"

Dr. Gordon and Attorney Pillars held their tongues in deference to President Brookman. "That's what I would do, Dr. Hancock. If I had put as much time and effort into the study as you have, and so profoundly believed it would advance medicine and save lives, I'd act immediately. Good luck."

Handshakes were exchanged all around and Charles and Bobbie strolled back to the parking lot to get their car and return home.

The research paper had already been prepared for submission to JAMA, but Charles didn't expect it to be published. It was too radical, too new and too controversial. However, if Charles could've have offered some advice to JAMA, it would have been that you are well advised to publish the paper. If you don't you'll wish you had done so when the opportunity presented itself. A wry smile crossed his face as he thought about what JAMA would do. He unlocked the car for Bobbie.

CHAPTER THREE

Monday, October 17

Headquarters, Journal of the American Medical Association, Boston, Massachusetts

Dr. Morton P. Bruken believed that the Journal of American Medical Association was the official representative and flagship publication of the medical profession. As Editor-in-Chief, and principal advisor to the Board of Directors, he championed JAMA as the most authoritative medical journal and the "world's most widely read" medical journal. He publicly acknowledged that other medical journals contributed to advances in medicine, but never considered them anything other than second-best. Occasionally, he even complimented what he considered his chief rival, the New England Journal of Medicine - a magazine that he knew was helpful to medicine but a magazine that he privately considered the best of the also-rans. There was no doubt whatsoever in his mind that JAMA was number one and wore the purple mantle of the physician and the medical profession. Normally, when an article was sent to him for publication it was well researched, and usually a finding that was generally known in the medical research community. Its submission to JAMA was for public announcement and to recognize the researchers for their work. It's was extremely rare that there was anything unknown submitted for publication.

In recent years, tobacco was about the most controversial subject and controversy was something JAMA preferred to avoid. The article received from Dr. Charles Hancock three weeks ago was very different from anything he had received in the past. First, it was very controversial. Second, the science seemed solid and he couldn't conceive of another explanation for the results that were reported. Not that good science was unusual, but it was rare when it was so simple and fundamental. He had read the article many times since he received it and several more times over the past weekend. He once actually turned the radio on and off, and pondered the radio waves that were still in the room after the radio went silent. But publishing Charles' submission, 'Radical Cancer Prevention,' would set off a firestorm of controversy and certainly have broadcasting companies, medical lobby groups, physician groups, hospital groups and other organizations reacting strongly. If Morton published it in JAMA it would perceptually identify the Medical Association as supporting the conclusions. Not publishing it, and later finding it true, would harm the reputation of JAMA and jeopardize its reputation as the premier publication in medicine.

Morton, quite frankly, didn't know what to do and could only think of calling Ohio State to see what their thoughts were. He had met Dr. Sheila Gordon in the past and had several conversations with her over the years. She had once invited him to be a guest lecturer at the Medical School, but his schedule wouldn't permit him to attend.

He finally got a phone call through to her after lunch. The report wasn't the answer he had hoped for and he remembered her exact words: "Morton," said Dr. Gordon, "I've put together a broad-based scientific team of professionals to review the work that Dr. Hancock performed. We are very early in the review of the work, but our preliminary results are that it's accurate. We still have a lot of work to do, but we're devoting considerable resources to this project and will be finished as quickly as possible. If the science can be verified to our satisfaction, the University intends to support Dr. Hancock." After a few more minutes of technical discussion, Morton thanked his colleague and dejectedly slumped in his $2,000 leather chair and tried to sort out an answer.

Medical advisors and editors at the New York Times, Philadelphia Inquirer, Washington Post and the Atlanta Constitution had also received copies of the paper on the prior Friday. The predicament at JAMA wasn't the same for these mainline newspapers. The news was of a very technical nature, and they rarely ran any stories of this type, unless they had local impact, or they could be verified through the local medical community. Dramatic announcements of this nature were usually covered after they were published in leading medical journals such as JAMA. The newspaper decision was no story until confirmed by the medical community. One reporter for the Philadelphia Inquirer had a friend who was a newscaster at a local television station, WPIL. The reporter gave his friend the paper as an example of something that he viewed as tabloid news "along with little green alien." The WPIL newsman passed it on to the station manager and it was the first opportunity the broadcasting community had to see the research report that would cause so much turmoil in the future. It was a chance for the scoop of the year. However, the station manager was much more interested in the upcoming Philadelphia Eagles game than the article. He read the article and realized it accused broadcasting, like the kind his station did every day, of causing cancer. He knew there was no way he was putting a story like that on the air and immediately went back to his concerns about the football game.

Late in the evening at JAMA Headquarters, Dr. Morton Bruken did what he got paid to do – he made a decision. After reading the article once more along with the recommendations by his staff, he decided to not publish the article or refer it to the technical group for peer review. He had reached the conclusion that 'Radical Cancer Prevention' wasn't scientific enough and he wasn't going to endanger the reputation of JAMA with such a paper.

CHAPTER FOUR

Monday, October 24

<u>Headquarters, Journal of the American Medical Association, Boston, Massachusetts</u>

"This is Marty Osborn, editor of the 'Real News'. I'd like to talk to Dr. Morton Bruken, editor of JAMA. Is he available?"

The secretary put Marty Osborn on hold and buzzed Dr. Bruken, fully expecting him to refuse the call. Morton was still uneasy about his decision not to submit Dr. Hancock's article for peer review. Now he had a call from 'Real News,' the most responsible of the tabloids – but still a tabloid. He hoped the call was unrelated to the cancer article, but he had a premonition. If he took the call he couldn't be sure how any comment he made would be used. He had to protect the reputation of JAMA. If he didn't take the call it would be reported that JAMA was contacted and refused to comment. Either way was a problem.

He decided to take the call and reluctantly picked up the telephone. "This is Dr. Bruken. What can I do for you, Mr. Osborn?" What he was about to hear over the scratchy connection would confirm his premonition.

"Dr. Bruken," started Marty Osborn, "thank you for taking my call. I won't take much of your time. I understand that you were given the opportunity to publish a paper entitled 'Radical Cancer Prevention' by Dr. Charles Hancock from Ohio State University. Can you confirm that?"

Morton Bruken thought to himself that he should have followed his first instinct and not accepted the call. He responded, "That's correct, Mr. Osborne. We've received a copy of the paper but haven't published it in this month's issue."

"Any particular reason?" asked Osborn.

Bruken assumed the JAMA mantle of superiority. "Mr. Osborne, we don't provide reasons to anyone when we don't publish a paper. As you may guess, we receive numerous papers and each must be evaluated for publication. The process takes time…"

Osborne interrupted, "Then you are evaluating the paper for publication, is that correct?"

Dr. Bruken again lamented taking the call. "Mr. Osborne, our policy is not to comment when we don't publish any particular paper or what action we are taking on papers we receive."

Osborne continued, "But, Dr. Bruken, this paper is very believable and Dr. Hancock claims to have found a very clear cause of cancer. JAMA doesn't think something like that should be published?"

Dr. Bruken got more official. "I've said all I can say, Mr. Osborne. Thank you for your call." There was a click before Osborne could say goodbye. Dr. Bruken pounded his desk, a rare form of expression for him, and mumbled, "I knew I shouldn't have taken that call."

Columbus, Ohio

The kitchen phone rang while Bobbie was making a salad for lunch. With little perfunctory introduction and in a semi-rude manner she heard, "Can I speak to Dr. Hancock please?"

"May I ask who's calling?"

"Yes, this is Marty Osborn, editor of 'Real News.' I'd like to talk to him about the research he did regarding the prevention of cancer."

With a bemused smile Bobbie called to Charles who was reading the paper in the living room. "It's for you, honey."

Charles picked up the phone next to his chair. "This is Dr. Hancock"

"Good evening Doctor, this is Marty Osborne, the editor of 'Real News.' Are you the Dr. Charles Hancock who wrote the paper 'Radical Cancer Prevention?'"

"Yes, I am," replied Charles.

"Is it possible to talk to you for a few minutes?"

Charles put his paper down and looked out the window. "Of course, Mr. Osborne. What would you like to know?"

"Doctor, I'm calling about your paper, 'Radical Cancer Prevention,' that was submitted to JAMA. It's the study that you did where you found that electromagnetic rays cause cancer in humans. I have a copy of it and it seems to make a lot of sense. It will be a big breakthrough in cancer research and prevention. Can I ask you a few questions, Doctor?"

"Certainly," replied Charles.

Osborne continued, "How long have you been studying this subject?"

Charles sipped his coffee. "I've been working on this for about three years."

"Did you do the research alone or did you have a partner or a team?"

Charles responded, "Initially I worked alone, but after I had some preliminary results I asked colleagues to do the same experiment to see if they could replicate my findings. They agree and their studies confirmed what I had already discovered."

"What's been the reaction by the university to your work?"

Charles paused to sip his coffee again. "The University is running their own confirmatory review of the work, but so far they have been very supportive of my efforts."

Then Osborne asked a question Charles hadn't expected. "What do you expect to happen next?"

Charles was surprised by the direct approach. "What happens next is not something that I have much control over. I did the research and provided my findings. I now expect that responsible people will read, analyze and verify the work I did. After confirming the validity of my findings, I expect officials who have the authority to make changes and do what's necessary to prevent people from getting cancer."

"What kind of prevention do you expect, Dr. Hancock?"

Charles' gaze was still on the shedding tree outside his window. He had expected this question and had given it considerable thought. He didn't want to minimize his work, but he also didn't want to be the one who started problems with the organization affected by his research, primarily the broadcast industry. "The remedy to the problem, Mr. Osborne, is very complicated. One obvious solution is the elimination of the electromagnetic rays. That's only one possible solution. The physicists and other scientists may have any number of additional ways to eliminate the threat, such as methods to protect the body, modification of the electromagnetic rays or methods I'm unaware of. However, there is clearly a very real threat and immediate action is required. People are getting cancer and dying every day. We need that to end immediately."

After a few more clarifying questions, Mr. Osborne asked his last question "Dr. Hancock, did you know that the Journal of the American Medical Association is not publishing your study?"

Charles didn't change his expression. "I'd heard that JAMA had decided not to publish the paper. I'm disappointed. I'd also be interested in how you got a copy of the paper. You must have some good sources."

Osborne didn't intend to confess that he had received the paper anonymously. "We have well-developed sources, Dr. Hancock. They're very necessary for us to be competitive. For obvious reasons we have to keep them confidential.

Charles smiled. "Well, I suppose I can understand that, Mr. Osborne. Do you intend to publish my paper?"

"We're not going to publish the entire paper, Dr. Hancock. But we intend to do a full story on your research. Your work looks like a major breakthrough and we intend to put it in front of America in our next issue. I think we'll be speaking again, Dr. Hancock. Thanks for the interview and thanks for the time and effort you put into this research. You've made a major contribution to medicine. I'd compare it to the prevention of polio by Dr. Jonas Salk. In fact, I may use that as the headline. How does that sound to you?"

"It's very complimentary for any physician to be compared to the great Jonas Salk. It's your paper, Mr. Osborne. I'm sure you'll do what you think is best."

"I appreciate you taking time to talk to me, Dr. Hancock. I may want to call you back again."

"That's fine with me, Mr. Osborne. Goodbye."

"Goodbye, Dr. Hancock."

Bobbie had been standing nearby during the conversation and the grinning Charles looked at her when he hung up the phone. "It seems Bobbie, that the 'Real News" is more interested in my research than JAMA. And, I have bad news for you. I don't think he's going to use the headline you wrote. It seems he wants to compare me to Dr. Jonas Salk." They both laughed.

CHAPTER FIVE

Wednesday, October 26

Nationwide

REAL NEWS

THE NEXT JONAS SALK?? DOCTOR DISCOVERS CAUSE OF CANCER!!

In 1953, Dr. Jonas Salk of the University of Pittsburgh discovered the serum that prevented polio. Is there another Dr. Salk?? The answer is YES! But this newest medical researcher is not in Pittsburgh, he's in Columbus, Ohio.

Dr. Charles Hancock, a research physician and faculty member of the Ohio State University School of Medicine, has published a paper entitled 'Radical Cancer Prevention.' In his paper, which is supported by the University, Dr. Hancock claims, very simply and in a very straightforward manner, that daily exposure of the body to electromagnetic rays causes cancer. Electromagnetic rays, often called EM rays, are the ones that are used by television, radio, cell phones, satellites, and other wireless devices. Dr. Hancock acknowledged that we've always considered these rays harmless in small amounts. However, he's now found that the proliferation of the frequencies being used and the constant exposure are responsible for certain kinds of cancer.

Dr. Hancock compared the rays to the proverbial saying regarding the 'straw that broke the camel's back.' One straw is nothing to worry about, but as you constantly pile on the straw it becomes too heavy on the camel and eventually will break the camel's back. Another cancer specialist used the example of exposure to the sun. In small amounts it's harmless, but prolonged exposure has been proven to cause skin cancer. This physician, who wished to remain anonymous, said the same thing applies to EM Rays. Another cancer specialist said, "I've read the work and it's right on target. I've seen for some time many of the results Dr.

23

Hancock described in autopsies. I simply never linked it to exposure to EM rays. This is an exciting breakthrough in the fight against cancer."

In our call to the Journal of the American Medical Association, we spoke to Editor, Dr. Morton Bruken, who confirmed that JAMA had received a copy of Dr. Hancock's study, but had decided not to publish it. Dr. Bruken cited the policy of JAMA that they don't discuss why they don't publish studies. The 'Real News' asks the following question to JAMA: 'If you don't publish a scientific work on the prevention of cancer, what do you publish?????' We got no answer!! It's a good thing the 'Real News' is real, JAMA certainly isn't.

Fort Valley, Georgia

Vonda Fluellen didn't believe what she read in the tabloids, but she always suspected that there was at least some truth in all of the stories. When she read the story in the latest edition of the 'Real News,' she was fascinated. She always had a suspicion that there was currently more cancer than in the past and the experience of cancer having killed her husband only strengthened her beliefs. Now, here was scientific proof that identified a significant cause of cancer. She read the article several times and was intrigued by the comparison of Dr. Hancock to Dr. Jonas Salk. She wasn't really sure who Dr. Salk was but she once knew a Charles Hancock from Ohio who said he was going to be a doctor. Was this the same Charles Hancock? It was an intriguing question. But without a picture, it was impossible to do more than guess.

Los Angeles, California

The second of the series of treatments aggravated Joey's sickness and had little effect on the rapidly spreading cancer. His mother and grandmother could do nothing for the youngster. The doctors had advised from the beginning that the treatments would be a painful and debilitating experience. It was doubly painful when the patient was a child because the parents also suffer. All they can do is comfort, reassure, cheer-up and sometimes just stay away. It was all very sad. Grandpa called every day but Laurie wished that her father could also be there. Joey adored his grandfather and he was the only adult male in the young boy's life. Being separated from Grandpa when they moved to California was traumatic and now the anguish was worse. Grandpa had planned to be there for the weekend, but business wouldn't let him get away. He promised to try again next weekend.

<u>The White House</u>

The President had been briefed by his press officer of the contents of the 'Real News.' He chuckled about the story. While there had been times when the tabloid stories had resulted in something real, it was very unusual. The White House press officer read each of the tabloids but usually didn't waste too much time on their stories.

CHAPTER SIX

Saturday, October 29

The United States

The fervor of interest in the cancer prevention news had intensified to white-hot nationally just a few short days after the 'Real News' broke the story. At JAMA Headquarters, Dr. Morton Bruken had stopped taking calls except from the Board Members who were all uniformly irate about the tabloid story and his actions. They wanted an explanation.

Other newspapers around the country had been in contact with Dr. Hancock and were preparing major stories on him, EM rays and cancer. Ohio State University Medical School was flooded with questions concerning the study and whether the University agreed with the findings. People were also asking questions about the little-known Dr. Charles Hancock who had authored the study. The OSU medical staff joked that they were working the same hours that the athletic department had to work when Archie Griffin was named the Heisman trophy winner for the second time. The staff finally put a quick biography of Dr. Hancock together and started making it available to anyone who called.

One of those asking for the biography was Mr. John Mahoney, Director of the Council of Broadcasters. Mr. Mahoney had retired early from a prestigious law firm in Washington, D.C. to take the Director's position. He enjoyed the job and especially the lack of pressure he always had while at the law office.

Congressional offices were also being deluged with letters and telephone calls seeking more information on the cancer study. It seemed that everyone had an interest in how to prevent cancer.

The White House

President Jenkins had started taking the cancer story seriously when the reaction from the American public became so great. The President had been briefed several times by the Surgeon General and it was an item of discussion each morning with his political advisors each morning since the news article. Everyone understood all of the complications associated with the article and they were being very careful in handling the White House response. Staffers and Cabinet members had been instructed to make no comments. All responses would come either from the President or Surgeon General, Dr. Ralph Gardner. The President thought that Dr. Gardner would be a very effective spokesman for any White House statement since he was an oncologist by profession and had survived colon cancer just two years earlier. Dr. Gardner had been to the White House each of the last three days to consult with the President. The President's political advisors were adamant that a press conference had to be held today at the latest. The President understood the need for a response, but neither he nor his advisors could agree on a position. Eventually, it was decided that Dr. Gardner would hold the press conference and assure the public that the report was considered serious and would be reviewed by government and private medical and scientific experts.

It was a somewhat nervous Dr. Gardner who stood behind the lectern in front of the wall with the words, 'THE WHITE HOUSE', behind him. Dr. Gardner had a soft voice that was very effective with patients, but lacked the authority of a deeper voice when holding a press conference. The pressroom was crowded when Dr. Gardner began his press conference. "Good afternoon ladies and gentlemen. I have a brief statement and then I'll take questions. The President and I, along with various advisors, have reviewed the recently published work by Dr. Charles Hancock entitled 'Radical Cancer Prevention.' The information in that study is certainly an encouraging step forward in the war on cancer in America. We appreciate all the effort that Dr. Hancock has put into this research. At this time, the details of the study have just been received and we're in the process of developing a research staff to review the work. We expect to have a comprehensive response to the report in the next few days. The President is encouraged with these developments and assures the American people that anything that might lead to the eradicate cancer in America, and in the world, will be doggedly pursued. Cancer is a scourge in our country and we need to do everything possible to prevent it. We also need to detect it early when it occurs, and cure it quickly and completely. I'll take questions now."

The Washington Post reporter was acknowledged. "Dr. Gardner, you didn't say that either you or the President agreed with the study. Do you have a position?"

Easy question thought Dr. Gardner. "Agreeing or disagreeing with the study is premature at this point. Like all research, it needs to be studied and evaluated. However, I can say that the President and I are encouraged with the preliminary information and look forward to the comprehensive review of the report."

The Atlanta Constitution was next. "Just who is doing the review, Dr. Gardner?"

This question was a little tougher since the Surgeon General had really done nothing yet. "I'm forming a Blue-Ribbon Committee in cooperation with the Centers for Disease Control to study the paper authored by Dr. Hancock

The follow-up question was a surprise. "Do you intend to include forensic pathologists in his study?"

"Of course," replied Dr. Gardner. "We'll have professionals from every applicable field of science necessary to review this study."

The Miami Herald reporter was recognized. "Is the President prepared to pull FCC permits from TV and radio stations if your review shows that their broadcast transmissions cause cancer?"

Dr. Gardner was well prepared for this question also. "It's much too early to answer a question like that. That's a major policy decision that can't be approached until we have all supporting and ancillary facts."

The LA Times was next. "Do you intend to invite Dr. Hancock to be a part of your Blue-Ribbon Committee?"

Dr. Gardner had been unprepared for this question and inexplicably blundered and blurted out, "Yes, I intend to invite Dr. Hancock to be on the Committee"

The room hushed for a brief moment as reporters made notes and the President's advisors wondered how long it would take the press to call Dr. Hancock to get his reaction. The President was watching the press conference and noticed the miscue. He thought to himself that we can get by this one, but he hoped it wasn't a glimpse of things to come.

Dr. Gardener indicated he would take one last question and it was the reporter for the American Bar Association.

"Have you consulted with the Justice Department regarding the legality of withdrawing FCC licenses for broadcasters?"

James Gardener could see the battle lines being drawn. "Not yet. Thank you all for your attention," concluded Dr. Gardner. He left the stage and hustled behind the curtain for a review of how the conference had gone. Long faces by the staff were his first sign that there was a problem and a 'correction' might have to be released.

Columbus, Ohio

Charles Hancock was also watching the live press conference expecting very little real information. He was startled to hear one particular answer. The Surgeon General wants the author of the study to be on the Blue-Ribbon Committee? Interesting! He was waiting for the next question to Dr. Gardner when the phone rang for what would be a long afternoon of telephone calls. Almost every newspaper that carried the original story called to ask his reaction to being on the Blue-Ribbon Committee reviewing his own research. His response was the same. "I haven't been contacted by the Surgeon General and wasn't aware that he had selected me to participate. I would certainly be available to serve, but it's unusual for the researcher to evaluate his own work. It could be that the Surgeon General wants me to consult on the evaluation but not as a participant. That would be fully acceptable to me."

Washington, DC

The staff director of the American College of Oncology had been on the telephone almost non-stop since the 'Real News' published the story. Because of patient caseloads and appointments, it was difficult to schedule an emergency meeting of the executive committee of the Board of Directors. Preventing cancer is good news, but not to the same degree for everyone. After all, the invention of sheetrock was good news, but not for the plasterers' union. Preventing cancer has serious consequences for that part of the medical profession that specializes in curing cancer. Crafting the proper response without appearing to be self-serving or greedy was critical. A second priority was to get at least one representative on the Surgeon General's Blue-Ribbon Committee.

The United States

The Atlanta Constitution was a mirror copy of every other major newspaper in America when it covered the story. The headline, 'CANCER CURED?' was in giant size type and three-quarters of the front page was devoted to the lead story. A picture of Dr. Charles Hancock was prominently displayed in the upper left hand part of the page. The Constitution covered the main highlights of the story and then referred readers to a rare eight-page insert that covered many details of what was known. There was an extensive story about Charles Hancock that traced his life, education, and career at Ohio State University.

There was also a biography of Bobbie that talked about her childhood, and her competition and success in beauty pageants. The story also mentioned her piano skills and career as a small business owner. There were even a couple of paragraphs related to her courtship by Charles and their days at Ohio State.

Their older son, Jeff, had a short story about his career as a lawyer in Ohio. The legal reporters also dug up a few cases he had won to add details to the story.

Their younger son, Harold, and his home protection company were also included. The story described his rocky start in the home security business, but put a Horatio Alger emphasis on the story with his ultimate success. One reporter remembered that his company had been 'tested' by the paper's investigative reporter a couple of years ago and had been lauded for its honesty and integrity.

A major part of the insert discussed cancer. Emphasis was on the different types of cancer and the various types of treatment. Special attention was paid to the kinds of cancers that strike the organs that Charles had identified in his research as the most vulnerable to EM rays.

However, the main story was what Charles had discovered. The stories discussed his methods of research, his findings, and his conclusions. The paper spent considerable space describing the kinds of EM rays that existed and the intensity and proliferation of the rays in the atmosphere. Readers, who may have been nonchalant about the subject before reading it, were worried when they finished.

There were also reports about what the government was doing and several first-hand reports from cancer survivors who wished the research had been done before they were stricken. The insert also carried a rather extensive interview with OSU President Randall Brookman. He was quoted extensively praising the work that Charles had done and how proud the University was to have such an accomplished scientist as a member of the faculty.

The remaining article outlined the rise in cancers in the world and the rise of cancers in the organs that Dr. Hancock had identified as being targets for EM rays. The cancer increases were shown in chart form and were very dramatic. The comment was made that increases in medical technology and better and earlier diagnosis still couldn't stop the growth of the cancer. America was losing the struggle with cancer.

To the casual reader the biography of Dr. Hancock looked very normal and only a trained and interested observer would notice any discrepancy. A close examination revealed a missing year after he graduated from high school until he enrolled at Ohio State. Charles had never discussed this year but when forced to comment, he chuckled and said he was 'finding himself' and asked if that wasn't what the growing up was all about.

John Mahoney at the Council of Broadcasters noticed the date discrepancy immediately. Vonda Fluellen realized when she read the biography that Dr. Charles Hancock was the same Charles Hancock that she knew. She also knew what had happened during the missing year. Or, at least, she knew part of it.

The United States

For the next three weeks the country was reacting to the news and the principal players were developing their positions. The print journalists realized that they had a story that was intensely interesting to all Americans and very unfavorable to their chief competitors, the broadcast media. Extensive newspaper coverage provided the information that America wanted and editors exploited this advantage to the maximum. Routinely, there were newspaper stories about the research, including interviews with prominent scientists and researchers. Opinions were expressed and evaluations were made as to the danger the EM rays posed to the citizens of America. Each of these articles was carefully written to dramatize the effect of the electromagnetic rays on the general population. Dissenting opinions were occasionally offered, but they were generally inconclusive and weak since there was scant conflicting research.

Over the years there had been research that showed cancer could be caused by some radiation such as ionizing radiation (x-rays, radon, etc.) and ultraviolet (the sun). Electromagnetic radiation at frequencies below ionizing and ultraviolet levels was rarely connected to cancer. While there were some studies suggesting a connection, the findings were very tenuous and not considered seriously. Other studies showed no connection. Related studies on low frequency electromagnetic rays from power lines, electrical appliances and power transmitters could not identify any cause of cancer. Specific studies on cell phones showed some connection when tests were done on mice, but the only firm conclusion was that more research was necessary.

All major newspapers did extensive Sunday supplements including interviews with Dr. Hancock, various scientists, and government officials regarding the dangers of continued exposure to EM rays.

Weekly magazines carried similar stories which continued to concern the public. The tabloids, which had originally broken the story, continued their drumbeat of information with specific stories of numerous people in the past that had been injured or killed by exposure. These stories usually centered on military members or government civilian workers who had repaired or operated transmitters and had been exposed to massive amounts of direct exposure to EM rays when the equipment was operating.

One recurring story had to do with an Air Force sergeant who had been assigned to one of the early warning sites that had been set up years ago to detect the launch of Soviet missiles. The sergeant was reportedly working on a part of the building known as 'The grid,' where the electromagnetic rays were emitted. The stories alleged a mix-up in signals resulting in the system being turned on and the sergeant being literally cooked alive. The stories always claimed that the government covered up the incident with a more believable story. Nevertheless, there were always other GIs who claimed they knew of the stories from their service and could attest that they were true. There was little proof, other than anecdotal testimony, that these incidents actually took place. However, the stories sold copies of the 'Real News' and readership was soaring. A tag-along advantage that was also occurring was that the 'Real News' was earning some grudging recognition as a legitimate newspaper!

The broadcasters for the most part had hunkered down and were trying to ride out the storm by relying on the public's fickle allegiance to any story. They continued to provide other news, with a heavy emphasis on gossip. They hoped viewers and listeners would soon forget the research that indicated they were in personal danger. As professional journalists, they had no choice except to cover the story, but they covered it in as little detail as possible and always provided any information they could find that failed to support the findings.

Nightly news broadcasts relied heavily on the use of words like 'alleged,' 'purported,' 'apparently,' 'unproven' and 'unnamed sources' to qualify and diminish any story on the effects of EM rays. There was constant reference to past cancer studies that showed little danger to humans from EM rays.

Sunday morning talk shows devoted a small part of each program to this story but focused on other stories that made the news that week. Dr. Hancock had not been invited to be a guest on any of these shows.

The radio talk show hosts for the most part were quick to point out to their callers that neither the host nor the caller had the expertise to fully understand the subject. Thus, any comments were without foundation and simply opinion. They also interviewed other scientists and doctors who did not openly refute the findings of Dr. Hancock, but continually cast doubts on the suspicion that must be part of all research until it can be verified. There were few supporting facts to back up anything, but the broadcasters put a lot of smoke in the air to confuse the listening public.

Washington, D.C.

The evening TV talk shows were much the same as the radio talk shows. The Barry Burlington Show was the acknowledged leader in evening talk shows and was seen nightly at nine o'clock Eastern standard time. Barry Burlington had been receiving increasing pressure by advertisers, producers and fans to have Charles Hancock on the show. There were even two live comments from callers asking why Dr. Hancock had not been invited to appear. Burlington ultimately relented to the pressure and invited Dr. Hancock to appear. Charles accepted. In order to build the biggest viewer base for the show, Burlington announced a week in advance that the 'cancer Doctor' would be appearing one week hence.

Understandably, Mr. Mahoney of the Council of Broadcasters was busy at work earning his very generous salary. He retained a small army of reputable and not so reputable investigators.

The reputable investigators were charged to look into every aspect of Dr. Hancock, Bobbie Hancock, their two sons, and everything about their lives. They were also looking at other related things such as the University and any research it had sponsored in the past. Specifically they were interested in knowing if Ohio State University had ever supported research findings in the past that were wrong. One team was looking at that question. Mahoney had no choice but to look at the research. He expected little in return for that investment except possibly embarrassing Ohio State University and weakening the University support for the work that Charles had done.

The second group enlisted to help with the research was broadcast station employees around the country and overseas. They were scouring news broadcasts and archives for any information available that could be related to the case. One of these employees worked at a small radio station in Macon, Georgia.

A disreputable group of investigators, with blemished reputations, was known as the 'undertakers.' The name was associated with their nefarious reputation of digging up dirt to destroy the careers of those they were targeting. For this group, Mahoney worked with the group through a contact point and never directly met face-to-face with any of the 'undertakers.' The contact point for Mahoney was a shadowy, rat-faced character known only as 'Smoke.'

Neither of the groups knew of the specific existence of the others but the "undertakers" were certain that there were other people working on the same case - a fact they couldn't care less about.

Initial reports were for the most part disappointing. Ohio State University had done a good job over the years of selecting research projects to endorse and those to avoid. If the University had a clunker in its background it was either minor or deeply buried in the records.

The background of Bobbie Hancock was also disappointing. There wasn't a hint of anything that could be useful. It was so good that Mr. Mahoney just 'knew' there was something there. That suspicion would ultimately cost him a lot of money.

Charles Hancock seemed like the perfect match for Bobbie. Initial reviews also showed no apparent character flaws and he seemed to be as squeaky clean as Bobbie. In fact, Mr. Mahoney thought that Dr. Hancock seemed to be the kind of doctor and researcher that the medical profession, and sick Americans, should be thankful for. After reading the report Mr. Mahoney made a personal note to himself to see Dr. Hancock, or someone Dr. Hancock recommended, if he ever had a cancer problem.

But, there was still that one period in Dr. Hancock's life that was suspect – that one missing year. Mr. Mahoney had the same intuition about that year as he had about Bobbie. He 'knew' there was something there, but whether he could find it or not was the big question. If he did find something, would it be worth anything? The investigators were asking for approval and money to dig deeper. Mr. Mahoney didn't think it would yield much, but it was all there was, so he approved the costs.

The legal community, on the other hand, could see a cash cow when it walked into their offices. Attorneys by the hundreds were interviewed all over America by newspapers, radio talk shows and in public forums. The focus of those interviews usually had constitutional aspects.

The first issue was a question regarding whether the citizens of America could sue the government (the deepest pockets) for failing to protect them. A related issue to this question was whether they could sue the radio and TV stations for endangering them. Of course, all the lawyers agreed that anybody could be sued, but held out little hope for success. Interestingly, only the print media interviewed the lawyers. A common comparison was with the tobacco cases but the more reputable lawyers quickly pointed out that there was no assurance that EM rays were causing cancer. Even if it was accurate, nobody had known there was any danger until now. So, winning a case would be difficult since the broadcast industry and the government would simply cite that they had no knowledge of any danger. And, in fact, there was some research to the effect that it was not dangerous. Naturally, some people with real or perceived medical problems that were not explainable in any other manner responded by calling their family lawyer and the legal cases started to collect in local courthouses around America. After someone filed a lawsuit, they then became a person to be interviewed and the newspapers had no shortage of people who had filed lawsuits to interview.

There was always the second constitutional issue. The radio and TV stations had a right to free speech and any termination of their right to broadcast would be a violation of their constitutional right. These interviews were especially prevalent on the radio talk shows. The broadcast industry liked this issue because it was 'safe' and people consistently supported free-speech issues. There was little discussion of the research and lots of opinions that people could identify with. A side benefit to the radio stations was that they could claim how fair they were in covering this issue.

One very smart lawyer on Mr. Mahoney's staff noted that at some point the Federal Communication Commission was going to become very involved in all this and it would be helpful for the broadcast media to work with the FCC and not be too critical. Mr. Mahoney sent a memo to all subscribers immediately on this issue. Stations overwhelmingly tended to support the constitutional right to free speech and invited lawyers who supported that view to be guests on the talk shows. Unfortunately, they could not fully control other lawyers who had a more balanced view of the world, or the general public who all knew of the Supreme Court decision that said you can't yell fire in a crowded theater. So the lawyers, the callers, and the radio hosts would argue back and forth as to whether or not broadcast journalism was protected by the constitution if EM rays might be harmful to individual citizens. There were the usual reminders that the government protects the public in the areas of food, drugs, consumer products, etc. The vast majority of lawyers interviewed on the air disagreed with further regulation of the airwaves unless there was a clear and convincing danger, and no such thing had been proven.

During these three weeks, the government had its own problems and couldn't seem to develop a good position. President Jenkins mouthed the usual platitudes and concerns about how serious cancer was, and stated that anything the government could do to prevent cancer was topmost on his agenda. He didn't have a live press conference and his comments were usually made during other events when reporters raised the questions.

Dr. Gardner was the government's spokesman but, frankly, wasn't doing a very good job. His too frequent references to his own cancer to support his commitment were having the opposite effect. He came across to his listeners as a whiner and not someone who was concentrating his efforts on the issue at hand. He had been initially embarrassed when he said Dr. Hancock should serve on the Blue-Ribbon Committee to review the research. He had to reverse himself when virtually everyone, including Dr. Hancock, said it was inappropriate. He had little to report on the efforts of the Blue-Ribbon Committee he had selected to review all of the evidence and couldn't seem to re-establish the credibility he should have as Surgeon General. At his press conferences he was unable to clearly articulate the government's position on its responsibility to protect the public.

During an interview with a weekly magazine, he blundered and brought up the Thalidomide scandal of the 50's. He was trying to make the point that things had improved. The comments backfired badly when the magazine linked the EM rays and Thalidomide together on the front cover. The resultant uproar across the country had the phones and mailboxes of the administration and Congress busy again. Dr. Gardner's press conferences were always well attended. Reporters didn't want to miss the show!

The military also contributed to the governments' problems. They were unable, for unknown reasons, to emphatically state that the anecdotal testimony regarding members being killed by EM rays was untrue. Their responses were that they had no record of any such happenings, or when they had an explanation their efforts were unconvincing. The service papers (Army Times, Air Force Times, etc.), which were commercially published and not controlled by the military, started to fill up with letters to the editors of specific instances. The tabloids monitoring these publications included the stories each week in their newspapers.

The general public was a different story. The guy on the street easily understood the research that Dr. Hancock described and could understand the lab rats living in metal boxes and not getting cancer. They believed Dr. Hancock's research was accurate, and they believed they were in immediate danger. Letters to the editors in all newspapers across the country overwhelmingly expressed fear that they were being exposed to cancer-causing rays and demanded something be done. They were expressing those views in every conceivable way. Letters to members of

Congress and the FCC were at an all time high. The Post Office reported that business in the Washington postal district was higher than at Christmas. Letters, telephone calls and e-mails to Congressmen in Washington and their home districts were unrelenting and were overwhelming staff members.

Unfortunately, the Congress was baffled about what to do. Members did little more than to assure their constituents of their concern, and that they would seek answers. Unfortunately, when Congress seeks answers, it takes lots of time, and the American people are not very patient. They weren't accepting the customary Congressional responses. Americans wanted action and the Congress was sadly inept, incompetent and unable to respond.

The President, without any reliable analysis of the research that Charles had done, could do little. There was paralysis in Washington. People were getting increasingly more vocal and talk of big demonstrations had started.

Small local groups were beginning to protest what they believed to be dangerous conditions and had started to picket radio and TV stations. The groups were small, but momentum was growing and it included letters to TV and radio advertisers.

Businesses were starting to review their commercial advertising practices because of the letters they received indicating further advertisement would result in a boycott of their product. In New Orleans, a particularly strong group of activists picketed a large car dealer who heavily advertised on the local television station. The picketing was not covered by the TV news team, but it was front-page news in all the local papers. The car dealer quickly got the message and dropped his TV commercials.

All in all, it was a tense few weeks and a very violent mixture was approaching the boiling point.

CHAPTER SEVEN

Friday, November 25

Washington, D.C.

Charles and Bobbie, along with Jeff, who was representing his father, made their way to the studios of the Barry Burlington Show. While it was advertised as coming from the nation's capital, the actual location of the studio was in Alexandria, Virginia. When Bobbie learned the location of the show, she suggested they get to Alexandria early and have dinner at a Greek restaurant she had heard about from one of her customers in Columbus. The comment was that eating at the 'Taverna Kritiki' was like being in Athens. Bobbie had never been to Athens and was looking forward to enjoying authentic Greek cuisine and atmosphere. The dinner was wonderful and she suggested to Charles that a vacation in Greece would be a great idea. After dinner they walked to the studio where the Barry Burlington Show was being broadcast. They arrived at eight-thirty to a polite but chilly reception.

Because of the subject and the advertising, interest in the show was high across the country. The Council of Broadcasters believed that Burlington would do a good job of handling Charles, and it would put the broadcasting industry in a favorable light with the public since they supported the appearance. Station executives expected that the number of viewers could possibly exceed records set by Super Bowl games.

After arrival Charles was advised that there would be other physicians and journalists on the show. Charles assumed this meant that they weren't supporters of his research, but he wasn't told exactly what part they would play during the interview. He wasn't surprised, and was glad for the preparation that he and Jeff had done over the past several days. Charles asked that both Jeff and Bobbie appear on camera with him, but the producer objected. Charles insisted and when he threatened to leave, the producer reluctantly agreed. After all the advance advertising, the show simply couldn't have a no-show of Dr. Hancock simply because he wanted his family to be with him.

About ten minutes before airtime, Barry Burlington appeared and greeted his guests. He said they would be on the air shortly and he would start the interview with an introduction of Charles and his family. Burlington would also alert the audience to the other guests who would appear later and then begin discussion of Charles's research.

At precisely ten seconds after the show went live, Barry Burlington began his show just like he did every night by greeting the audience. "Good evening, everyone. This is a very special night on the Barry Burlington Show. We've all heard of the cancer research done by Dr. Charles Hancock. His findings have been heavily reported by all the news organization for the past several weeks and have stirred considerable controversy. We are very fortunate to have Dr. Hancock with us this evening. With Dr. Hancock are his wife Bobbie and son Jeff."

The camera panned to the three guests seated across the table from Barry Burlington. "Thank you, Mr. Burlington," replied Charles. "My family and I appreciate your invitation to be on the show and to discuss the research that I've done. I hope this appearance will help everyone to understand the findings I've made."

Burlington was unhappy about the little snit over Bobbie and Jeff appearing. The family picture automatically tipped the scales on truthfulness and sincerity toward the Doctor. Also, the Doctor's unassuming thank-you comments further tilted audience reaction toward supporting him.

The first question from Burlington was an easy one. "Dr. Hancock, please tell our audience a little about your research."

Charles avoided a lot of the details and explained in about six minutes what research he had done and what he discovered. The next series of questions were very general in nature regarding Charles' background, how he liked working in a University, and how he liked being a doctor.

Then Barry Burlington asked, "There's been a lot of comment in the press that your research isn't being covered adequately, especially by the broadcast press. What do you think of that?"

Charles paused and then began a reply to a question that he had anticipated but hoped would not be asked. He had given considerable thought to his answer on the trip to Washington. "Actually, Mr. Burlington, what I think of the press coverage isn't really important. I'm a physician specializing in cancer research. I've no real expertise in media relations, so my opinion isn't worth very much. However, I can tell you a little factual information about media coverage. Each day I have to set aside part of my day to respond to the press. I do that each morning at the studio we have at Ohio State University. Almost exclusively, the reporters that attend are from the printed press, and they come from around the world. Rarely are there representatives from major TV networks to interview me. As an example, one evening I watched the most famous of those newscasters and found that my research occupied less than a minute of the news, and the commentator used five different qualifying words such as 'purported' and 'alleged' when describing my work. In contrast, a mentally disturbed truck driver who took his family hostage in New Jersey received coverage of over two minutes including film footage. Additionally, Mr. Burlington, yours is the only TV or radio talk show that's invited me to be a guest. Based on the experiences I've just described, I think your viewers can draw their own conclusion as to the importance that the broadcast and printed press are giving to this story."

Barry Burlington was noticeably agitated. "Are you suggesting, Dr. Hancock, that the broadcast coverage is intentionally underreported or slanted?"

A relaxed Charles was once again prepared for the question. "Mr. Burlington, I was advised when I agreed to appear on this show that the broadcast media didn't want me discussing my research to a live audience. An audience that I know has a very real and a very personal interest in preventing cancer. After all, most Americans have been personally touched by cancer or had cancer in their immediate families. I was told that to deflect criticism that the broadcast media is avoiding me, I would be invited, but the focus of the interview would be shifted from the work that I've done to the coverage by the media. It appears that is what you're doing here. Let me be very direct, Mr. Burlington. If you want to talk about media coverage of my research, you should get people who are skilled at that subject. That's not me. If, on the other hand, you want to talk about my research and my finding that exposure to electromagnetic rays is harming each and every person by causing cancer, then I'm more than happy to be part of this program."

Barry Burlington quickly went to a commercial break.

After they returned, the remainder of the show was chilly, formal and a disaster for Barry Burlington and the network. Charles would only discuss his work, but the producer had lined up two journalists and one other physician as guests. Although the journalists agreed that the media coverage was balanced and fair, their analysis was woefully inadequate after the comments by Charles. And since Charles wouldn't discuss the media coverage the show faded fast for Barry Burlington. The only other guest was the other physician, who also happened to be a cancer specialist. Incredibly, he had only read an executive summary of the original research paper and relied on newspaper accounts to fill in the details of what Charles had written.

During the discussion, there were some technical descriptions of what Charles had found and the guest physician acknowledged he had seen similar results during autopsies and generally agreed with Charles. The hour for the show had more than its normal commercial breaks, and there were no handshakes or even a thank you for Charles or his family when they left.

Jeff was ecstatic when they got to the taxicab. "I told you, Dad! I told you! It was the trick we all expected. I thought for a minute or so there that Burlington was going to try to punch you. He was one unhappy man. Imagine those mutts trying a trick like that? I hope they get ripped to shreds by the newspapers for what they tried. They deserve every critical word. I certainly wouldn't want to be around Burlington right now. Great job, Dad!!"

Charles and Bobbie were both smiling at the enthusiasm of their son and at how the show went.

CHAPTER EIGHT

Saturday, November 26

<u>Columbus, Ohio</u>

The next day was festive in the Hancock household. The local and national newspapers had covered the Barry Burlington interview, and they reported it like what it was - a botched ambush. Charles' comments during the show were directly quoted, and the print media had another big news day. The television and radio news covered the show but very briefly and with few details. There was no direct mention made of Charles' comments about the Burlington show trying to shift the focus of the show. As usual, there was no mention or coverage whatsoever of the findings of the cancer research! Much to Charles' satisfaction, the University continued to enjoy no negative or controversial comments from any of the publicity to date. The expectation that the University would be drawn into any controversy simply hadn't happened. In those instances where the University was mentioned, it always seemed to be a favorable comment. A certain amount of thanks was due to Dr. Hancock, since he never missed a chance to mention the laudable academic excellence and accomplishments of his alma mater and employer. Some of the other Big Ten 'sister' schools were irked with all the attention that Ohio State was getting, but they knew it would also help them. And, of course, football season wasn't over.

<u>Fort Valley, Georgia</u>

The answering machine had gone on the fritz last week, and Vonda now had to get up immediately and answer each call or wonder who it was. This particular caller was persistent, and it wasn't until the eighth ring that Vonda finally answered the call from her sister. "Vonda, I was watching the Barry Burlington Show last night and there was a Charles Hancock from Ohio on as a guest."

Vonda had also watched the show but didn't mention it. "Yes?"

Her sister was unstoppable once she got started. "You used to date a Charles Hancock from Ohio, and the one on TV looked exactly like the one you were with. Is it the same one?" Without waiting for a reply, she asked another question, "Are you going to call him?"

Vonda pondered a moment or so but couldn't hide her irritation "Look. First of all, you couldn't recognize him. You never saw him. All you saw was a picture I showed you thirty years ago. The chances of it being the same Charles Hancock are very remote. I'm sure there are many men in Ohio named Charles Hancock. It's a relatively common name. Second, even if it was him, we haven't seen each other or been in contact with each other since 1972. We had a few laughs, but it was over a long time ago. A lot of water has passed under the bridge. He has his life and I have mine. It's history and that's all it is. There's no reason to disturb it." Vonda changed the subject as best she could and then ended the conversation as soon as she could without being rude. "Thanks for calling, but I have work to do and I'm behind schedule. I'll see you in a few days." Vonda knew it was the same Charles Hancock from her past. The show last night had revived many of her fond memories of Charles before he became a doctor.

She fantasized more than she should then actually went into her closet where she kept some 'old' stuff and took out a dress she had saved from her single days. It was one of three she cherished. The others were her wedding dress and her prom dress. She brushed her hair, put on some make-up and tried on the dress. It fit perfectly. Her figure hadn't changed much from the old days. She pranced around for a while in front of the mirror for a few minutes then slowly took off the dress and put on her blue jeans and prepared for the day's work.

She never thought that her sister would be calling about an old boyfriend, and she certainly never expected that she would be telling everyone else. One of those people her sister talked to was a reporter for Channel 10 in Macon. He had only mild interest in the story, but it seemed to generate some interest when he discussed it with the program director, but there was no coverage.

There was, however, a call to the Council of Broadcasters. It was a call that was very interesting to Mr. Mahoney and one that he would follow up on.

Washington, D.C.

Barry Burlington was still in a rage at 9 a.m. in the morning after the show with Charles Hancock. Burlington could not bring himself to mention the name any more and simply referred to Charles as 'that doctor.' He and the producer had assembled the staff, including the publicists, to do a recap of last night's show.

"I still don't understand why 'that doctor' thought we were trying to set him up," fumed an irate Burlington. "Is there anyone here who ever considered that?"

Not surprisingly, there weren't any volunteers to answer that question.

Burlington continued, "God damn it! We've always run our show as a straight-up, professional, no-hidden-agenda operation. We never try to get guests here and surprise them or embarrass them. That's been our reputation. I've watched last night's show several times, and we come off just the opposite. What the hell happened? After the comments by 'that doctor,' it prevented me from talking to the journalists since it would only reinforce what he said. The only other person left was the other doctor and he was a damn flunk if there ever was one. He either agreed with 'the doctor,' or said he didn't know. That show was a disaster, and we need to get something quick to redeem our reputation. I want the damn publicity people to get yakking to the papers about how great the show was and emphasize that we never duck controversy." After a pause, he continued, "I also want to accelerate those real quality interviews that we've scheduled. I know our viewing audience likes cement-head starlets, but we need to get some quality guests on, and quickly. We need something meatier so we can get this episode with 'that doctor' behind us. Get me some ideas by later today!" he screamed as he stomped from the room.

The White House

President Jenkins was meeting with the Secretary of Defense, Chairman of the FCC, the Attorney General, the Surgeon General, two Congressmen, two Senators, and several political advisors.

"I watched last night's interview of Dr. Hancock on the Barry Burlington Show. I'm not sure what Burlington had planned, but the doctor turned the interview into an embarrassing scolding of Burlington. It came across to me that Dr. Hancock was right. Why would he have more journalists than doctors to discuss Hancock's research? I think the good Doctor sniffed out that trap and put his own trap out successfully. I have to hand it to Hancock; he was prepared and did a good job. I don't like seeing Barry sandpapered like he was, but he asked for it. He's generally been a friend to us and may be looking for some help with the show to get some credibility back. If he asks for someone from your department to be on the show, I think we should help him out, but let me know first. The latter part of the show was focused on Hancock's research, and the only other physician there agreed with him. This can only add more fuel to the fire in the country that something needs to be done. I'm getting an awful lot of mail from all over the country, and even some foreign countries, demanding that I take actions to protect the lives of citizens. I know the FCC is swamped with citizen demands for action. How about the Congress?"

Both Senators started to answer at once, but eventually the senator from Nebraska, who was the senior of the two, replied, "Mr. President, there's nobody in the Congress who can remember a time when we got more mail. It's coming in every conceivable way. Most of my colleagues have turned off their fax machines. Those with e-mail addresses are reporting that their mailboxes fill up immediately after they're emptied. The comments are virtually the same message. 'What is the government going to do to protect us from getting cancer from EM rays?' My view is Mr. President, that we don't have much time before people will start taking their own action. As I see it, there are three things they can do.

"First, they can pressure us to do something, and that's their preferred solution. Please believe me Mr. President; they're putting pressure on the Congress like never before.

"Second, they can pressure the radio and TV stations to shut down, and they can do that through pressure on sponsors. I don't think the second possibility is much of an option. It takes time to impact sponsors and the nation's impatient. It's also an incomplete solution because many of the sources of the EM rays are not commercial. But, there was an inordinately aggressive group in Louisiana that demonstrated against a car dealer who eventually withdrew his ads at a local TV station.

"Third, the people will take direct actions themselves. Everything from picketing Washington, like they did to Nixon during the Vietnam war days, to burning down radio and TV stations or assaulting anyone who has anything to do with the industry. It could get very dangerous. We have to remember that we have a lot of crazies out there with guns and causes. We also have a lot of mothers trying to protect their children from getting cancer. This is a situation with some substance to it, and it could unite a lot of disjointed characters and ordinary people to bring about lot of serious trouble."

The Attorney General picked up where the Senator left off. "Mr. President, I don't have to tell you that there are several legal questions involved in addition to the concerns that the Senator has just listed. We control access to the airwaves through the FCC. That agency could revoke all but the most necessary broadcast permits, such as police, fire, military, aircraft control, and similar essential services. In doing so, we can expect serious disruptions in communications mainly through the loss of all cell phones. People complain about a need to be protected from these harmful rays, but it's another thing when they lose their cell phones and satellite TV. They will also lose some cable TV. Most people don't know that a lot of the cable TV they have in their homes gets to the cable company by satellite or other airborne transmission.

"Of course, we can expect a death struggle with the communications industry if we try to eliminate their broadcasts. To them it's a true First Amendment right, and any alteration will be a constitutional challenge. We will be flooded in every court in the country with challenges. We need to think through our approach to this. Our actions have to be sound and possibly along the lines of the challenge to President Nikon's 'executive privilege' assertions during Watergate. While nobody will publicly admit it, the Supreme Court was involved informally. The Court was not an active planner in what went on; the court was fully informed and was asked to make suggestions. The ultimate legal decision was theirs alone, but it was a unanimous decision if you remember. The management of that decision was part of the overall handling of the controversy. We can learn from that.

"Lastly, we have a smaller problem, but one that's a part of the overall consideration. That's the ham operators in this country. There's a lot of them and they would be very difficult to police. In terms of harmful rays, there won't be much danger, but there's the problem of your neighbor illegally broadcasting while you can't watch your favorite show on cable or satellite TV."

The President had been listening for the past forty-five minutes to their comments and, as usual, saw no easy solution. He knew well that if there were any easy solutions, these kinds of problems would have been solved long before they got to him. "Thank you for all your comments and thoughts. I'm going to consider this further for the better part of today, and I hope we can get together in the next day or so with a plan. I want all of you to be thinking of the pros and cons of any government action and be prepared to address all of your concerns, including military action, when we return. Thank you."

The President went upstairs to the living quarters for a cup of coffee.

46

While the other members of the meeting were leaving, the Secretary of Defense grabbed Attorney General Crobin by the arm and whispered, "Military action? Do you know anything about any military action?"

The Attorney General whispered back, "No, I assumed you knew what he was talking about?"

Neither man said anything else and returned to their respective offices.

Miramar, Florida

Jacky Jones was one of those guys who was always a delight to be around. He had moved to South Florida from Pittsburgh about ten years ago and found what he believed to be the "good life". After graduating from culinary school and learning his trade in some of the finer restaurants in Pittsburgh, he secured a job with the prestigious Fountain Bleu Hotel. It offered him a chance to do what he liked to do best, create and cook. He was always happiest when he was asked to create something unique. After working his way up to senior chef, he was able to establish a unique service where he actually met with customers before dinner. He established a following and he now had a number of customers who simply called him to the table and they "discussed" dinner. After review of suggestions and what seafood and vegetables were fresh that day, Jacky went to the kitchen to prepare the food. Patrons never looked at the menu, and the meal was a creation. Naturally, price was never a consideration.

Jacky had also met one of the desk clerks and after a seven month courtship, had married. He had recently learned that he was to become a father. They purchased a small house in Miramar and life was wonderful. Kitchen work is naturally very physical, and after a normal shift, Jacky was tired when he got home. To relax late in the evening, he liked to sit on his back patio and look at the ever changing Florida sky.

One particularly harmless mind game he played with himself was to see if he could determine the blinking pattern of the red aircraft warning lights on the three distant radio towers that rose into the night about ten miles south. He had been watching the towers and the blinking patterns for several months now and actually had almost convinced himself that they were random and uncoordinated. However, he still wasn't ready to totally concede that there wasn't some pattern to the lighting sequence.

So, once again, he had gotten home late from work, opened a bottle of Heineken beer, and settled back to enjoy the crystal clear Florida skies and see if he could break the code on the lights. He noticed a small hole in the screen on the front door and made a mental note to fix it on his next day off. He had been watching the blinking red lights for about fifteen minutes when he heard the six booms that sounded like explosions. He knew they couldn't be explosions, but he couldn't imagine what would cause such a loud and seemingly organized series of noises that late at night.

Then a surrealistic feeling came over him as he watched. It seemed like something from television in slow motion. The red light on the very left tower started to get lower until it disappeared from sight. What could make the light lower? He understood when the other two light towers both fell to the right. All three towers had gone down, and there were no lights or towers blinking their warnings into the clear night sky! The source of the explosions was now clear. A few minutes later he heard the sounds of numerous sirens filling the night air and knew what had happened. But why? And by whom?

Gray, Georgia

Two hours later in a suburb of Macon, Georgia, neighbors reported two explosions near the cemetery, the location of the broadcasting tower for radio station 'WAXY 99, Home of the Golden Oldies.' Responding police officers found the same as the police in Miramar had found earlier. Two of the four supporting legs of the transmission towers had been dynamited, and the towers crashed forward into twisted, grotesque, metal spaghetti. In both cases, there were no injuries, and the explosives were placed in such a way that the towers fell in a direction to do the least damage, except to the towers.

Within hours of each explosion, local reporters and stringers of national newspapers were on the scene. Pictures of both towers were in all afternoon newspapers the next day. No one claimed responsibility for the tower in Macon, Georgia. In Florida a group called 'Killing-Cancer" had letters delivered to all the local newspapers acknowledging that they were responsible for the towers being destroyed and that all other towers were in danger. "Killing-Cancer" had written letters in the past, and their existence was well known. In this letter they referred to themselves as 'KC's' and the TV journalists would ultimately refer to them as the 'Caseys.'

The term "Casey" stuck. It was soon adopted and well known to most Americans and to all law enforcement and government leaders.

CHAPTER NINE

Monday, November 28

<u>Columbus, Ohio</u>

Charles was shocked and saddened to see the Columbus Dispatch headline reporting the bombings of the broadcast towers in Florida and Georgia.

"I expected some problems, Bobbie, but nothing like this. I thought there would be letter-writing campaigns, maybe some protests, but it looks like the people are going back to the revolutionary days and taking matters into their own hands."

Bobbie was sipping her coffee and still reading the story. "It looks that way… this is awful. But there's not much that can be done by anyone in Columbus. Only the Government can do something, and from the looks of this, it's only a matter of time before someone gets hurt."

<u>The White House</u>

As a result of the bombings, the same group that had met with the President the previous day was called back to an emergency meeting. In addition to the original members, the director of the CIA, William 'Bill' Hughes was also in attendance.

"Thank you for coming on such short notice," remarked a grim President Jenkins. "Last night's bombings of the transmission towers in Florida and Georgia are serious matters. Before we begin, let me get something straight. This 'Casey' group isn't a single group? It's more of a generic name that has surfaced around the country, and their cause is stopping the radio broadcasting. Right?"

Attorney General Ken Crobin nodded his head. "That's generally correct, Mr. President. The original 'Killing-Cancer' group is from the Miami area, but other groups around the country are calling themselves 'Caseys.' But, as far as we can tell, there's no organization or communication between the groups."

"OK," continued the President. "Let's review where we are. First, we haven't completed the analysis of the paper by Dr. Hancock, so we don't know if his science is accurate. Second, we have massive letter-writing campaigns going on to the Congress, to the Administration and particularly to the Federal Communication Commission. We also have some grass-roots activity by activists across America protesting the continued broadcasting. And we have intense lobbying from affected groups, most notably the broadcasting industry, the medical community and all organizations that are primary suppliers to those organizations, like the pharmaceutical companies. We have also had demonstrations here in Washington, and in selected cities in the country, all aimed at stopping the EM rays. These demonstrations have been increasing over the last couple of days. Fortunately, so far they have all been peaceful. We now have two clear instances of direct violent action from, at least in one case, a group dedicated to stopping the EM transmissions. We have no information regarding the 'Caseys' and little hope of solving anything quickly. Did I get it all right?"

Heads nodded again around the room and CIA Director Hughes spoke up. "One more thing, Mr. President. We have increasing indications that the public protests are escalating around the world. A massive rally is scheduled tomorrow in Berlin led by members of the Green Party. That's the environmental group. We have another rally identified in London, and they expect Hyde Park to be filled with demonstrators and sympathizers. We also expect action in the next few days in Japan, Greece, Spain and Canada."

"OK – thanks," groaned the President. "Let's get on to new business. What can we add to what's just been said?"

The Attorney General went first. "Mr. President," he began, "we've dispatched additional FBI agents to Miami and Macon for investigation. If we're successful in arresting the culprits quickly, it will deter others. However, as you so accurately pointed out, the initial indication is that we won't catch anybody soon, or perhaps ever. The towers are all in sparsely populated areas, they have no protection, and there are no witnesses or clues. It's a simple task of putting bombs of some sort under two of the supporting legs and setting them off. They don't even have to go off at the same time, and the perpetrator can be long gone when they do go off. Once two of the four legs are weakened, the tower falls toward those weakened legs and self-destructs. For the most part, the towers are not insured and they're expensive to replace. Bottom line, the radio and TV stations are out of business unless they can find an already existing facility to put another transmitter on top of. Given the latest bombings, it seems unlikely that anyone will volunteer to rent space to a company that wants to put up a transmitting antenna."

The President had another strained and painful look on his face, but the Attorney General continued. "There are two other complicating factors. Number one, many antennas, especially in the south, don't have a wide base for support. They're simply put on a small concrete pad and held up with guy wires. Any schoolboy with a set of heavy-duty snips can cut those wires and bring those towers down. There's virtually no way to protect all the transmission towers, but I'll have more on that later. A second problem is that over the years the telephone companies have been avoiding the cost of building towers and are renting space on existing tall buildings. In fact, even some churches have rented space. These are primarily for communication repeaters and transmission equipment for cell phones. The problems here are twofold. First, many are on occupied buildings that could endanger people and, second, many of these locations are affixed to community water towers. If anyone targets these sites, we'll have problems far beyond a single tower falling in a field. If these bombings continue, we'll have very serious problems."

The President's expression soured.

"Second is the possibility of protecting these tower sites. It's almost impossible for the local police to do, since there are so many towers and the locations are so remote. There simply aren't enough police to protect local communities and these broadcast sites. A possible work around to the protection problem is to hire private guards. It's expensive and the broadcast industry claims they can't afford to stay in business if they have to guard their towers twenty-four hours a day. As an aside to the problem, we don't think there are many private firms that will take the job. We quickly surveyed some of the larger security companies, and they indicated they would have trouble getting employees to work so closely to the transmission towers. They liken it to guarding Chernobyl. Protection could be provided to the guards, but adequate protection means metal sealed buildings without windows. No windows means closed circuit TV; that means more expense. Guarding the towers is simply not a viable option at this time. Of course, we could have the National Guard protect the facilities and the Secretary of Defense will speak to that issue. That's all I have, Mr. President."

The President nodded and looked at the Secretary of Defense.

"Good morning, Mr. President," started the Secretary. "All of the problems that have already been discussed about guarding the towers with security forces apply to the National Guard with a number of qualifications. I believe we already have the adequate equipment to protect any guards with tanks and armored personnel carriers. They're shielded from the EM waves, and we could easily outfit them with closed circuit cameras. Heating, air conditioning and toilet facilities would have to be provided. While that's possible, I don't think I need to go into detail regarding the problem of the American public seeing the offending towers protected by the Army. Additionally, it will be expensive if we use either the National Guard or the regular Army. If the Guard provides the coverage, we'll have to reimburse the States. I'm not sure how much support we'll get from the State Governors either.

"With regard to what the Defense Department can do in the future, there are some possible actions that we can take now. I can immediately reduce the number of EM transmissions we generate. In those areas where we have our own broadcast stations, we can shut them down. We can order the military to reduce the use of cell phones to emergencies only. We can also temporarily scale back our exercises, which will reduce the use of the airways, but we can't do this for any long period of time. We can also cancel the agreements we have with private companies that have leased space on our bases for their transmission equipment. We'll get sued for contract violation, but most of our contracts have a clause that says we can terminate contracts during emergencies. The courts will have to decide if it's an emergency."

The President nodded and looked at the Congressional delegation.

The senior Senator from Nebraska was acting as spokesman for the Congress again today. "Good morning, Mr. President. After our meeting yesterday, I polled over two hundred Congressmen and Senators to get their thoughts on the situation. They were unanimous in their concern for the country. They're being inundated through every conceivable method of communication you can think of, all saying that something needs to be done immediately. One even had a brick thrown through his window with a note saying 'stop the EM rays!' There doesn't seem to be any comparison of what is going on now to anything in recent history. It seems to be the clear sense of Congress that you need to immediately end the use of the airwaves except for essential services such as military use, aircraft control, etc. Now, does that mean they'll support you if you turn off the TVs? Regretfully, each will put his or her own interpretation on how it should be handled. With no TV advertisement, incumbent Congressmen have a clear advantage over any challenger. However, if you're known as the congressman that turned off the TV, you'll have a tough time getting re-elected. So, they want something done, but publicly I don't think anyone in the House of Representatives will stand up and say you did the right thing. Your strongest support will come from Senators who have two or four years remaining on their terms. They'll be more helpful and have pledged to do the best they can to support and endorse your actions."

The Secretary of Commerce spoke next. "Good morning, Mr. President. Since Dr. Hancock's study was originally published, I've been in close contact with the broadcast industry and the large and small TV and radio stations. I've also talked to a few Governors who asked about shutting down Public Television. The overwhelming feeling of the broadcasters is no surprise. They believe that there should be no restrictions on their right to broadcast, and their reasons aren't anything new.

"First they point out the economic impact, which they estimate will be the loss of billions of dollars of income in the next year alone, and the loss of over one million jobs. They're referring to the on-air personalities, technical staffs of all the stations, the suppliers to the stations and the advertisers. As an example, they point out that the loss of revenues if they don't broadcast the Super Bowl to be over fifty million dollars. They also mention the loss of millions of dollars invested in equipment and facilities.

"The telephone companies share some of the same problems. They've spent billions on outer space satellite deployments and ground based stations to handle millions of calls every hour. If they can't recoup those sunk costs, they'll have to consider bankruptcy. Even the automobile industry is voicing an opinion. They spent a lot of money outfitting their cars and trucks with radios, telephones, Global-Positioning receivers and locators. Those costs won't be recovered and profits will turn to losses. I've also been in touch with all kinds of other industries that rely on wireless communication for success. Folks like the parcel delivery companies, grocers, utility companies, even the post office. They've all built infrastructures in their organizations that rely on wireless communications. If there's a shutdown, they'll lose big bucks. Unanimously, they are saying to leave everything alone and do nothing until you've completed your studies on the validity of the research, and you're absolutely sure that Hancock is correct.

"Naturally, all the broadcasters and the broadcasting companies pointed out that any restriction on the use of the airwaves was a clear violation of their first amendment rights. They promised that any restrictions whatsoever will be met with immediate lawsuits and instant petitions to the Supreme Court to halt enforcement of any decision you make that is unfavorable to them."

President Jenkins thought of the wisdom of the sign old Harry Truman kept on his desk that said "The Buck Stops Here". The President certainly had a "buck" in the middle of his desk this time.

After several more minutes of discussion and questions, a tired-looking President looked at each of his advisors. "Thank you, ladies and gentlemen. I'm going to take some time to think this over and consult with some other folks I think might be helpful. I'd like to meet back here at the same time tomorrow. Thank you for coming."

The President left the meeting room, and his advisors again started talking amongst themselves as they left.

Washington, D.C. (Across town)

"Good evening, ladies and gentlemen," intoned a serious Barry Burlington. "This is the Barry Burlington Show and we have a very exciting show for you tonight. I think all Americans are aware of a study by Dr. Charles Hancock that has been in the news lately. We had Dr. Hancock on last night. For those of you that might have missed that show, we have more information on the subject tonight. We have several experts in the field and will devote the entire hour to this subject. We'll be back after a word from our sponsors."

The camera cut away and Barry Burlington got comfortable in his chair. Ninety-three seconds later the red light came on again and Barry Burlington began:

"Tonight ladies and gentlemen, we have a panel of experts with us to discuss the effects of electromagnetic rays on the human body. With us in the studio is Dr. Lamont Turks, a Professor at Ohio State Medical School and a colleague of Dr. Hancock. In our Chicago studio is Dr. Chester Kidd, an oncologist and cancer specialist for the past 40 years and still in active practice. Good evening, gentlemen."

Both physicians mumbled a good evening and smiled.

"Let me begin with Dr. Turks since he's a colleague of Dr. Hancock. I take it you know Dr. Hancock?"

A smiling Dr. Turks looked directly into the camera, "Yes. Dr. Hancock and I have been on the faculty at Ohio State for many years. He was already at Ohio State when I arrived twenty years ago, and we've been colleagues since that time.

54

Burlington asked a few more mundane questions and then got to the part of the interview he had been building up to. "Dr. Turk, can I ask you what you think of Dr. Hancock's cancer research?"

"Of course, Mr. Burlington," replied Dr. Turk smiling with a Cheshire cat grin. "Dr. Hancock has done remarkable work during his tenure at Ohio State, and I commend and laud him for his contribution to medicine. The University is very fortunate to have a physician and researcher of his caliber on the staff. His latest research is a major breakthrough, even if it's created a controversy here and overseas. However, I'm sure that he and the University expected this kind of controversy."

Barry Burlington jumped right in. "What do you mean, controversy?"

"Well, his findings haven't been verified by the government's Blue Ribbon Committee yet. I don't know if he appreciated what would happen when he released this preliminary information, but it sure has caused a problem."

Barry Burlington went to the next guest. "Dr. Chester Kidd is an oncologist who has practiced medicine for the past forty years. What do you think of the research, Dr. Kidd?"

"Well, Mr. Burlington, I can't help but admire Dr. Hancock for his efforts. We all know the misery that cancer has been causing to individuals and families over the years. Any research, and especially research that identifies ways to prevent cancer, is very welcome. I'm very interested in seeing the results of the Blue Ribbon Committee that's reviewing the research."

Barry Burlington interrupted, "Have you reviewed his work, Dr. Kidd?" After a short pause, Dr. Kidd resumed. "I have, Mr. Burlington, and I'm a little bit surprised. I'm certainly not saying that Dr. Hancock has reached improper conclusions, but, I've been treating cancer patients and seeing autopsy reports for years and years, and I just can't confirm from my experience what he's reported. It may be there, but I haven't seen it. For example, Dr. Hancock's research has been done on mice and primates. While the monkeys are close to humans in many ways, they're not identical. Also, the details of the autopsies on human remains aren't conclusive in my opinion. I've witnessed many autopsies, and the condition of the internal organs and inner body parts very simply aren't as described by Dr. Hancock. I pray that Dr. Hancock is correct in his finding. We need to help people beat cancer, and the best way to do that, of course, is to prevent cancer."

Once the two doctors had finished their comments, the phone lines were opened and they answered questions. Answers to viewers' questions were to the effect that they couldn't verify what Dr. Hancock had found in his studies. There was no denial or refutation of the work, just scholarly questions as to its veracity.

Columbus, Ohio

Charles was fuming and bordering on rage. He finally couldn't contain himself any longer. He picked up the phone at about 9:30 and called the Barry Burlington show. He surprisingly got through and identified himself.

The operator said, "Please hold, Dr. Hancock. I'll put you through."

After waiting for about fifteen minutes, Charles had calmed down. He wished he hadn't called and wanted to hang up. He would have to accept that if he did, Barry Burlington would say that he was on the line but wouldn't hold. It would seem like Charles thought he was too good to wait, so he held on. With about six minutes left in the program, he heard the voice of Barry Burlington.

"We would now like to welcome Dr. Charles Hancock from Ohio State University to the discussion. Dr. Hancock is the author of the research that we've been discussing. Good evening, Dr. Hancock."

"Good evening, Mr. Burlington, and good evening to your guests. I'll be brief, Mr. Burlington, and I'd like to address my comments to my colleague, Dr. Turks."

Dr. Turks kept smiling. "Lamont, you and I have been colleagues for many years, and we've known each other almost twenty years. It would seem to me that another physician commenting on the work of a colleague, should be neutral until he can examine the work in question. Wouldn't you agree?"

"Of course, I agree Charles," replied Dr. Turks.

Barry Burlington liked the reply by Dr. Turks but had a feeling in his stomach that there was something going to happen that he wasn't going to like. He glanced at the producer with that 'have a commercial ready on short notice' look.

"Good," continued Charles Hancock. "Maybe to ensure that everyone knows your degree of neutrality, you should discuss what happened between us about five years ago?"

Dr. Turks was slow in responding, "I don't see any need to bring anything up like that, Dr. Hancock."

Charles wasn't giving up. "Do you have any objections if I bring it up?"

Dr. Turks disliked speaking to Charles. In fact, except at formal meeting, he hadn't spoken to him in five years. With his grin gone he replied. "I don't think there's any need to bring that up, Dr. Hancock, and I object to your doing so."

Charles had known Lamont wouldn't agree. When Dr. Turk had plagiarized an article Charles had written five years ago, the University had reprimanded him. It was all kept private, and Lamont wouldn't want to bring that out in the open. With the refusal, Charles continued. "OK, Mr. Burlington, since my colleague objects to discussing this incident in our past, I can only say that his motives are not neutral and maybe he'll discuss it with you after I hang up. Then you, and your audience, can make your own judgments."

The camera was showing a very stern Dr. Turks and a bewildered Barry Burlington.

After a short pause Dr. Hancock began again, "I have one other question for Dr. Turks. Lamont, we all know that one of the ways to protect yourself from EM rays is to put a metal shield around your house. This generally means relatively thick metal siding, a metal barrier between the roof and the house, and protective coating for the windows." Dr. Hancock paused for a longer period of time. "Dr. Turks, are you now having those kinds of protective shields put on your home in Columbus?"

Dr. Turks didn't answer, and Barry Burlington went ashen.

After a seemingly endless pause, Barry Burlington finally spoke. "Are you going to answer, Dr. Turks?"

Finally Dr. Turks answered in a very low voice. "I'm in the process of having extensive renovations done on my house, but those renovations are unrelated to electromagnetic rays.

Barry Burlington stared in disbelief, waiting for more information.

Dr. Turks said no more. Barry Burlington, barely able to speak, sputtered, "Do you have anything else to say, Dr. Turks? Dr. Turks?"

Dr. Lamont Turks had risen from his chair and left the studio.

There were two minutes of airtime left in the show. Suddenly Barry Burlington blurted out, "That's about it for our show tonight. Thank you for watching and good night." The producer went to an immediate commercial.

Burlington didn't bother to thank his guests and stormed out of the studio, once again shouting and cursing because of 'that doctor.'

The telephone rang when Vonda was standing nearby and she answered, "Hello."

"Good morning, Miss Fluellen," intoned the unknown voice of someone who could have been a radio personality.

"Good morning," replied Vonda.

"Excuse me for bothering you this morning, Ms. Fluellen. My name is Sam Forbet. I'm a special Agent with the FBI. I'm currently looking into the recent bombing of the radio tower on Gray Highway. Do you have a moment to talk?"

Vonda was scared. She'd never had any dealings with the FBI and certainly didn't know anything about any bombings. "Yes, I have some time, Mr. Forbet. What would you like to ask me?"

Agent Forbet began and tried to put her at ease. "First, Ms. Fluellen, you're not suspected in any way of having anything to do with the bombing. The reason we called you is because we believe the bombing was a reaction to recent newspaper reports regarding the possible harmful nature of electromagnetic rays that the towers broadcast. A Dr. Charles Hancock wrote that article, and we understand you know Dr. Hancock. Is that correct? Do you know Dr. Hancock?"

Vonda was amazed that the FBI knew that and that they were calling her so soon. "Yes, I suppose you could say I know him. I dated him when I was single, about thirty years ago."

"Have you seen or heard from him recently?" asked Forbet.

Vonda smiled slightly, "No, Mr. Forbet. I haven't seen or heard from him since we stopped seeing each other years ago. I wasn't even sure it was the same Charles Hancock that I dated when I saw the name. After I saw his picture I'm fairly sure, but not positive, that it's the same person. I've only seen a picture in the newspaper of someone I knew thirty years ago."

"Miss Fluellen," replied Forbet, "Do you have any information about the bombing of the tower, or any idea who may have been responsible... or any information that you think the FBI might be interested in knowing?"

Vonda was still nervous that the FBI was calling her. "No, Mr. Forbet, I have no idea at all. As you probably know, I manage a peach orchard in Fort Valley, and I'm not active in very much of anything except running the business and activities in my church. I don't know anything."

After a few more questions, Agent Forbet had nothing else to add either. "Thank you, Ms. Fluellen, for talking to me. We may send an agent to see you later if something develops that you may be able to help with; but for now, that's about all. Again, thank you."

"OK, Mr. Forbet, if there's anything you think I can do to assist the FBI, please call me again. I'm willing to help." After hanging up the phone, Agent Forbet made a note of the conversation in the file and a note that she should not be contacted again unless her name somehow surfaced again. Years of being in the investigation business had given Agent Forbet the nose for evidence. He had made up his mind that Ms. Fluellen had nothing to offer and even wondered why her name was involved in the case at all.

Vonda hung up the phone a little shaken and wondering how they had learned about her. If she knew about her sisters recent phone calls she would be surprised that the Macon Telegraph wasn't calling for an interview.

Children's Hospital, Los Angeles, California

It had been four weeks since the cancer treatments had been completed on Joey, and the results were grim. The cancer was not in remission and Joey's condition was deteriorating. Steve Parson's life had been a living hell for the last month. Whenever he had the opportunity, he left Washington and went to his grandson's bedside and tried to cheer up little Joey. His daughter, Laurie, cried all the time and only managed to stop when she visited Joey in the hospital. Beyond visiting Joey she was unable to do anything whatsoever. Steve's wife was staying in Los Angeles and trying to keep some semblance of order, but not really doing a much better job than their daughter.

At the hospital, Steve had a meeting with the Director of the Hospital, the Chief of Staff and the attending oncologist. It was a little more consultation than most patients get – but then, Steve Parson was not just another grandfather. Steve Parson was well known in America and got VIP treatment wherever he went. The report was that Joey had not responded to the treatments. Anything beyond what had been done was considered radical experimentation, and no estimates could be given regarding success. Complicating future treatment was that anything radical was not covered by medical insurance and was always very expensive. Steve Parson's least worry was the cost. His only concern was Joey. The attending oncologist indicated several courses of action and emphasized the extreme danger, stressing that there was no assurance of any success.

Steve Parson stopped by to see Joey after his consultation and found a very sick but relatively happy little guy. Joey adored his grandfather and if anyone could make him smile, it was Steve Parson.

Steve smiled when he saw his grandson. "Hi, Joey. How ya' doing?"

Joey offered a pained smile when he saw his grandfather. "Hi grandpa!"

"How's the food, Joey? Are they giving you lots of ice cream?"

Joey's eyes lowered a bit. "Nah, I don't get much ice cream, Grandpa, but they give me Jell-O, and I guess that's OK."

"Guess what, Joey?"

"What?"

Steve Parson took the box from behind his back. "I talked to the President last week and he sent you a present." He handed the box to Joey who extended his weakened arms to get it. He slowly opened the box and took out a model of a Coast Guard Cutter. The white boat with the red strip on the bow was the same kind that the President had served on when he was in the Coast Guard. On the base was a glass case under which was a note that said, 'Best wishes and get well soon, Joey - Harrison Jenkins.' Joey obviously liked the boat and started moving it up and down like it was in heavy seas. Steve stayed for the maximum thirty minutes and talked about Joey's favorite football team, the UCLA Bruins.

After leaving the room, he quickly walked past his VIP escort and hot-footed it to his car, where he broke down and cried. He kept crying while he drove back to his wife and daughter.

CHAPTER TEN

Tuesday, November 29

Washington D.C.

The President's advisors all rose when he entered the situation room in the basement of the White House. "Please sit down, ladies and gentlemen," he remarked. Everyone took their seats. It was very clear that the President wasn't happy and there wouldn't be any small talk.

"I talked to Surgeon General Gardner, and he's advised me that his Blue Ribbon Committee still can't offer any opinions as to the quality of the research conducted by Dr. Hancock. Their preliminary work has so far failed to identify any flaws in the research, but there's a lot of work to be done and it takes time. I've given a lot of thought to each of your recommendations, and I've decided to do the following. To begin, I'm delaying any direct action to reduce the amount of electromagnetic rays in the atmosphere. I'm simply not convinced that it's the right time to take any action like this. I believe that more evidence must be identified. However, I'm going to recommend that the public, as a precautionary step, take voluntary measures. This will have some effect on commerce, but it won't generate the kind of legal and commercial turmoil that a government restriction would generate. I'm also going to issue an executive order to all federal employees and the military to reduce the use of any device that would generate EM rays. I've actually never been convinced that we need everyone and their brothers running around the government with phones and beepers. My order will be to the effect that phones and beepers can be used if essential, and I'll expect a 50% reduction. This order will remain in effect until further instructions from me. And lastly, I'm going on television the day after tomorrow with a request to the American people asking for voluntary restraints. These tower bombings must stop before someone is injured and a lot of equipment is destroyed. I'm also going to ask Dr. Gardner and Dr. Hancock to join me. I haven't spoken to Dr. Hancock, but I believe he'll support my course of action and recommend restraint to the American people."

The President looked around the room. "Comments?"

Heads nodded and the only person who spoke was the Attorney General. "I agree with your plan, Mr. President, and I agree with your analysis of the impact. I believe we'll still get some suits filed against us, but since all actions are either voluntary or taken through executive order, there's little chance of any success. There's another possibility that we'll get lawsuits claiming that we need to do more. But those will lack evidence and not reach any kind of decision until long after you have settled on a permanent solution for this situation."

"Thanks, Ken," acknowledged the President. "I see the situation the same way."

There were no other comments from the advisors. "OK," said the President, "I'll call Dr. Hancock and see if he can help me, and I'll make arrangements with the Press Office to schedule an address to the American people the day after tomorrow. I'd appreciate it if you would all keep this plan of action to yourselves until I have everything firmed up. When that's taken care of, I'll send you each a press release as to what you can say and how you can help me. Thank you."

The President rose and left the room. Small conversations started amongst the advisors as was normal after each meeting with the President. Generally, there was agreement that the course of action was sound.

Fort Valley, Georgia

David McDonald, the only investigator that didn't live in Washington, had taken the red-eye morning flight from Philadelphia to Atlanta and gotten his rental car. The drive from Atlanta to Macon, and then to Fort Valley, had been pleasurable, and more scenic than most stretches of interstate he was accustomed to seeing around Philadelphia. There were the usual billboards, but there weren't as many and there were stretches where signs were almost non-existent. When he turned off the interstate and went west on Georgia 96, he saw his first peach orchards. The trees were dormant this time of year, but he could imagine them in blossom from pictures he had seen. The rural two-lane highway twisted and turned until he got to the outside of town where he looked for Peach Orchard Lane. He missed the turn and ended up in the town of Fort Valley where he saw a huge American flag flying over some sort of building. Out of curiosity, he turned on the main road and drove toward the flag. It turned out to be the assembly plant of the Bluebird Bus

Company. Buses were assembled on one side of the road and the recreational vehicles were assembled on the other side. Next to the plant was a storage lot with school buses as far as he could see. After taking a look he turned around and retraced his steps, again looking for Peach Orchard Lane. He had driven just about a mile back when he saw the washed-out sign. He turned right and drove the half-mile to the large colonial house with the circle driveway and manicured lawn - and the dog.

It seemed that Vonda Fluellen had exquisite taste for gracious southern living, but she also kept some protection nearby. The large German shepherd was occasionally barking very loudly, but continually showing its teeth outside his driver's side window. An older black man in excellent physical condition came from the house, walked to the car and said to the dog, "Hush." The dog quieted down but didn't take his eyes off the driver of the car.

"Good morning, my name is Marcus. Can I help you, sir," asked the serious, but not unpleasant man.

"Yes," replied David. "My name is David McDonald and I'm an investigator. I'd like to talk to Ms. Vonda Fluellen if possible."

"One minute," he said as he went back in the house. The dog stayed next to the car. Inside the house, Marcus found Vonda in the library.

"Miss Vonda," he began. "Excuse me for interrupting, but there's a man here who says he's an investigator and wants to talk with you."

Vonda stopped typing and her mind remembered her conversation with FBI Special Agent Forbet the day before. "An investigator? I thought they wouldn't want to talk to me again. I wonder what happened? Uhhhh, show him in Marcus, and invite him to wait in the den. I'll be there shortly."

Marcus returned to the car and escorted David McDonald to the den. The dog followed close behind and David was reconsidering the need to get a gun permit in every state. Inside the den, David was offered a place to sit.

"Would you care for a glass of tea, sir?" Marcus offered.

"No thanks," he said, thinking to himself that he hadn't had any iced tea in years. It was about fifteen minutes before Vonda came to the den. It seemed longer because his mind kept going back to the dog and wondering if it was in the house or outside. David McDonald was a tough guy who had served his military time in the Marine Corps. But all his life he hadn't liked dogs and was uncomfortable around them.

Vonda entered the den wearing blue jeans and a baggy red shirt. She was not a young woman, but she was remarkably attractive and shapely. "Good afternoon, Mr. McDonald. I didn't think you would be here so soon. Those tower bombings are terrible, and it's good to see the FBI working on the case so quickly. I don't really know what I can add to the interview I had with Mr. Forbet yesterday, but I'll do what I can to help." She appeared calm and confident on the outside, but Vonda harbored some of the suspicions of the federal government that were held by many southerners. She was as nervous today as she had been yesterday talking to the FBI agent.

David McDonald didn't understand fully her comments about the FBI, but he didn't see any need to clarify who he was. If Vonda wanted to believe he was from the FBI, it was fine with him. He just had to be on his guard that he didn't represent himself as an agent.

"Thank you for your time, Ms. Fluellen. Your home is beautiful."

Vonda nodded her head.

David smiled. "But I didn't come here to talk about your house and I know you're busy, so I'll be brief. I'm trying to learn as much as I can about all the circumstances regarding the situation with the transmission of electromagnetic rays that's been in the news so much lately."

Vonda interrupted. "I believe I told Agent Forbet yesterday as much as I know…which is nothing. I have no information or even any suspicion of who would bomb radio towers."

"I understand that Ms. Fluellen, but we've found that often little bits of information that seem unimportant can help us solve cases and put the bad guys behind bars. So, if you could just indulge me for a few minutes, it may help stop some of these acts before anyone gets hurt."

He had a few general questions that Vonda easily answered. After gaining as much of her confidence as possible, he eased his way into some of the personal questions.

"Now, Miss Fluellen, you and Charles Hancock dated for about a year. Is that right?"

"Not exactly a year, Mr. McDonald, but almost."

David mustered up a little smile, "I'll bet it was difficult for an Ohio boy to get comfortable here in Fort Valley."

Vonda looked a little surprised. "Oh no, Mr. McDonald, we didn't live here. We met in Miami and we both lived there for about a year."

David showed slight surprise. "Oh. I guess I thought that Charles lived here for that year."

"Oh no," replied Vonda. "We lived at the Ocean Ranch Hotel in Miami, Florida. It was really very nice and very enjoyable."

McDonald knew from his review of Charles Hancock's background that his family didn't have the kind of money to support a son for a year in Miami. "I didn't know that," he remarked, "I guess you both had jobs in the area?"

"When we first met Charles had a job at the hotel and I was a guest. Then I decided to get a job and one was available at the hotel. So, for a while, we both worked at the hotel. After Thanksgiving, we both quit our jobs but still lived in the hotel. I think Charles still had a job, but I'm not very sure about that. It wasn't a full time job."

McDermott was perplexed. "You're not sure if he had a job?"

Vonda had sort of let her guard down and was remembering the fun she and Charles had in Miami. "Well, he said he had a job. Once or twice a week, he took the suitcase from under the bed and left the room. He came back about noon with the suitcase. After that we went to the beach or to the pool or sightseeing, or whatever we wanted."

McDonald was interested now. "He took a suitcase from under the bed and left for a couple of hours and then returned? Do you know what was in the suitcase?"

Vonda thought for a minute. "I don't know for sure, but I think it was money. Charles was secretive about the suitcase and kept it locked. One morning he needed to open if for some reason, and I briefly noticed money inside. He quickly closed it and left. That was the only time I saw anything."

"You didn't see anything else in the suitcase?"

"No, that was the only look I ever had."

David was interested in more detail but thought he had to be cautious before she got suspicious and wouldn't talk any more.

"You must have wondered what he was doing."

"For some reason, Mr. McDonald, I believed it had something to do with buying and selling stocks," replied Vonda. "Once when we were downtown he pointed out the building where the stock market was and said it was an important building. When he left he said he was going downtown to take care of some business." Then Vonda seemed more in control and added, "But what has that to do with the tower bombings?"

David smiled the fake smile he practiced often to look sincere. "You know how it is during these investigations, Ms. Fluellen. We want to know everything. As I said before, often a piece of information that doesn't seem very important becomes important when another piece of information is matched up with it."

Vonda nodded her head like she understood, but she didn't. She thought to herself, 'How can what happened in Miami so long ago be connected to the bombing of radio towers?' She was now suspicious and didn't trust McDonald. David could sense the change and thought it was time to end the interview. He had gotten little information, but he might need to come back sometime and he'd like as friendly a reception as possible.

"Miss Fluellen, you've been most helpful and I appreciate your cooperation. Is there anything else you could tell me that might be useful or is there anyone else that you think could provide any information to help us?"

"There's nothing, Mr. McDonald. I, quite honestly, don't see why anyone is talking to me. It all seems like a waste of time, but you fellows know best how to do these things." The interview had ended and Vonda was escorting Mr. McDonald to the door. "If there's anything else I can do, Mr. McDonald, please call me."

David was trying to concentrate on being polite, but was more intent on looking for the dog.

"Thank you, Miss Fluellen for your time and cooperation. I don't think I need anything else, but someone will call you if we do."

David looked around. "Uhhhhh, there was a dog out there when I came in."

Vonda smiled. "Don't worry, Mr. McDonald. You're safe. Go ahead to your car. There's nothing to worry about unless you try to hurt me." She had the coquettish smile of someone who knew an inside joke.

Mr. McDonald got in his car and headed back to Hartsfield Airport in Atlanta.

He had learned something, but what?

CHAPTER ELEVEN

Thursday, December 1

<u>Washington, D.C.</u>
The evening call from the President of the United States two days before was an unforgettable event. Bobbie had picked up the phone to hear a voice say, "Good evening, this is the White House calling. Is Dr. Hancock available to talk to the President?" Bobbie quickly got Charles and stood by his side while he talked to the President. Of course, she could only hear one side of the conversation.

"And good evening to you, Mr. President…"

"And I like the work that you're doing too…"

"Yes sir, it is a big problem…"

"I agree with you…"

"Yes sir. I certainly can…"

"Absolutely, Bobbie would be delighted…"

"Yes sir… we look forward to it…"

"Thank you for calling, Mr. President."

Charles was still reaching to put the phone down and Bobbie was already peppering him with questions. "Well…what was that all about? Why did the President call you? What would I be delighted about? What's going on?"

Charles had a big smile on his face. "Bobbie, the President wants me to come to Washington to be on television with him. He's going to make an address to the American people, and he wants the Surgeon General and me to be with him in the Oval Office while he makes the address. So…. we're going to Washington!"

Bobbie could only say, "Oh my!"

The two days flew by and it was time to go.

Charles and Bobbie had been to Washington before but not with such VIP treatment. When the President invites you, it's a very nice way to visit the nation's Capital. Charles and Bobbie were met at the airport by a White House car and taken to the Ritz Carlton in Crystal City. Bobbie was very impressed. She had never been in a hotel room with three telephones, including one in the bathroom. After arrival they were given a couple of hours to freshen up and then taken to the White House to meet with President and Mrs. Jenkins. The meeting was very amicable, and they had a lot in common since three of them were Ohio State graduates. As it turned out, they had all been to the University of Georgia campus at least once and Charles several times in connection with medical seminars.

After the small talk was complete, the discussion changed to the President's plan. Charles concurred with the President's approach and agreed to appear with him the following evening. Charles clearly stipulated that he wouldn't acknowledge any flaws in his research and the President didn't object.

After the meeting, it was back to the Ritz Carlton and an early dinner at the Cafe de Italia, an Italian restaurant several blocks away that a colleague at Ohio State had recommended. The hotel provided pick-up and delivery service for hotel guests eating at local restaurants.

The small restaurant had both an inside and outside dining areas but, of course, the outside area was closed due to the weather. Inside it was like being in Italy. The atmosphere, food and ambiance were authentic. The restaurant recommendation was excellent and the meal was superb. After a cup of cappuccino, Charles and Bobbie called the hotel for a ride and headed back. Bobbie said she wanted to do a little shopping, but didn't have time for much more than a look at what shops were available.

During the day, the White House had delivered a draft of the President's remarks for Charles to review and offer comments. Charles made a couple of notes and called the telephone number provided with the speech and suggested some changes. He was reminded that the car would be back to pick him up at 7:30 that evening and that the President planned to speak to the nation at 9:00 Eastern Time. Charles would need some time for makeup and to participate in the preparation for the telecast. Charles had to admit to himself that he was a little nervous. After all, he was going to the White House to be on national TV with the Surgeon General and the President of the United States. It was certainly a big jump from stopping at Kroger's grocery store on his way home from work and getting a couple cans of soup!

At precisely 7:30 p.m., Charles and Bobbie got into the car waiting at the entrance to the Ritz Carlton and departed for the White House. It was a clear night and the drive across the Potomac was enjoyable. Traffic in Washington is always heavy, and it was no different this evening. After about thirty minutes, their car was stopped at the guard station at the White House. After the guard inspected the credentials of the limo driver and checked their visitors' log, the car was permitted to enter the White House grounds.

Charles and Bobbie were met by a protocol officer and escorted through the metal detectors. When they were ushered into the waiting room near the Oval Office, Bobbie accepted a cup of tea while Charles looked over the final statement that had been given to him for review. He was surprised to note that all of the suggestions he had made were accepted. He mentioned it to Bobbie and she responded that maybe his next career would be Presidential speech writer. They both laughed.

A little after 8:15 p.m., two women in smocks came in and asked Charles and Bobbie to join them in the Oval Office. After walking the short distance they entered the Oval Office and were surprised. The office was much smaller than either of them anticipated. It was jammed full with TV lights, cameras, and cables all over the office. From the camera's eye it looked like the office normally looks, but a total view showed a hodgepodge of technical equipment. It was planned that the President would sit behind his desk, as he normally did, and that Surgeon General Gardner and Dr. Hancock would sit off to the President's left. Two chairs were already in position, and pieces of tape had names designating where Charles and Dr. Gardner would sit. One of the women asked Charles to take a seat in the chair with "CH" on it so she could do some make-up work. Charles took his seat and the woman opened a case and began to get the shine off Charles face and sprayed his hair to keep it in place.

At about twenty minutes to nine, Dr. Gardner arrived and exchanged pleasantries with Charles and Bobbie. The President followed him about five minutes later. All three took their places while the makeup specialists completed their finishing touches. The sound technicians kept asking the President to talk so they could get the proper sound levels for the broadcast, and the lighting technicians made an occasional change of a lamp to eliminate newly found shadows. At five minutes to nine, the office became hushed. The broadcast director assumed the position of a maestro in front of a symphony orchestra. All eyes watched him as he fretted and looked at the clock.

At one minute he started the countdown. "OK, one minute to telecast." He did the same at thirty seconds, ten seconds and then counted: "five…four…three…two…one…go!"

President Jenkins looked in the television monitor and began. "Good evening. Thank you for allowing me to spend some time with you this evening. On those occasions that I ask for broadcast time to talk to you, it's because there's a message that I believe to be very important to everyone. That's the case now. I want to talk about the research conducted by Dr. Charles Hancock of Ohio State University. His work has been widely publicized in the press and is a concern to many Americans. Dr. Hancock's findings indicate that electromagnetic rays that are transmitted into the atmosphere are a primary cause of cancer. There's significant debate on this finding. The government, along with many other researchers, is now conducting validating research. Regretfully, this validation can't be done quickly. This type of work takes time. The people of this country are concerned and anxious for action. I fully understand that. Dr. Hancock is joining me this evening, along with Surgeon General Gardner, to announce to the American people what action the government is taking."

The President paused while the camera panned to his guests.

"Dr. Hancock, Dr. Gardner and I have discussed this research and what impact it could have on the current and future health of the American people. The findings that Dr. Hancock has made are serious. However, as with all research, one finding is normally insufficient to draw conclusions and make drastic changes. Research must be duplicated by independent researchers to ensure the findings are accurate. The Surgeon General, Dr. Ralph Gardner, has appointed a blue-ribbon committee to evaluate the findings of Dr. Hancock. This group has been dedicated to this task since Dr. Hancock's research became available. Their findings are not yet ready for publication, but we expect an answer soon. Until that time, it's premature for anyone to draw definite conclusions. Before the government can direct any action, we must be sure. Corrective action in regard to the reduction of electromagnetic rays will be drastic and will profoundly affect our nation. If that's the course of action indicated, then you can be assured the government will take the appropriate action. Until Dr. Gardner's committee completes their work, we need to be prudent. Most of you know that some people have taken matters into their own hands and caused destruction of radio and TV broadcasting towers. This is wrong! I ask that all of us act in a restrained manner until we have confirmation of Dr. Hancock's research. This is a request that Dr. Hancock supports."

When the President made this comment, the camera pointed toward Dr. Hancock so he could be seen there slightly nodding his head in agreement. The Surgeon General sat unmoved.

"So," continued the President, "I ask the following of all Americans. As a precaution, I would like to ask each of you to voluntarily reduce the amount of electromagnetic rays you generate. Please look at all of the electromagnetic generating devices you have in your office and home and reduce where you can. This is strictly voluntary. When we have final evaluation of Dr. Hancock's work, we will most likely need stronger measures or possibly none at all, depending on the results of the evaluation. Of course, I can't ask the American people to sacrifice without asking the federal government to do likewise. I'm doing the same thing here in the White House, and I'm also issuing an executive order to the government tomorrow directing the minimum use of any devices that generate electromagnetic rays. I have also asked the Surgeon General to set up a hot line for anyone to call for information. That number will be displayed on the screen at the end of this broadcast."

"In conclusion, I would again ask for the support of the American people in taking these preliminary and precautionary steps, and to avoid any further destruction of equipment or property until we have solid facts. Thank you for listening, and God bless you."

The camera's red lights went out and the director yelled, "We're off the air."

The President stood up and shook hands with Surgeon General Gardner, Charles, and Bobbie. He then thanked everyone in the Oval Office and left. The protocol officer assigned to Charles and Bobbie appeared and offered the nearby men's room if Charles wished to get some of the powder off of his face. After a minute or two in the men's room, Charles returned and he and Bobbie were escorted to the pick-up point for travel back to their hotel.

In the car Charles started to laugh. "Pretty impressive, huh? Do you think this will be the beginning of a movie career? My first role was to sit and watch. I did a good job of that and I didn't forget a line."

He and Bobbie had a hearty laugh. When they got back to the hotel room, they realized that while they hadn't done much, they were both exhausted. They looked forward to getting back to Columbus, Ohio the next day.

<u>Washington, D.C.</u>

Throughout offices in the city, there were emotions from agreement, to incredulity to total disgust at the President's actions. The telephone industry knew that cell phone use was going to take a dive and profits would be lost immediately. Just the reduction in the government income would be noticeable and harmful. It was also a sure loser for the communications industry. At worst, there would be no more cell phones and pagers. The best that could come out of it would be getting back to business-as-usual if the research wasn't validated.

Even then, customers might realize that they don't really need to be connected to each other constantly. The result would be a drop in business for however long it would take to convince customers that they need more instant communication.

The broadcast industry was facing devastation if a permanent ban was enacted. Radio and television broadcasting were major contributors to the EM rays in the atmosphere every day.

Of course, the cable TV industry was ecstatic. Their goal had always been to get all TV viewers hooked up to cable, and prospects of reaching that goal were greatly enhanced. They had significant success in TV but little with radio. If electromagnetic rays were ultimately found to be harmful, business would boom.

The car manufacturers were equally concerned. If there were no broadcast radio, America's drivers wouldn't be satisfied with the current CD arrangements in their cars. The trunk-mounted systems were not really popular, and a way would have to be found to allow drivers to play multiple disks from the driver's seat. All industry across America was evaluating the impact of a ban on EM generation on their businesses and their everyday lives.

At the American Medical Association Washington offices, the consternation continued. The AMA members were still up in arms because the tabloids had scooped JAMA, and the oncologists were frantic. Confirmation that EM rays cause cancer would result in less EM rays and less cancer.

Over at the Council of Broadcasters there was near panic, and it had been that way all month. Loss of broadcast television would be a terrible and fatal financial blow to the industry. Since television became the dominate provider of news back in the fifties, it had continued to grow and prosper. Many people had cable TV, but even cable was taken from stations that still broadcast on airwaves

Radio was another story. A ban on broadcasting would end radio. The only hope was cable radio which had never really caught on with the public.

Before the President's address to the nation, John Mahoney, the Director of Council of Broadcasters, spent the day going over the investigation with David McDonald. Mahoney had had no good days in the last month. His attorneys had been in touch with network attorneys and were poised as a team to act. The problem was, nothing could be done until the government acted. After all, how can you go to a judge and ask for a restraining order against the government if the government hasn't acted? What do you say? 'Your honor, we think the government is going to do something, and we want you to tell them not to for these reasons...'

Tonight's address by the President just compounded the problem and was very difficult to handle. How can you bring suit because of voluntary action? All the attorneys were dead in the water until the government did something and it looked now like it wouldn't happen anytime soon.

The meeting with Investigator McDonald was disappointing. After spending a considerable sum of money and digging deep into the life of Charles and Bobbie Hancock, there was nothing of substance. Both Charles and Bobbie were model citizens. They earned everything they had. They worked hard and they played by the all-American rules. Mahoney was disappointed because he firmly believed that everyone had something to hide. It was just a matter of digging deep enough to find it. Once that information was found, you gained a big advantage over any adversary; there was no doubt that Dr. Charles Hancock was an adversary. There were no scandals, no skeletons, nothing that they didn't want known. There had to be one thing. What was it?

When McDonald described the interview with Vonda Fluellen both Mahoney and McDonald were intrigued. Had she not thought McDonald was an FBI agent, he probably wouldn't have learned about the time in Miami. But, what did it mean? Charles and Vonda had spent almost a year in Miami living in a hotel. They both had jobs until around Thanksgiving of 1971 and then they both quit. Vonda thought Charles still had a job of some sort, but it wasn't full time. He left a couple of times each week with a suitcase and returned around noontime. Where he went and what he did was a mystery that had something to do with stocks. At least, that's what Vonda thought. Once, Vonda said she briefly saw him open the suitcase and there was money inside. After a year of playing house in Miami, Vonda goes back to Georgia and Charles enrolls in Ohio

State University and becomes a doctor. Who paid the bills? The questions were left hanging in the air.

Had it been two or three years ago, answers could be found. Trails go very cold after thirty some years. Nobody was around who could possibly know the truth. Suppose there was someone.....it would be difficult to find them.

Fort Valley, Georgia

Vonda watched the President's broadcast to the nation and saw Charles for the first time in over thirty years. She had to admit to herself that she was very impressed. He was one of those men that can take a girl's breath away when they are young, and Charles still had that impact on her. She had taped the broadcast and replayed that very short segment that they showed Charles. She had also taped the numerous analyses of the President's remarks and the clips of Charles and Bobbie going to the White House earlier in the evening. She thought back on her interviews and decided she had better make contact with Charles.

The computer in the library was only used for the peach business. The computer upstairs had all the latest equipment that her son had convinced her they "needed". Actually, she was quite happy with the computer and was fascinated by the information available on the Internet and the help that she sometimes got with small problems. After the computer had gone through its startup routines, she clicked on the icon that said 'internet,' entered her password, logged on to the search program, and typed in "Ohio State University". In about a minute she had the home page for the university and started to search around for the listing of the faculty members. After going down a few search trails with no results, she eventually found the Medical College and the faculty listing. There in the familiar blue hypertext was "Dr. Charles Hancock – Professor". She clicked on the name and a blank memo form came on the screen with Dr. Hancock's name already printed in the 'To' part. She had not intended to get in contact with Charles, but after she called the FBI earlier in the day and learned that the 'investigator' she had talked to wasn't from the FBI she became very concerned and decided Charles needed to be told.

After thinking awhile she began typing her e-mail.

'Charles

I've heard about the research you've done, and I saw you on TV tonight with the President. You looked exactly as I had thought you would look after a few years. You've caused a lot of excitement throughout the country, and I think that the work you are doing is wonderful.

I'm not writing for any personal reason. However, things have happened and I thought I had better tell you something that you might find useful. I know that you're happily married and have been that way for many years. I have no intention of trying to be a part of your life again, but there was an incident that you should know about.

After the story broke about your research, I had a call from my sister who had seen you on TV. I dismissed her comments as old news and thought the incident was closed. For reasons that I don't understand, the incident wasn't closed. I didn't hear anything again until after the two radio towers were bombed. The FBI had sent additional agents to the Macon area, and they were investigating the tower bombing here that took place on Gray Highway. I had a call from a local FBI agent, and I considered it not much more than a harmless chat. The agent said that he might send another agent out to see me, but probably wouldn't. The next day I had a visit from who I thought was another FBI agent. We talked and I tried to provide as much information as possible. During that conversation I mentioned our time in Miami and he was very interested. He was especially interested in how we lived. I told him that after we stopped working in the hotel, I thought you had some kind of part-time job, but that I really didn't know much about it. I also mentioned that you had a suitcase and I once saw you open it and there was money inside. I said I didn't know how much or what it was all about. When he asked more about your job, I speculated that it probably had something to do with the stock market since you mentioned something about that to me once.

I reminded him that I was a young girl at the time and life was a lark. He took notes and asked other questions like, 'Did I know you were going to college when you left,' 'How did you pay for college, and other similar questions. I said I didn't know anything about any of that.

After he left I was a little suspicious, so I called the local FBI office and learned that whoever I talked to wasn't an FBI agent. I had to admit that I hadn't seen any credentials and that the man never actually said he was FBI. When I mentioned that I was surprised to see the FBI at the house so soon after the *telephone call, he didn't disagree with me. At any rate, I don't know who it was and neither does the FBI. I can only assume it's someone who doesn't have your best interests at heart. I'm sorry if I caused any additional problems for you. It seemed innocent at the time, but I suspect it probably wasn't.*

I hope I didn't do anything terribly wrong, Charles. I'd never do that to you. I have nothing but the fondest memories of you, and I'm proud of what you've become and the contribution you're making. There's no need to reply to this note. I just wanted you to know what I had done.

Sincerely

Vonda

CHAPTER TWELVE

Monday, December 5

<u>Columbus, Ohio</u>
 Charles hadn't read his e-mail for several days, and he was anxious when he saw the note from Vonda. While her name brought back fond memories of their year in Miami, it concerned him that she was contacting him. After reading the note, he breathed a little easier and replied:

> *Vonda,*
> *It's nice to hear from you again. There have been times when I've wondered about you and hoped that everything had worked out for you. By now, you already know what's happened to me. I married after I started medical school and have remained married to a wonderful woman. We have two sons who also live here in Columbus. Until now, my life was that of medicine and research. It's all changed now, hasn't it? I'd be interested in hearing what's happened to you over the years. Drop me a line if you have a chance.*
> *Thanks for the note on the interview with the FBI. I warned my wife that the findings I've made could cause us some trouble. It sounds like some of the folks wanting to cause us problems have paid a visit to you. The interview with you is most likely part of an effort to discredit me. I expected it and I expect a lot more as time goes on. There are a lot of reputations and a lot of money involved in all this. The people with a lot to lose won't give up easily.*
> *Don't worry about anything. You haven't done anything wrong. Efforts to harm me may cause some grief, but those efforts will ultimately fail.*
> *The findings I've made are solid science and they'll have to be dealt with. Showing that my research is flawed is the only thing that can discredit me. I have no concerns about the research*

because everything I've said is truthful and factual. We have serious problems with electromagnetic rays, and they very simply cause cancer in human beings.

I'm disappointed at some of the violence and destruction of the transmitter towers, but I can fully understand how people can be motivated to do that. After all, parents who love their children do what they think is right to protect those children.

Again, drop me another note when you get some free time and let me know what you're doing.

Cheers,

Charles

<u>Washington D.C.</u>

The "undertakers" were busy at work with their first disinformation efforts. Mail-outs had been sent to the sleaziest of the tabloid publications, plus local and national television stations. They had been anonymously prepared and mailed from Columbus, Ohio. A sprinkling of what looked true was enough to make the letters believable. It was questionable if all of the publications would print anything, but if any did at all, the others would pick up the story. The story was craftily written to confuse the reader and cast as much doubt as possible on the squeaky clean reputation of Dr. Charles Hancock.

The headline of the least credible tabloid started the ball rolling:

SOUTHERN BELLE AND EAGER STUDENT ON RESEARCH STAFF OF NOTED CANCER DOCTOR?

This publication has learned that Dr. Charles Hancock, the researcher who found that electromagnetic rays are a cause of cancer, may have discovered more than cancer in his lab. Authoritative reports are swirling around him with allegations that he had a year-long affair with a 'Southern Belle' from Georgia. It's also rumored that he has accepted sexual favors from a student who has done 'what it takes' to get good grades from the noted researcher. The affair with the southern charmer is unknown to Hancock's wife and family or Ohio State University. The story of the student has been difficult to research, and the standard tactic of the University seems to be to 'deny-deny-deny.' The best information is that a certain comely student wasn't doing well in Dr. Hancock's class and offered to 'do-whatever-it-takes' to get a good grade.

Dr. Hancock reportedly accepted her offer. This publication will have more on these stories as they develop.

Ohio State University

It wasn't unusual for reporters to meet Charles when he arrived for work. It was, however, very unusual when they were at the doorway of the Medical Center when he went home because it was generally too late to get the story on the nightly news. Today was one of those very unusual days.

The University Public Relations Office called Charles and told him early in the afternoon that there was a lot of interest in talking to him when he left the office today. When he inquired why, he was told only that they had a story they wanted to check out but would provide no other information.

When he stepped out of the entrance of the Medical College Administrative Building, numerous reporters and several mini-cams met him. The Public Relations staff had set up a stand where reporters could put their microphones, and Dr. Hancock approached the stand.

"Good afternoon," he began. "What's happened to generate all this?"

The reporter for Television Station 7 in Columbus was the first to respond. "Dr. Hancock, several publications and TV stations have been sent an article today indicating that you've been having an affair with an unnamed southern belle. They also accuse you of increasing grades for a student in return for sexual favors. How do you respond to that?"

Charles was stunned! His normally glib tongue left him. At first it flashed through his mind that someone had read the e-mail he sent to Vonda earlier in the day. How? Collecting himself he started his reply. "You say someone has accused me of an affair with a southern belle and a student had grades increased in return for sexual favors? Who said that?"

The same reporter for Channel 7 replied, "It was anonymous, Dr. Hancock."

Charles started to reply and was somewhat flustered. "I've never heard of any of this before. I'm not sure exactly what to say. These allegations are untrue and invasive of my privacy. I'd like my accusers to say publicly what their allegations are and give me a chance to reply. That's all I have to say."

His answer was not the crisp replies he was known for, and it didn't completely dispel the possibility that the rumors were true. Charles got in his car and left, dreading the six o'clock news and possibly the national news.

When he arrived home, he told Bobbie what had happened and immediately called Jeff and Hal and asked them to come to the house as quickly as possible. Once everyone had arrived he began. "If you haven't seen the news tonight, you're in for a surprise. I was ambushed this afternoon when I left the medical school. It seems that there's a story floating around alleging that I had an affair with some 'southern belle;' and that some student has been given good grades for granting me sexual favors. Just so you all know, there is absolutely no truth to any allegation that any student got better grades for any reason at all. All of my students have been graded on their performance in my classes, period. There's never any other basis for grading their performance. Now, that doesn't mean someone won't claim otherwise. I'm going to call Randall Brookman and the Human Relations Director tonight to see if there have been any complaints. With regard to the allegation that I had an affair with a 'southern belle,' that's also completely untrue. I haven't had an affair with anyone, ever. However, like many other things, there's something to this that could make it a problem. Long before I met your mother, I had a girlfriend in Miami. She was a 'southern belle' in the sense that she was from Georgia. We stopped seeing each other when I started school at Ohio State, and I haven't been in touch with her…until today. When I got around to checking my e-mail today, I had a note from her. She started out by saying that she had no intention of getting back in my life but thought that I should know something that could affect me. It seems that the FBI somehow learned of our dating and called her in relation to the tower bombing in Macon. That part was harmless. Then a man she believed to be an FBI agent visited her. He had a lot of questions and she told him of our days in Miami. It turned out the investigator was not an FBI agent, and it's not known who it was. This allegation that I had a year-long affair with a 'southern bell' is probably rooted in that relationship thirty years ago. I told you that when this all started there would be serious efforts to discredit me because they can't discredit my work. This is part of that smear."

After pausing to think a moment or two, he resumed. "Now we have to decide what to do. I want to first make some calls to see what the University knows. Next, I want to call a press conference for tomorrow. I want each of your opinions before I do anything." Charles then explained his plan to the glee of both his sons and Bobbie and everyone agreed.

"Why don't you send out for a pizza and I'll make my phone calls and Jeff can start working on the statement?"

Charles went to his office to make his calls. As he expected, Randall Brookman knew nothing about any of the allegations and had never heard of any student making complaints or allegations against him. He said he would issue a statement to that effect in the morning. Charles asked him to hold off until noontime because Charles though he would probably have a press conference in the morning. Dr. Brookman agreed.

Charles's call to the Human Relations Director confirmed that there had never been any complaints about Dr. Hancock. Charles asked that the director be prepared to confirm that to the press if asked and he agreed.

Charles then called the Public Relations Director to discuss the press conference the next day. After the conversation, the Director was very angry and refused to do what Charles asked. Charles knew that a little 'rain from above' always helped, and he expected that Randall Brookman would see it Charles' way and not the PR Director's way.

Back in the kitchen the conversation was very hostile toward the anonymous source of the lies. Charles sat down, picked up a piece of pepperoni pizza and added some red pepper and parmesan cheese.

"OK," he started, "let's see what we have. I've talked to the university, and they know of nothing to support the allegations. The president is prepared to go to the press tomorrow and support me one hundred percent. I still like the idea of the press conference to take these charges on directly…has anyone changed their mind?"

The only person to talk was Jeff, the attorney. "We've been talking about it, Dad, and we agree fully. I wrote a preliminary statement and everyone agrees with it."

Charles was very proud of the support that his family was showing. He slowly read the statement that Jeff had written.

"Whoa…..I say, Whoa!! It looks like you all want to go to war. I know we can say everything here, but can we back it up?"

Jeff assured his father that it was legally sound and again recommended that he use it.

Charles re-read the statement. "OK, I'm in agreement with this almost totally. I want to make a couple of changes to suit my style, and I'll use it in the morning. This might even be a little fun." He smiled and took a bite of his pizza. "Thanks for all your help and support. I'll sleep better tonight, but others might have trouble sleeping tomorrow night."

Before retiring for the evening, Charles made another call to the University President. "Good evening, Randall, I'm sorry for calling so late but I wanted to talk to you once more." Randall Brookman looked at his watch and thought to himself - 'so late? It's only 9:30?

"It's not too late, Charles, what can I do for you?"

Charles started slowly. "It's about tomorrow, Randall. You know it's going to be a relatively big day and I need some help from the University. I already talked to the Public Relations people and they're very unhappy. So, I need a little arm-twisting, and I hope you can see your way to instruct the PR people to help me. Here's what I need..."

CHAPTER THIRTEEN

Tuesday, December 6

The White House

The political staff had briefed President Jenkins immediately when they learned about the allegations that Dr. Hancock had had an affair and was trading grades for sexual favors. The President was disappointed that something like this would be alleged and would be more disappointed if any of it were true. He had met Charles and was impressed. He looked like the all-American boy, and these allegations were troubling to the President. He pressed his advisors for details, but there were few. All that was known was that there had been allegations mailed to the tabloid press and legitimate press that Charles had had a year-long affair and that a student alleged that he had increased her grades for sexual favors. No other details were known.

The FBI had naturally done some background checks on Charles before he was permitted to visit the White House, and the investigator who did the check was shocked by the allegations. The FBI Director had reported this to the White House and the President was even more surprised. There was information that Charles would be conducting a press conference before the start of classes at Ohio State. President Jenkins had scheduled office work for the morning and asked the political staff to keep alert and let him know when the press conference would take place, since it was scheduled to be telecast live by a local affiliate of ABC in Columbus.

On the north side of Washington, the "undertakers" were suddenly worried. The plan to start a rumor about Dr. Hancock on the baseless comments of Vonda Fluellen no longer seemed like such a good idea. Dr. Hancock hadn't handled the questions by the press very well, but he did well enough to keep the story from taking off. There was almost no coverage on the evening news, and the doctor had a chance to review the allegations and prepare a response. How well would he do at refuting the charges? Everyone would find out at 10 a.m., EST.

<u>Fort Valley, Georgia</u>

Vonda Fluellen was physically sick from the stress and tension surrounding Charles. He was a man that she hadn't seen for over thirty years, but a man who had seemed to live an exemplary life and was now being attacked by somebody. She knew that the basis for the allegation of a year-long affair with a southern belle was based on her comments. She had read the e-mail from Charles and wondered if she should reply or simply stay out of the fray. Her sister had called and was all excited about the notoriety that Charles was getting, and Vonda had been very angry and impolite. She screamed at her sister that it was her doing that anyone in Georgia was involved in any way with Charles Hancock and she should be ashamed of what she had done. She ordered her to stop talking about Charles and her. In a rare burst of viciousness, she screamed "Keep your mouth shut! This is none of your business!" Then she cursed her. Vonda was depressed when she hung up the phone. She had never spoken to her sister like that, but she knew her sister was a busybody who caused some of the problems. They should be thankful that a man like Charles might have discovered a way to prevent cancer.

CHAPTER FOURTEEN

Wednesday, December 7

Ohio State University

The press conference was scheduled for ten o'clock, but the reporters and TV cameras started arriving at 9:15. At most press conferences, the radio and TV journalists were usually noticeably absent. Today was different. They smelled a scandal and were covering the press conference with enthusiasm. The University Public Relations staff was furious, just like their director. They didn't like to be told how to do things, especially if the instructions came from someone who was not a "journalist". When the instructions came from Dr. Hancock, they could be ignored. When orders came from the University President, they had little choice but to comply. Of course, they didn't have to comply in a friendly manner, but they must follow the instruction of the University President. For some reason, people in public relations think they are the guardians of the right to free speech and the first amendment of the Constitution. They tend to forget they're employees and paid by the administration. Any instruction they think violates a free press or suppression of free thought is unwelcome and resisted.

In this case, the orders were clear, and at exactly ten o'clock they made an announcement to the assembled reporters.

A stiff and formal Director of Public Relations asked for quiet. "Good morning, ladies and gentlemen. We have a change in the way we normally operate for today's press conference. If any service is planning on telecasting this press conference live, it won't be permitted."

"What?" shouted the local Columbus affiliate for ABC. "Why can't we broadcast live? Our subscribers are expecting to see this press conference."

The Public Relation Director agreed privately, but continued. "Dr. Hancock has indicated that the only way he'll hold a press conference is that it not be broadcast live or recorded, except by him. If you're not agreeable to that restriction, you'll not be permitted to attend. Also, each of you will have to sign in with your name, home address and organization, verified by picture identification."

The grumbling was loud, and a reporter from the Columbus Dispatch spoke up, "What's this all about? Why do you need our home addresses and identification?"

The Public Relation Director wasn't explaining anything. "I'm sorry if you don't like the ground rules. Dr. Hancock will not hold the press conference under any other rules. Perhaps you can ask him at the press conference."

"Does the University agree?" yelled the reporter from the Dayton Daily News.

The Public Relations Director snarled, "Yes."

After more grumbling, the reporters were asked to proceed to a room down the hall, which had uniformed university police standing behind tables at each of the two doors. When the reporters arrived they received further instructions from the Public Relations Director.

"OK. Please complete the sign-in sheet on the table and indicate the information requested – name, address, telephone work number, position and organization you represent."

More grumbling ensued and the PR Director was surprised when only one person walked away without any further comment. After constant criticism and veiled threats that the University would regret this, each of the reporters was inside the classroom waiting to start the press conference.

Fifteen minutes later the door opened and Charles, Jeff, Hal, and Bobbie arrived together. The lectern had been placed at the head of the classroom, and Jeff spoke to the reporters first.

"Good morning. My name is Jeff Hancock, and I'm Dr. Hancock's son and his attorney. You've all been briefed that you must sign in to attend the press conference. Is there anyone who has not signed in?"

No hands went up in the air, but a grumbled voice from the back could be heard, "I signed in, but I don't like it and it will be reflected in my story."

A slight bemused smile came to Jeff's face, but he ignored the comment and spoke again. "Another restriction on this press conference is that it not be televised live or recorded. Is anyone here transmitting live information or taping?"

There was no comment and Jeff was sure there wasn't because he recognized the equipment needed to telecast live, and none was in the room. There could be a recorder but it wasn't worth the trouble to try to assure it wasn't being taped. Actually, Jeff had recommended it be recorded so the tapes could be used in any court trial, if necessary. Besides, he would be taping his father's comments to have an accurate record.

"OK, since everything is ready, I'd like to introduce my father, Dr. Charles Hancock and my mother, Mrs. Bobbie Hancock."

Charles moved to the podium while Jeff stepped to the background. Charles stood mute at the podium for what seemed the longest time before he started.

"Good morning. Yesterday when I was leaving work, several reporters met me. They wanted to question me about rumors regarding my personal behavior. I consider these charges very serious, as I'm sure you do. I've asked my family to be here to hear my response firsthand to be sure there is no misunderstanding.

"I'd like to address each charge." Charles slowly surveyed the room of reporters.

"First, there's an anonymous charge that I've had a year-long affair with an unnamed woman referred to as a 'southern belle.' My cowardly accuser is anonymous and can't be confronted to provide the basis for this charge. As you can see, I'm not anonymous and I'll respond. This charge is completely...totally.... and utterly false. I married my wife, Bobbie, over 30 years ago and have been completely faithful to her during that entire time...no exceptions. There's been no affair, no other woman and no misconduct on my part whatsoever."

Charles paused again to allow the reporters to complete their notes.

He then continued. "The second charge is that a female student has received favorable treatment from me in exchange for sexual favors. Like the first charge, my cowardly accuser is anonymous, and no details are provided – just accusations. This charge is likewise completely, totally, and utterly false. There is no student that has received any grade from me except for the work that they have done in my classroom. No exceptions!"

After a brief pause, Charles continued. "I've also checked this allegation with the University President and the Human Resources Director, and neither one has any knowledge of any complaints against me. The University will officially confirm later today, that there's never, repeat never, been a complaint or hint of a complaint about my conduct with any student. No student has received a grade based on anything except class performance."

Charles paused once again to allow the reporters to complete their notes.

"A natural question is why would someone start such a charge against me or try to besmirch my reputation. I don't know the answer to that question. The concoction of these lies is nothing more than a criminal act to destroy a reputation I've been building for many years as a faculty member at Ohio State University."

Charles paused again. When he started to speak again his voice was noticeably raised and the raging anger in him was evident. Someone later remarked that his eyes were starting to mist.

"I won't permit this to happen. I won't stand for this, and I'll take harsh action against anyone that perpetrates these lies…this includes each of you! The reason I didn't want this press conference carried live is because I don't want these slanderous and cruel allegations against me circulated any further. On advice of my son, and attorney, I'm advised that I do not fit under the legal definition of a 'public person.' As such, anyone who prints this garbage, and these lies, is in peril under the libel laws of this country. The only defense anyone has under libel laws is that the subject of the lies is a 'public person' or the information is true. Neither of those defenses will prevail. I am not a 'public person,' and the information is totally baseless."

"Consequently, it's my very clear intention to take legal action against any organization that prints this information, or anything like it. By suing, I mean I intend to sue your organization and you, personally, if this story is published. You're the caretaker of the story and it's your organizational and personal responsibility to ensure that the laws are followed. Failure to do so will be at your own peril. Incidentally, when I say this story is slanderous and libelous if you print it, I also mean any related story or stories that say you know something about it but won't tell your audience."

Charles slowly scanned the reporters trying to make eye contact with each one. "In summary, I've worked very hard to build a reputation that my family and I could be proud of. I've done that, and I don't intend to see it ruined by some feckless coward who wants to do me harm. Thank you for coming."

Charles, Bobbie, Hal and Jeff strode from the room without any further comment, leaving a room full of gaping mouths and reporters worried that their station might run the story and set them up for a lawsuit.

John F. Kennedy Airport, New York City

The International Terminal at JFK Airport in New York City isn't pretty, and it's not as relaxed as the facilities at Port Columbus Airport. Nevertheless, today everything was beautiful to Charles and Bobbie. In just another two hours they would be off to Rome! It was the first trip to Italy for both of them and they were glad to put Columbus and everything going on in their lives aside for the time being. The intrigue of the press and the resistance of the country to change were difficult pressures to bear every day. Charles and Bobbie felt free and careless for tonight.

Tomorrow they would be enjoying pasta, a glass of Chianti, the Trevi Fountain and the romance of Rome. They expected jet lag and didn't have any real plans until after they had been there for a day. Rome was a city rich in history and one that Bobbie always wanted to visit. As a girl she never missed a movie that had scenes from Rome. She saw "Three Coins in a Fountain" so many times, she lost count. She knew she would be overwhelmed by a trip to the Vatican. She had seen so many pictures and heard so many stories of the Vatican, she would be ready to visit immediately when they arrived. She had heard of the bronze foot of St. Peter being worn away by the faithful touching and kissing it over the years. She also wanted to see the altar of St. Peter under that majestic cut glass window. But most exciting to her was Michelangelo's 'Pieta.' It was a sculpture of such impact that she considered it emotionally overwhelming when she had seen it in pictures. Charles was as excited as Bobbie, and he was looking forward to visiting the Sistine Chapel. He knew the pictures he had seen over the years wouldn't do it justice. So, like two lovebirds going on their honeymoon, Charles and Bobbie were sitting, having coffee in New York and waiting for their fantasy to begin.

Nobody knew they were leaving except Randall Brookman, Sheila Gordon, and their two sons. Nobody was exactly sure of where Charles and Bobbie were going. They knew that the first stop was New York and that Jeff would get a call where they could be reached in the event of a real emergency.

Everyone also understood that anything to do with the controversy in the States about the cancer research was not a real emergency unless the President of the University or the President of the United States was involved. Charles had arranged for a short vacation in his discussion with Randall Brookman, and nobody at Ohio State would know in advance that he would be gone. Charles planned to be back in a week.

The Ritz Carlton Hotel, Washington D.C.

An out-of-town salesman named Jerome O'Mally had rented a suite in the Crystal City Ritz Carlton and asked for the largest facility to accommodate his local clients later that evening. The credit card passed inspection and the credit card system gave Mr. O'Mally its 'best client' rating. Of course, there was no Mr. O'Mally, and all the information in the credit card file was fictitious. But, the account was large and always paid on time. Most of the "undertakers" were present for the meeting and they were all furious! With all of their contacts in the broadcasting industry, they knew what happened within minutes of the end of the press conference. Charles reaction to 'come out swinging' was totally unexpected. After all, they knew that Charles had the one, unexplained and very mysterious, year in Miami, and they knew that Vonda had been with him most of the time. They believed that something took place there, but they didn't know what it was. It was their calculation that there was "something" to the "southern belle" charge and Charles would be reluctant to be too forceful in a reply. The totally false charge of the student and the grades would tend to support a pattern of misconduct by Charles and make both stories more believable.

The "undertakers" were wrong. They never expected Charles to fight back so ferociously. They expected a docile academic to apologize and say nothing had happened. The threats of lawsuits against the media and against individual reporters were a shock. The reporters were personally worried about being sued, and the media organizations privately had been told by their lawyers that they were probably liable if they printed any harmful information about Dr. Hancock. The endless battle between the press and the government over the first amendment was rare in this particular set of circumstances. The question of whether Charles Hancock was a public figure and able to sue for libel was very unclear. On the surface they all concluded (as did their lawyers) that Charles Hancock was probably correct. Each of the publications and broadcasters came to the same conclusion, and there was no mention of the press conference or the allegations ever broadcast that day, or any other day. Even the 'REAL NEWS' learned of Charles' threats and also declined to publish any comments.

The lead "undertaker" - code name "digger"- started the meeting.

"It seems that our little plan to discredit Dr. Hancock didn't work. The mechanics that normally produce good results weren't the right ones for this operation. That doesn't mean we stop. We still have an assignment, and we still need to keep focused on our goal. The only blemish in the squeaky clean life of Dr. Charles Hancock is what we call the "Miami Year". The only thing I can see is to dig a lot deeper into it. We know that Charles was in Miami over thirty years ago with a woman by the name of Vonda Fluellen. She lives in Peach Country, Georgia, wherever the hell that is. She's the one that gave us the information on the Miami trip, and she's the one that told us about a suitcase filled with money. She mentioned, in passing, something about stocks, but we don't think there's anything to that. A kid from a poor family has no money to buy stocks and no investing experience. I think that was just her comment with no basis in fact. If, there's something to that year in Miami, it's the only weakness we've found. There's no explanation for a poor Ohio kid ending up in Miami with a pot of money, supporting himself and his girlfriend for about a year and then going to medical school. There's something there and we need to find it. I'm sending the "graybeards" to Miami for the next month to start investigating. Even at this late date, there must be someone in Miami who remembers this Ocean Ranch Hotel and what went on there."

The "digger" didn't know it, but he was right.

"The next thing we have to do is dig deeper into his family. His wife Bobbie is simply too perfect. I'm assigning other investigators to this project. We'll go to Columbus and dig into Bobbie's past, in detail. We'll also look at their kids. It's hard to believe that those two kids are clean. One's in the personal security business and the other's a lawyer. Not exactly what we would call 'clean' professions. We need to do an in-depth investigation at both places. In Miami we also have to do door-to-door interviews. I think we can find something in Miami, but it's going to be time-consuming and expensive. Don't worry about money. We're well financed."

The "digger" paused and sipped on his expensive glass of wine.

Then he continued. "Just for your information, I'm meeting with the 'Legal Eagles' tomorrow night. I expect we'll have some local legal problems, and we need to be sure we are covered when that happens. Any questions?"

No one around the suite moved or raised a hand.

"OK, help yourself to some refreshments, compliments of the American broadcasting industry and let's get to work first thing in the morning."

<u>Children's Hospital, Los Angeles, California</u>

The hoped-for results of the experimental cancer treatments were failing badly. Joey was getting progressively weaker and sicker. Nobody would say it, but Joey was dying. It looked to Steve Parson like Joey's death would be soon.

Steve spent the minimum amount of time on the job and the maximum amount of time with his wife, daughter and Joey. It was a difficult time for everyone and talk was rare. There simply weren't the words to explain what was happening and the wrenching and agonizing emotions that they bore every minute. Joey was now only able to sit up in bed with the help of the bed elevating his frail body. He could still talk, but he lacked any spirit and was listless most of the time. He still tried to smile when his grandfather visited, but it was increasingly harder. His diet had been changed to only soft foods and all the ice cream he could or wanted to eat. It was a deathwatch of the most profound kind.

Steve Parson knew of Charles Hancock as the cancer doctor at Ohio State University. At one point, he tried to call him but was told that Charles was on vacation and nobody was sure when he would be returning. Steve Parson never called back. He really believed that he had excellent medical advice available and was getting the best there was.

Unfortunately, the facts were that there was no cure and a small boy was going to die shortly.

CHAPTER FIFTEEN

Sunday, December 11

Rome, Italy

After four days Charles and Bobbie decided they had seen enough of Rome and were ready to leave. They decided they should spend the remainder of their vacation somewhere else in Europe and booked a flight to London. The trip started with a bus ride through the crowded and lively Italian city to the airport, which was a microcosm of the city. Every tourist at some point says, "Arrivederci, Roma" when they leave. It was Bobbie who said it aloud to Charles in the taxi on the way to the airport. After driving and gesturing his way through the city, the taxi driver finally dropped them off for their British Airways flight that was leaving shortly after noon.

The change from Italian culture to British was noticeable immediately, and Bobbie delighted in the contrast between American and British English. She was slightly envious of the British accents that the stewardesses on the jetliner had. A light lunch was served and the flight was the best kind – uneventful. Bobbie and Charles made it a point to use the restroom before they arrived at Heathrow airport. The stories of long lines at the customs inspection may have been just stories, but they weren't taking a chance.

When they arrived they found that the reports of long lines at the customs counters weren't true and they passed through quickly. Then it was on to the train for the short ride to Victoria Station in the heart of London. Friends had told them of the London Elizabeth Hotel near Hyde Park, so it was over to the "tube" for the Marble Arch exit. After a short crisp walk, they were registered at the London Elizabeth. Charles suggested dinner in the hotel so they would have lots of energy for tomorrow's sightseeing. Bobbie thought the "Swan" Pub next to the hotel might be a little more fun and Charles relented. They had beer that was chilled, but not cold beer by American standards and shepherds pie for dinner. Neither Charles nor Bobbie was familiar with the European custom of strangers sitting at your table. During their meal a British couple asked if the empty chairs at their table were taken. Bobbie expected them to take the chairs to another table and was surprised when they sat down. Feeling somewhat awkward, Bobbie introduced herself as did Charles. The couple responded in a friendly manner, and they struck up an enjoyable dinnertime conversation. After dinner they had another round of drinks and discussed everything from the difference in American universities to the traffic in all cities. They all stayed in the pub until almost ten o'clock. The other couple was only in London for the day and they were headed back to Kent that evening. Everyone exchanged addresses and promised to keep in touch.

Charles and Bobbie had a delightful evening. They were looking forward to the next day and quickly fell asleep when they got back to the room.

The White House

President Jenkins had a ritual of waking up by listening to his clock radio. This morning he was on schedule like he was most other mornings. The 'Oldie-Goldie' station awakened the President to the sounds of the Mamas and Papas singing 'Mama Mia.' He liked the song and stayed in bed until it was finished. On this particular day, it would turn out to be the best part of his day. After a stop in the bathroom, he shuffled to the dining area where a pot of coffee, half a grapefruit, and three newspapers were on the table. The newspapers went to press in the very early morning hours and routinely missed stories that developed late at night or early morning. The newspapers would give him some background on what had happened while he was asleep. Of course, an aide had already read the papers and highlighted any stories that the President might be interested in reading. At the "stand-up" meeting with his staff, he would learn what had happened since the papers went to press. There would also be a political analysis of any overnight activity plus an intelligence briefing compiled by the CIA. After finishing his breakfast, he then dressed in his usual dark suit for the start of his day.

Twenty-five minutes later, he arrived at the Oval Office and was met by his secretary and immediate staff.

"Good morning," greeted the President. "The papers looked benign today; let's hope it stays that way."

President Jenkins could tell by the reaction that there was something else that he didn't know about yet.

His Chief of Staff answered, "Good morning, Mr. President. You're right that the papers didn't have much today, but there are events that didn't make it to the papers, yet. It seems that in Biloxi, Mississippi, there were two radio towers bombed last night. This time there were causalities. The explosive device went off prematurely when the bomber placed it on the leg of the tower. The blast toppled the tower and killed the bomber. Preliminary reports are that the bomber was a local businessman with a family of four and a Boy Scout leader. He'd been very vocal in recent weeks about how the EM rays were killing the scouts. He organized several demonstrations in the downtown area of Biloxi and routinely demanded that all radio and TV stations be shut down. Seems he couldn't get results that way, but last night he was able to get two radio stations off the air, but at fatal expense."

The President's face showed disappointment. "Well, we knew when we asked that the bombing stop there was a good chance that it wouldn't work. It didn't."

The Chief of Staff interjected before the President could say anything else. "There's more, Mr. President. In Kansas City a group calling themselves the 'KC-Casey's,' which means the 'Kansas City Cancer Killers, killed a guard last night and occupied a local radio station. They broadcast for about an hour until law enforcement had the electric company turn off the power. They're holding three station employees as hostages and demanding that the radio station be turned back on. Management is still negotiating with them, but they intend to turn the station back on since the 'Casey's' have threatened to harm the hostages. We have communications people standing by to pipe the actual broadcast here when they get back on the air. Unfortunately, the broadcast will also be live to most of the people in America. It's a tough situation."

A more dejected President gazed at the portrait of Alexander Hamilton that he had put in the Oval Office when he became President. He asked, "What's the Governor doing about the takeover?"

The Chief of Staff responded. "At this point, local police have sealed off the area around the radio station and are attempting to deal with the intruders. The Governor has provided back-up police and emergency services if needed. The state police have also sent their hostage negotiation team and it's being used. The rest of the state police have been put on alert for more back-up, if needed. Additional patrols by both state and local police have been increased around other radio and TV stations, plus keeping an eye on the broadcasting towers. We probably have until about noon today before we have to make some comments on this."

The President continued to gaze at the portrait of Hamilton. "I think I'd like to talk to Dr. Hancock. I think it would be helpful if I can say I talked to him since he was with me when we asked that these terrorist acts not take place."

The Chief of Staff replied again, "I'm sorry Mr. President, but we don't know where Dr. Hancock is right now. He and his wife left after his press conference four days ago and went to Rome. We obtained a hotel address from his son, but he's already checked out. Nobody is sure of where he went. We think it was to London because he made a comment to that effect when he was leaving. Nobody, including his son, is sure right now. Dr. Hancock told his son he would stay in touch, and we expect some communication from him today."

The President hunched forward in his chair. "Do we have anything substantive yet from the Surgeon General?"

The Chief of Staff shook his head from side to side.

"OK," continued the President. "Let's do this. Please get the Surgeon General here as early as possible this morning with a full progress report. Next, prepare a statement to the effect that I asked, and Dr. Hancock agreed, that we need time to review the research conclusions that he reported. During that time, I've reduced the number of transmissions from the federal government, and many other corporations also voluntarily agreed to reduce EM transmissions. We'll need to add whatever the Surgeon General has at this point. Third, we again strongly request that all Americans not panic and give us time to determine what course of action is best. We need to look strong and positive when we make this statement. Lastly, call the Governor and offer him whatever help we can be to him. Any questions?"

The room was silent.

"OK, good. Now what about other communications? Do we need to send some folks to the talk shows tonight and tomorrow?"

The Chief of Staff answered, "Yeah, we should. I think the Secretary of Defense would be good. He can cite the reduction that the military has made in their EM transmissions. I don't think we should send Dr. Gardner. He simply doesn't make a good enough impression on television. We could also send the Vice President. He's knowledgeable on the subject and makes an excellent impression."

"OK," said the President as he pushed back his chair and rose to leave. Everyone else left immediately and quickly went to do what was needed to comply with the President's decisions.

<u>Children's Hospital, Los Angeles, California</u>

Little Joey died at 9:15 on Sunday morning. His mother, grandfather and grandmother were with him at the end. The hospital chaplain conducted a short memorial service, and private internment arrangements were made in the Los Angeles area. Steve Parson wanted the child buried in the Washington area, but his wife and daughter thought it would be better if Joey were closer to his mother who intended to stay in California.

Attempts were made to tell Joey's father without success. One telegram and two messages on the telephone answering machine were unanswered. Only three people said goodbye to Joey.

CHAPTER SIXTEEN

Monday, December 12

<u>The White House</u>

The meeting in the situation room was attended only by "principles"; no aides or assistants were permitted. Around the table sat the President, the Secretary of Defense, Chairman of the Federal Communication Commission, and the Attorney General. Noticeably absent was the Vice-President.

The President spoke first. "Gentlemen, I'm sure you are all aware of the tower bombings last night in Mississippi and the radio station take-over in Missouri. The radio station has now been retaken but only after the Governor ordered it back on the air for fifteen minutes so that the protesters could broadcast their message. Their message was very persuasive and will get headlines in all of the national papers. The TV stations won't carry as much of it, but the American people seem to have switched to newspapers for their news since this EM scare became so real. It won't be long before it will be the only talk in America. References to the bombings and the loss of life in Kansas City make the message even more powerful. That alone requires that we act and that we act quickly and forcefully. However, there are other developments."

President Jenkins looked toward Surgeon General Gardner. After clearing his throat and shifting noticeably in his chair, a nervous Dr. Gardner started his report. "As each of you already know, the Centers for Disease Control did the leg work and set up the Blue Ribbon Committee to verify the claims of Dr. Hancock that exposure to electromagnetic rays causes cancer. Dr. Hancock spent years on his research, and Ohio State University put a team together to review the findings. That Ohio State team confirmed the findings, and the University is standing behind Dr. Hancock. Our committee has conducted an extensive audit of Dr. Hancock's findings and did some accelerated tests on laboratory animals by exposing them to large amounts of EM rays."

Dr. Gardner shifted in his seat again and once more cleared his throat before he started again. "Our findings as of midnight last night are that Dr. Hancock's research is correct. His findings are valid and legitimate. We believe it's solid science that exposure to EM rays causes cancer to specific parts of the body. We can't confirm these beliefs with 100% reliability, but we're in the 80% area. We need to do the experiment on larger animals though their lifetimes and do further tests on humans to reach a 100% conclusion. We've looked at humans in New York and Tierra del Fuego like Dr. Hancock did, and we found the exact findings he reported. We also verified the level of EM rays in both places to be valid. In a nutshell, Dr. Hancock is correct. EM rays cause cancer in human beings."

The room was shocked into silence momentarily and no words were spoken for almost a minute. Attorney General Crobin broke the silence. "That's the most dramatic statement I've ever heard. This is a turning point in the history of the United States. We need to be extremely careful and deliberate in how we handle our actions."

The President spoke next and addressed the Attorney General. "You're right, Ken. This moment will be in the history books, and our actions will be put under a microscope forever. Any suggestions?"

A more confident sounding Surgeon General spoke again. "There's no question that the financial repercussions and national defense aspects of this information are alarming. Notwithstanding that, the health of all Americans is overriding and must be our primary concern."

Attorney General Crobin spoke again. "This is a health issue but it's also a legal issue. Our constitution mandates that the government must provide for the common good. There can be little misinterpretation that protecting our citizens from being subject to a known killer is primary and certainly would be considered to be in the common good."

The President looked around the room for more comments but there were none. Most were in a state of awe at being present at such a major turning point in history. President Jenkins looked at the empty seat reserved for Vice President Solomon Lee, and briefly thought of how inappropriately named he was. The President considered Lee to be a political hack whose chief interests had always been looking good and his next conquest in the bedroom. He was good at both and considered extremely lucky considering the scrutiny that elected officials were subject to since the Clinton administration. President Jenkins then looked at his longtime friend and confidant, Secretary of Defense Samuel Ulysses Gray. They had been friends since high school and roommates at Ohio State.

Sam had gone into politics in Ohio and served as Lieutenant Governor before being elected to the Senate. His advice and support helped elect Harrison Jenkins President of the United States, and his wisdom was unexcelled.

The President spoke as he looked at Secretary Gray. "What I want to do is as follows, Sam. First, I want you to head a classified task force to examine what happens if we end all EM transmissions in America. Start your examination by ending all EM transmissions and then building back those you believe are essential and an acceptable risk to resume. I'd like the Attorney General and Chairman of the FCC to be vice-chairmen. I would also like you to include the Vice President, the Secretary of Commerce and the CIA Director. Regretfully for the task force, I want a preliminary report in 48 hours so I can go to the American people with a statement".

Secretary Gray cringed internally at the thought of working with the bubble-headed Vice President, who would work to make the panel a platform for self promotion, and the Director of Central Intelligence, who was generally considered to be the crankiest man in Government.

Before replying, Secretary Gray made a mental note to talk to the President about those two. "Mr. President, it's a difficult task you've assigned me, but given the urgency of the assignment I'll need to get to work on it immediately".

President Jenkins nodded. "OK, gentlemen, we know what we have to do. Let's get to work. Ahhh…Sam, could you stay another moment. I need to talk to you about a defense issue?"

After the room had cleared and the door closed, the President raised his hand with the palm toward the Secretary. "Don't say it Sam, I know! I know! Let me give you some helpful advice. The Vice-President is leaving shortly to give a speech in Atlanta tonight. Give him about an hour and then contact his office. When they tell you he's out of town, say thanks and start your meeting. Just about the same with the DCI. He's out of the country right now, and there's no way he can get back in time. Call that Admiral who's the deputy and order him to come to your meeting today. He's solid, but very loyal to the Director. If he balks, tell him I instructed it and he can call me if he wants…Uhhh, on second thought, never mind. I'll call him myself and direct him to attend your meeting and not discuss it with his boss until he returns. At the meeting you be sure to tell him that he, and only he, can represent the Intelligence Community. I'll deal with the DCI when he gripes to me. And between you and me, I'm getting a little prickly myself about all his bellyaching.

He's a good man, but starting to wear thin with the non-stop carping about everything he doesn't like".

A smiling Secretary of Defense started to back out of the room. "Thank you, Mr. President".

After everyone had left, the President returned to the Oval Office and asked his secretary to set up a meeting with the leadership of the Congress for later in the afternoon. He also asked that the Surgeon General be included. The day that began so nicely with music from the sixties suddenly deteriorated into an ugly mess that only seemed like it would get worse. He was reminded of a comment that he had heard when he was in the Coast Guard. A sailor from Georgia once described a very bad situation by saying, 'that dog will just get more fleas.'

<u>London, England</u>

After a full day of sightseeing, Bobbie and Charles had dinner at a small Indian restaurant several blocks from their hotel. Neither of them had much appreciation for Indian food, but they enjoyed the meal as a change of fare.

Bobbie's comment that, 'I've had about as much curry today as I'll need for the next year' summed up their meal. It was enjoyable, but they wouldn't be back. Unsure as to the wisdom of walking back to the hotel, they hailed a cab and rode the short distance to the hotel. When they picked up their key, they found a note from Jeff asking that they call when they returned. Charles noted it was 10:00 PM local time, so it was early afternoon in the States. He could return the call when he got to his room.

The call was placed easily and he found his son in his law office at a time when he didn't have any clients. After Charles reported all of their activities over the last two days he added how happy Jeff's mother was, and how much she enjoyed London. Then he asked why Jeff had called him.

"The reason I called, Dad, was that the White House called and was trying to get a hold of you. They wouldn't tell me what they wanted, but said it was important and would like you to call."

Charles actually stroked his chin and wondered what they wanted. "I've given them everything I have. What's the number I'm supposed to call and who do I ask for?"

Jeff quickly gave the number to his father and then added, "Ask for the President; he wants to talk to you."

Charles was surprised, but having met the President, he knew him to be a hands-on kind of guy. "OK, I'll call him," said Charles.

"Wait, wait, Dad," Jeff hurried to say. "There's more that you might be interested in. Nothing is confirmed, but all the papers are carrying stories that the Surgeon General's Blue Ribbon Committee has agreed with your findings and reported that to the President. Speculation is rampant that the government is going to close down all the radio and television stations, plus pull a lot of other permits for telephones, ham operators and stuff like that. There's almost a panic here on the television stations.

"The other rumor is that the Congress is going to hold hearings, and quickly. The newspapers speculate that it's a farce to delay any action and are alleging that Congress will bring in so-called experts who will testify that there's no danger. Things are really popping here. You're missing all the fun while you and mom are looking at the crown jewels and getting a daily portion of shepherd's pie." Jeff was laughing as he finished.

Charles was also chuckling when he replied, "Actually, the shepherd's pie is good, but what's interesting is something called 'Bubble & Squeak.' It looks like leftovers that were fried in a pan and it tastes like cardboard that they somehow got all of the taste out of!"

Both men laughed heartily.

"OK," said Charles. "I'll call the President and see what he wants."

"OK," replied Jeff.

"Thanks for the call. We're probably leaving here in a day or so. Don't give out my number, but you can reach me here at the London Elizabeth. You mother wants to have tea with the Queen tomorrow, but has agreed to settle for a trip to Stratford-on-Avon if the Queen is busy."

There was still time, so he placed a call to the White House.

Charles called the number that Jeff had given to him and was surprised when the President's personal secretary answered the telephone.

"Good morning, this is Dr. Charles Hancock and I'm returning a telephone call from the President."

"One minute, Dr. Hancock; I'll see if the President's available."

After a short wait there was a click and Harrison Jenkins was on the telephone. "Good afternoon, Charles, how's London?"

"London's fine, Mr. President. Bobbie and I are having a wonderful time."

"Good, good," replied the President. "Before we talk about something important, I wanted your opinion of the bowl situation this year."

Charles chuckled. "Mr. President, since we thumped Michigan this year, it's already a successful year. We should be going to the championship game, but I guess we missed out on that when Penn State upset us. But we're going to a bowl, so it's still a successful season. With a good passing game and a tough defense, we're one of the best teams in the country this year and ranked number 4. Are you going to the game?"

"Actually, I'm looking into it," replied the President. "Of course, I'll have to sit on the other side of the field for one half…. maybe you and Bobbie would like to go with us?"

Charles smiled. "That would be wonderful, Mr. President."

After a short pause, the President spoke again. "Charles, it's hard to believe there's something more important than Buckeye football, but there is. I recently had a meeting with the Surgeon General and we discussed your research. It seems that his Blue Ribbon Committee has confirmed your research. As usual, they won't confirm totally, but Dr. Gardner says they are in the eighty-plus range of accuracy and that's good enough for me. We're looking at what action to take next. I'm sure you can appreciate that any action we take will have a very significant impact on the country, and on the world. The broadcast industry will be hit the hardest, but they're not alone. There are many other industries and countless jobs at stake. Naturally, I want to do the best for the country and minimize any adverse impact my actions cause. I've also met with some senior members of Congress regarding a course of action. Many of them are in a very tight spot. It would seem that the best interests of the people would take priority over any other interests, but that's, regretfully, not how it works in Washington. The broadcast industry in particular has been making hefty contributions to campaigns over the years and it's payback time. Members of Congress have been getting visits by the top fat-cats over the past week refreshing memories of their past generosity and what the loss of jobs in the industry will do. They also remind members that they can support any candidate in the future that they think best serves their interests. Most importantly, they control the pictures and sound bites that are broadcast nightly on the news. They can show a candidate at his very best or picking his nose. These guys are a tough bunch of cookies and a very powerful and well-financed group. If I pull FCC permits, it will result in millions of dollars of financial losses. Any action we take will be very traumatic to our economy."

Charles interrupted, "I certainly understand that, Mr. President, and I hope and pray that you find the right solution."

The President continued, "One of the suggestions that the Congress offered was that hearings be held on this issue. They want to sensitize the American public to the importance of this situation and gain their acceptance of the clearly emerging solutions. For that reason I think it's a good idea. As you can imagine it has a down side, also. It could be used to convince the American people that there isn't a problem that requires turning off the TV and radio stations. I really don't have much choice except to agree to the hearing. If I don't agree the Congress will point to me as the problem, and it will only further delay things. Also, I really can't stop the hearing. Congress can do whatever it pleases without my approval. By agreeing, I can keep the pressure on to move the hearing quickly and keep the focus on their efforts. So, that's the status of what's going on in Washington on your research today. In connection with these hearings, I expect that you'll be invited to testify before Congress, and it will probably happen very quickly."

"I'm ready to testify now, Mr. President," replied Charles. "If there's an error in my work, we need to know it. However, as I believe, and as all reliable scientists so far have found, there's no error."

"I think you're right, Charles, and I appreciate your attitude and cooperation in this matter," replied President Jenkins. "However, there is one other part of this you should be aware of. Before I say this, I need your assurance that this call is not being recorded."

"It's not as far as I know, Mr. President. I'm in my room at the hotel and I dialed the call directly myself."

"Good," continued the President. "One thing about the hearings is that there's a reliable expectation that everyone isn't interested in supporting you. Some Senators have a strong interest in supporting the broadcast industry, and you can expect strong efforts to discredit or cast doubt on your work. Senator Trevor Mitchell is heading the inquiry, and the broadcast people have funded him very generously over the years. He and other Senators also have large numbers of broadcast industry jobs in their districts that will be lost if FCC broadcasting permits are pulled."

Charles replied in a serious voice, "I understand that, Mr. President. But, I can assure you that no respectable scientist will testify that what I've done is wrong, or that I've reached false conclusions. They have too much invested in their professional reputations to be part of some tawdry affair like this. There will probably be a couple of lightweights available but even they won't be able to refute my work. All they'll be able to do will be to cast doubt on my work. That won't work...you need hard science and they don't have it. The American people are too smart, and the newspapers will show them for what they really are. Now, having said that, I want you to be assured that I won't take any of this lightly. I'll be fully prepared. After my appearance and phone call to the Burlington show, I think everyone knows me well. I'll be OK."

The President continued, "I'm not worried, Charles, but there's a little more. Washington is a barracuda town. It tears apart anything that it doesn't like. You can also expect in-depth investigations into you and your family. If there is a skeleton in your closet, you can expect it to be found."

"That's already started, Mr. President," replied Charles. "I'm sure you know about the fabrications regarding my affair with a southern belle and my trading grades for sexual favors. It was all nothing but pure lies. I've learned that suspicious investigators are interviewing people I knew over thirty years ago. I had a friend once in law enforcement that said he could have anyone arrested and charged with a crime. That may be true, but I'm not worried. I've been dedicating my life to medicine and prevention of disease for many years. That dedication and accomplishment will overshadow anything that's alleged from my past. Bobbie and I discussed this and we're prepared for whatever happens. I appreciate your words of caution."

The President wondered why Charles mentioned being arrested and charged with a crime but assumed it was a figure of speech. "Thanks for your help. I'm sure I'll be talking to you again. Goodbye, Charles."

"Goodbye, Mr. President."

CHAPTER SEVENTEEN

Wednesday, December 14

Washington, D.C.

Senator Trevor Mitchell got to be a senior Senator because he knew when to look at things and most importantly, when not to look. His ample campaign finances always looked clean, and he never spent any time checking them out. It had worked for three campaigns and had earned him eighteen years in the Senate. The contributors always came around when they needed something, and it was easy for Senator Mitchell to help out his friends. The recent visits from representatives of the major broadcasting networks and the Director for the Council of Broadcasters were very clear about their need for help. They gently but clearly reminded him of all the generous financial support they had provided, and how they had always made him look good when they covered his voting record and campaigns. They were adamant about action on the question of EM rays and would not take 'no' for an answer. This issue was their only item of interest, and they were calling in all the IOUs they had built up over the years. Trevor was under more pressure than ever before and hoped his meeting with representatives of those organizations this morning would assuage some of their concerns.

As they sat down in the private dining room of a local hotel in Washington, Trevor began his remarks. "I had a late night meeting yesterday with the Senate majority leader. He had met with the President earlier in the day and the President was seeking advice. It seems that the test the government has run on the electromagnetic wave supports the findings of Dr. Hancock – the EM rays cause cancer in human beings. The results are not 100% according to the majority leader, but they're in the 80% range. The President has already reduced the amount of EMs that are being put into the atmosphere by the government and now he's planning to seriously curtail the amount of EMs that are generated by commercial organizations. In fact, he's considering pulling all FCC permits!"

A glove across the cheek couldn't have caused more shock on everyone's face. Nobody replied immediately.

Senator Mitchell finally answered, "Considering that, the President is faced with a situation of pulling the FCC broadcasting permits or letting the American people be exposed to EM rays that cause cancer, he has very limited options. The majority leader saw none. I suggested that the congress could hold hearings with members of the Senate and House of Representatives and elicit other comments. It's about the only opportunity that's available. The majority leader has asked me to chair those joint hearings, but we have very little time. The President can act without Congress on this matter, but it's considered unlikely that he will if the Congress can guarantee speedy hearings. We'll have to get busy and develop a strategy, or all of the television, radio and telephone FCC licenses could be pulled within the next two weeks. If you're to save your industry, you need to provide a case that is supportable and believable by the American people. If you can't do that, the broadcast tickets will be pulled."

Acting for the broadcasting industry, John Mahoney spoke first. "I believe we can provide you and your committee with enough facts and data to show that the EM rays are not harmful and that licenses shouldn't be pulled. We have experts that will testify that their research doesn't support the findings of Dr. Hancock. Also, any conclusions on his findings must be verified in detail, which will take years.

"We also believe that Dr. Hancock is suspect, but we don't have the details yet. Possibly the committee could be helpful. I assume you would call Dr. Hancock if you held hearings?"

Senator Mitchell nodded.

There were other comments from the major broadcasting companies, and it was agreed that full background papers, recommended questions and specific areas to examine would be provided to Senator Mitchell as quickly as possible. Senator Mitchell agreed to hold the hearings as late as possible so that a defense could be mounted. More questions and answers followed, but the deal had been cut. Each participant went their own way to hold up their end of this bargain of the devil.

London, England

Charles and Bobbie had risen early and were enjoying the famed 'English breakfast' in the small dining room of the London Elizabeth

Hotel. After a third cup of coffee, Charles was preparing for a day of sightseeing around downtown London.

Washington, D.C.

The President invited the congressional leaders to the Oval Office, and the White House kitchen provided coffee and chocolate chip cookies for refreshments.

After everyone was seated, the President began, "I want to start by thanking each of you for being available on such short notice. What I have to talk about is a very serious situation for our country, and I hope that we can work on it in a bipartisan way – it's truly an issue that's unrelated to party or ideology. It's an issue that's related to money, and that could be a factor. I ask that you keep the bigger issue in mind when considering your options."

The Congressmen seemed confused. "You're all aware of the situation with the impact of electromagnetic rays on the human body. Dr. Hancock published his article and concluded that those EM rays cause cancer. There's been no credible evidence, or any evidence at all, refuting Dr. Hancock's conclusions. The Surgeon General and the Blue Ribbon Committee have done a review of Dr. Hancock's work, and they've concluded that Dr. Hancock is correct. EM rays cause cancer."

The members were stunned and sat in silence.

"As you know," the President continued, "I've reduced EM transmissions somewhat in the government, but it's really only been a dent in what needs to be done. Much more is mandated. We can't continue to kill our citizens! We must act! You all know that any action we take will cause a storm of protest because it will affect many of our vital industries, most noticeably commercial television and radio. We can also expect residual economic fallout in the radio and television manufacturing industry, as well as the automobile industry. Whatever action we take will be extremely unpopular, but we must act."

None of the assembled political leaders ventured a comment.

The President continued, "The natural course of action is to withdraw all FCC broadcasting licenses from the radio and television stations in America. We would still have cable TV and, undoubtedly, an increase in the floundering cable radio industry. Nevertheless, it will be traumatic for the country and politically difficult. I'm soliciting your comments and advice about how to handle this situation.

108

"The leadership of the Congress has commented that they believe congressional hearings are appropriate and have even identified Senator Trevor Mitchell as the chairman. That hasn't been announced, but I'd also like your thoughts on that issue. I don't need an answer right now; late afternoon tomorrow will be fine."

Substantial discussion continued for another 45 minutes, with each of the Congressmen agreeing with the President's assessment of the problem.

The President concluded the meeting by again asking cach of the legislators to submit their comments in writing or by a telephone call sometime tomorrow.

CHAPTER EIGHTEEN

Thursday, December 15

Washington, D.C.

THE WASHINGTON POST
CONGRESS TO HOLD HEARINGS ON DANGER OF
ELECTROMAGNETIC RAYS

In a rare bipartisan move, the President and the leaders of both parties in Congress announced today that hearings will be held in two weeks concerning the danger of electromagnetic rays (EM) in the atmosphere. Flanked by majority and minority leaders of the Senate and the House of Representatives, President Jenkins announced at a press conference today that a committee of the Congress would be formed to hold hearings. Senator Trevor Mitchell of New York will chair the committee. The committee will be composed of eight members of the House of Representatives and four Senators, including the Chairman. The hearings are expected to take one or two weeks and the panel is charged to write a public report outlining their findings.

Dr. Charles Hancock of Ohio State University first raised the dangers of electromagnetic rays when he published findings that showed that the EM rays cause cancer in human beings.

In his paper titled 'Radical Cancer Prevention,' Dr. Hancock discussed the effects of EM rays on various experimental animals when they were exposed to the rays and the absence of effects when they were not exposed to the rays. He found significant differences, primarily increased cancer incidents in those animals that were exposed to the same amount of EM rays that human beings are exposed to. His research was duplicated by other scientists in Australia and London and reportedly has been confirmed by the Blue Ribbon Committee appointed by the President. No formal announcement has been made by the President's committee to date.

Controversy has been swirling since Dr. Hancock's paper was rejected by the American Medical Association's Journal of Medicine and initially leaked by a weekly tabloid, the 'Real News'. While the AMA has yet to publish anything on this subject, they have acknowledged the importance of Dr. Hancock's work and will send a representative to the hearings.

Groups contending that there's insufficient evidence to support the findings of Dr. Hancock have indicated that they look forward to the hearings. Director and spokesman for the Council of Broadcasters, John Mahoney, said, "I look forward to a full airing of all facts regarding this subject. The evidence of harm to humans is insufficient to warrant any action at this time. Quite simply, we don't believe that the information developed to date supports the conclusion that EMs cause cancer."

Dr. Hancock is currently out of the country on vacation and could not be reached for comment. His son and spokesman, Jeff, was quoted as saying that his father was aware of the hearing and looks forward to presenting the results of his work to the Congressional committee if invited to attend.

Senator Mitchell indicated that he expected Dr. Hancock to be the first of many witnesses scheduled to testify. Other witnesses include numerous cancer specialists and researchers. When asked if the Surgeon General would testify, Senator Mitchell indicated that the final witness list had not yet been approved.

This is the first time that a joint effort by the Congress supported by the President has occurred. Both sides are lauding the bipartisan efforts of all concerned and plan to have a comprehensive report for the American public.

Commercial television stations and C-SPAN have not indicated if they'll carry the hearing live.

For more on this story, see page three which has the names of expected members of the committee, dates for the hearings and possible witnesses.

The Ritz Carlton Hotel, Washington D.C.

The "undertakers" were having another meeting to review the progress to date. The investigators in Columbus had sent a preliminary report and reported that they found absolutely nothing.

Both of the Hancock children were squeaky clean.

Jeff, the lawyer, was a rising and respected member of the profession. He specialized primarily in estate law and had little controversy surrounding his work. He volunteered to represent indigent criminal defendants and had a reputation for working hard to assure that they got a fair trial. He also did volunteer work with his church and was an active member of the Ohio State Alumni Association.

Harold was the entrepreneur in the family. After graduation from Ohio State, he went to work for a security firm in Columbus. In a short time, he was dissatisfied with the firm and the way they did business. He resigned and opened his own firm and has achieved a notable amount of recognition. A secret investigation last year by the Columbus Dispatch contacted several local security firms for assistance and published the results. Harold's firm was found to be the most honest and most forthright by the newspaper. After that investigation and report in the newspaper, business boomed and Harold had to hire more employees.

Bobbie's background was also crystal clear. She grew up in small town and did all the things that little girls dream of. She was pretty, had lots of dates and was a cheerleader in high school. Going to Ohio State was her dream, which only got better when she met Charles Hancock. After their first meeting, she went home and told her roommate that she had met the man she was going to marry. She was right and the marriage was one from the story books. More digging could be done in Ohio, but the investigators opined that their work would be futile. There was simply nothing to find.

The investigators in Miami also provided disappointing results. The Ocean Ranch Hotel had been razed years ago, and they couldn't find anybody who could remember anything of any substance. They hadn't canvassed the neighborhood to talk to every single resident, and would need more help if that action were required.

The past owners had been contacted, but during the time that Charles and Vonda were there, the hotel had been in receivership. Both receivers had passed away and left nothing about the short period they were in charge.

Two employees were located, but they both reported that there were so many guests and residents over the years that they had no specific recall of Charles and Vonda. They further indicated that if there been something suspicious going on, they would have known about it. The hotel had its share of hustlers, con men and ne'er-do-wells that they remembered. One employee recounted a story about a pool hustler that would shoot eight-ball pool for fifty dollars a game and shoot with only one hand. There was also the alleged Mafia hit man that lived in the hotel for over a year. Nobody had any recall of a specific young kid and his girlfriend who lived there for a year.

The "digger" was naturally very disappointed in the results. "Our production of information to date is paltry. We need to get some results. I've decided to pull the investigators out of Columbus and send them to Miami. We have two weeks to get something on that year Charles spent in Miami. We don't have much time. If we don't have something when the hearings start, we'll have wasted a lot of money and we won't be much help to discredit these findings."

"OK?"

Nobody replied.

"Well, that's how it is. So, for now, help yourselves to the snacks provided by the American broadcasting industry and hope that they'll still be providing these goodies, and our paychecks, this time next month."

Council of Broadcasters, Washington D.C.

The mood was grim around the table. With the announced hearings, most broadcast journalists saw an uphill fight to convince the American people that there wasn't a danger from the EMs. The President believed it as well as the Blue Ribbon Committee at the Centers for Disease Control. Finding a respected physician or scientist to dispute the results would be almost impossible. Mounting an offense against the report would be extremely difficult. The facts simply weren't there; and the credible experts weren't available. They all had seen the Barry Burlington talk shows where the effort was made to discredit Dr. Hancock and the dreadful results of those efforts.

The public's opposition to the broadcasts continued to grow. Americans all over the States were in somewhat of a dilemma. They wanted to keep their TV, radio and cell phones, but they didn't want to get cancer. When the citizens balanced everything, ending the broadcasts was the most acceptable solution and they were expected to reluctantly agree.

What was available to the broadcasters was the law. All lawyers know the old saying, "When the facts support your case, argue the facts. When the facts don't support your case, argue the law."

John Mahoney believed he had a decent-to-good case on the facts. He could produce a number of cancer physicians to testify that the results were too preliminary and unverified in a detailed clinical and scientific sense. He had enough doctors available to say that, based on their experience, they couldn't agree with the results. Of course, they would not testify that they disagreed either. Unfortunately, they might also testify that they had seen similar autopsy results that had been reported by Charles in his research.

Mahoney thought he had a better case on the law based on the freedom of the press clause contained in the first amendment to the Constitution. There was considerable research done by the staff and Mahoney believed a serious and credible offense could be made that if the government withdrew all FCC permits, it was a complete repudiation of the Constitution. There were, of course, numerous problems. First and foremost was the Supreme Court finding that yelling fire in a theater, if there was no fire, was not constitutionally-protected free speech. This case had ominous comparisons to that case. The case was also easy to understand, which meant the average citizen could easily understand both sides of the argument and easily side with the protection of themselves from something that would give them cancer.

There were also many more academic arguments. The Bill of Rights says that the government will not restrict free speech. It doesn't say that the government has to provide a vehicle for that free speech to be transmitted. The government's only obligation is not to prohibit free speech. Even with the words of the constitution, there are limits and the government can restrict speech. The fire in the theater comment is one along with any comments that cause panic or fear, or release restricted and classified information. Another problem was the context of the Bill of Rights. It was written at a time when there was only the written press. Later cases extended coverage to the broadcast press, but there was no a guarantee that the justices would see it that same way again. The lawyers will contend that over the last hundred years the broadcast press had attained the same legitimacy as the written press and had to be protected. They could point out that the majority of Americans got their news each day from the TV, not the newspaper. While they candidly didn't expect this argument to be successful, it would confuse the action and be another hurdle for the opposition to overcome.

If the government decided to revoke broadcasting licenses, the broadcast industry would have to immediately get a restraining order to prevent that from happening until they could get into court. The proper way would be to go to a lower court and seek a Temporary Restraining Order (TRO). This would run the risk of the court not ruling in their favor and they'd have to appeal. It was also likely that any lower court would decline to hear the case since it had national impact or would rule and have their decision affect only the jurisdiction of the court. Time was very short and the legal system worked slowly. The Broadcasters Council needed a TRO quickly. Also, going to lower courts would be seen by everyone involved as a delay tactic and could hurt them in the long run. It was John Mahoney's recommendation that the request for a temporary restraining order be submitted directly to the Supreme Court.

Mahoney had the papers ready to submit directly to the Supreme Court if the government decided to withdraw FCC permits. He would ask for an immediate temporary restraining order and ask for a speedy trial on the merits of the case. He actually didn't want a speedy trial or any trial at all. If the case languished in some law clerk's in-basket for the next twenty years, Mahoney would be happy. However, to get a restraining order, you must ask for a speedy trial.

Mahoney had been in touch with administrators at the court and convinced them that the case had all of the ingredients for immediate Supreme Court involvement. It was clearly a national emergency situation which affected Americans in every state in the union. It was also very clearly a constitutional issue since the essence of the broadcasters defense was the Bill of Rights. Mahoney was very confident the Supreme Court would approve a temporary restraining order and then order a speedy trial.

Fort Valley, Georgia

Vonda couldn't decide if she was getting paranoid or going crazy. She felt that she was being followed. While it wasn't possible to specify who was following her, it seemed that every time she went anyplace there was someone watching. Once when she went to the Peach Mall in nearby Byron, Georgia, she saw a man pull into the parking lot after her and not leave his car. When she drove out, the man stayed in the parking lot, but another suspicious car seemed to follow her until she returned to the orchard.

She also thought her telephone calls were being monitored. She stopped using the cordless phone except for routine business. Personal calls and any discussions regarding her schedule were taken on the corded phone in the bedroom and she spoke very little.

Once, just to satisfy herself, she left the house at 11 p.m. and headed toward Warner Robins, Georgia on State Road 96. She had not been away from the house more than 10 minutes when a car was behind her. She drove over the interstate overpass and slowed. The car didn't pass until she abruptly pulled into the parking lot of the new high school. The car kept going. She immediately pulled out and sped toward home. When she passed the curve in the road, she pulled into the entrance of the new housing development and turned off her lights. Minutes later the same car that had passed her while she was parked in the high school parking lot passed again. She knew she was being followed now! It was a mystery that was never solved. Vonda never found out who it was, or why anyone was following her.

Miami, Florida

Ray Echeveria had lived in the same apartment on SW 4th Street since he left Castro's Cuba in 1961. The first job he had in America was as night auditor in the Ocean Ranch Hotel. When it finally closed and was razed, he found work at the El Hambra hotel where he worked until retirement. With the money he invested from his jobs, his Social Security check, and the untaxed money he received from the Cuban government over the years, he had a nice retirement. He still lived just one block from the old Ocean Ranch Hotel and walked or took the bus everywhere he went. He had no family anymore and passed the days fishing in the bay.

One evening several months earlier, Ray had a young visitor who introduced himself as Roberto Alvarez. Alvarez indicated that he was from the Cuban government and that a Mr. Palance had asked him to visit. Ray shuddered imperceptibly, and invited him in for coffee. What else could he do? Minutes later Ray Echeveria was dead from a knife in the chest. Two days later the neighbors knocked on his door to see if he was s OK. When they didn't get a reply they called police who found the body. The yellow police tape was still around the apartment when one of the "undertaker" investigators came down the street knocking on every door under the guise of a survey. When he saw the police, the investigator kept going and didn't return for another week. Ray Echeveria had known Charles Hancock well and knew all about what he was doing while living in the Ocean Ranch Hotel. Ray had a direct hand in making the arrangement. He had been following the developments regarding the EM rays very carefully. Apparently Mr. Palance was also following developments closely. For reasons that Ray Echeveria didn't understand, Roberto Alvarez had been given what the Cubans called a "terminal assignment." He completed that assignment in Ray Echeveria's apartment that night and assured that a long kept secret would stay that way.

Wheeling, West Virginia

The transmitter on Radio Hill was an obvious and easy target. Many in this riverfront town wondered why it hadn't been destroyed by some of the local groups that were demonstrating every weekend.

The concern about the transmitter tower ended about eleven o'clock in the evening. Apparently, the perpetrators wanted a grand show and had invested a little more money than necessary. They used fireworks and extra dynamite to set off three explosions instead of the necessary two. The first was a fireworks display that got the attention of local residents. While everyone was watching to see what all the excitement was about, there was another fireworks display that sent even more pyrotechnics into the air. The final act was three simultaneous explosions filled with lots of fire and smoke. The tower slowly tipped and then collapsed into a pile of twisted metal. The spectators cheered from their porches. It was the fourth tower destroyed in America that day.

Number 10 Downing Street, London, England

'Winston Churchill' Fletcher never expected to be elected to any public office, precisely because of his name. He believed it would be a handicap because of the fond memories the British people had for his namesake. He was surprised when he ran for his first public office and was elected. He asked around and found that the name actually attracted some voters and gave him "name-recognition," which is so necessary to be elected. After his first win he worked hard to represent his constituents and established a good name for himself as a responsive and hardworking representative. He then decided to campaign for the House of Commons and found that his name and his reputation made a nice combination; and he had been elected to his first term over ten years ago. He worked hard to represent his district and continued to build a reputation for himself. When his party obtained the majority of delegates in the House of Commons, he campaigned for the post of Prime Minister and won! It was one of those elections that surprised everyone. He had settled into reasonable comfort in the PM's house and thought he had a pretty good handle on governing the United Kingdom. His popularity with the ordinary citizen was healthy, and he had not suffered any of the scandals that seemed to have plagued politicians worldwide for the past ten years.

His circle of advisors had been hastily called to his residence for an emergency meeting.

Director of Scotland Yard, George Gilbert, was outlining developments. "It seems that it was more than just a few lads having a little fun. The first incident was in Mercyside on Old Daresbury Road. The radio transmitter tower was dynamited earlier today in broad daylight. That's a very congested area and the tower fell on some small cottages killing an elderly woman.

In Kent, there were two more bombings and both towers fell. Nobody was hurt in either of those incidents.

"Tomorrow the UK version of the American Caseys, will be marching in downtown London with a final rally at Trafalgar Square." Estimates run as high as thirty thousand people may show up and walk past Buckingham Palace on their way to Trafalgar Square. The London Police are on high alert; no trouble is expected, but we can never be sure. It's getting very serious. The newspapers are constantly running stories on the dangers of the electromagnetic rays, and everyone across the country is scared."

Prime Minister Fletcher looked at the other assembled advisors to see if any of them had anything to say. Several of the advisors made comments, but they were a repeat of the rhetoric made by the advisors to President Jenkins when he reviewed the situation. There was nothing that hadn't been said already in America and probably every other capital in the world.

The Prime Minister looked at the Scotland Yard director again. "Anything else, Mr. Gilbert?"

"Yes sir, there is. I've been in touch with my counterparts in Germany, Italy, Spain, and Belgium, plus representatives from Interpol. All report that there is unrest in each of their countries. You know that the French are always having demonstrations by farmers who drive their farm vehicles to town and block traffic. This time it's the opposite. They're getting reports of serious unrest in the city and are expecting a massive demonstration by Parisians sometime in the next week. The Germans have had some small demonstrations in Berlin, and they've also had several tower bombings. Even the government of the Netherlands is getting concerned because demonstrations are planned in Amsterdam within the week. That's a switch...the Dutch rarely worry about anything."

Prime Minister Fletcher leaned back in his chair and looked relaxed. He wasn't, and his advisors knew it. Finally, he spoke, "I'm going to call President Jenkins and see what the Americans are going to do about all this. Since they started it, maybe they have some thoughts about how to rectify it before we have problems that will make some of those soccer riots look like nursery playtime. I think we'll have to call an emergency session of the House of Commons and present a plan. Let's assume that the research by that American doctor is correct and plan accordingly. My guess is that we're going to have to turn off the BBC, all the tellies and the radio stations. This is what the Americans call a "no-win" situation. Whatever we do will cause problems, but we must act. If these EM rays are causing cancer, we need to stop them. And we need to pressure the Americans to clean up their part of it. After all, those satellites in space that are beaming down EM rays every day are theirs. We can only do so much here. I'll discuss that with President Jenkins when I talk to him later. Thank you for coming."

CHAPTER NINETEEN

Tuesday, January 3

Columbus, Ohio

The family meeting had been underway for about an hour, and everyone had reported what had happened to them.

Charles was trying to sort out details and tried to sum up. "So," he started slowly, "it seems that we've been targets of some sinister group for the last month or so. Bobbie and I have been the real focus of the activity, especially over the past two weeks. Friends, and strangers in some cases, have told us that they've been contacted about us. We don't know what they found, but it has to be very little and most likely not true. People have been to Bobbie's high school looking for anything they could find, and I've had the same snooping in my background. Harold and Jeff have had inquiries regarding their business practices that were likewise fruitless. But the last two weeks have been extremely difficult for me. I'm trying to keep up my schedule and meet my responsibilities at the University. Incredibly, the Congress has been the biggest problem." Charles shook his head in disbelief.

"I was advised that the Committee Chairman, Senator Mitchell, is in the hip pocket of the broadcasting industry and intent on blocking anything that will harm the industry. As Chairman of the committee, he has a lot to say about what happens. However, he still has to have substance to work with. He's digging into the meat of my research and I also believe he's one of the people digging into our lives. I've been badgered daily with increasing demands from the committee staff for all kinds of information. Originally, I tried to be helpful, but their demands never stopped. I'd get hourly calls for explanations of what I've already sent or they'd ask for more data.

"Then there was an incident that changed everything. When I was in med school I co-authored a paper with two other students. The paper earned an "A" for each of us and got published in the University medical journal. When it was published, the name of one student was omitted. It really didn't matter much and the student thought it was funny. Well, I was talking to a Senate staffer about some articles I had published; and I mentioned this little incident and the student's name. As it turns out, the guy did very well in life and went into semiretirement several years ago.

He moved to Mexico Beach, Florida, and is the only doctor in this small fishing village on the Florida Panhandle. He only treats the local residents, which takes a few hours each week. He also donates time to the local government when they have questions on medical issues. So, he's well known in the town. The day after I mentioned that his name was left off of the published article, my friend had a visit at his home from somebody calling himself an investigator.

When the investigator was somewhat vague about who he represented, my friend said he was going to call the police. The investigator became very nervous and indicated there was no need to do that. My friend insisted and the investigator got in his car and left.

Now, does anyone here think that an investigator for a Senate committee is afraid to talk to a police officer? If he were on legitimate Senate business, he would be glad to talk to the local police. Immediately after that he called me, and we laughed about the paper that he didn't get credit for and he told me how wonderful Mexico Beach was. He invited us to visit anytime and guaranteed the shrimp would be only one hour out of the water when they were served to us.

"Then he told me about the investigator. I was irked and called Senator Mitchell. After getting a lot of runaround by his staff, I was very emphatic that unless I talked to the Senator in the next hour he could read the newspaper to see what I wanted to talk to him about. Thirty minutes later I got a call back from a not-so-friendly Senator.

I asked him about this incident, and he denied they were doing any investigation like that. I asked him how it could be possible that I mention a friend to his staff that I've had nothing to do with for the past twenty-five years, and the very next day he gets a visit from someone who wants to know about me. An investigator, I reminded Senator Mitchell who ran away rather than talk to the police.

Mitchell then dismissed my comments and said I was imagining things. Since I wasn't in a good mood with him anyway, I told him that maybe his staff could start to imagine any further information they might need from me. It seems that giving information to them is the same as putting it on the front page of The Washington Post. He said he didn't think that was funny, and I told him I wasn't trying to be funny."

Charles had worked himself up and was clearly ticked off at Senator Mitchell.

"He reminded me that I was scheduled to testify before his committee in two days. I told him that I considered the appearance before his committee to be an invitation and I'd handle it like any other invitation. Then I hung up before he could reply."

Jeff was smiling. He enjoyed the way his father was handling the Senator.

"So," continued Charles. "I was immediately issued a subpoena to testify. It will be interesting to see how Mitchell explains why he had to subpoena me to testify. I'm sure he'll say its standard procedure, but he knows I'll get my chance to reply to the press, and in front of his committee, which will be well covered by the media. Ultimately, I think their real agenda is to discredit my work and me. I intend to appear, but I hope they've reformed their ways before I get there. From the treatment I've gotten from those folks, you would think I was Charles Manson instead of Charles Hancock. I'm really irritated!"

Bobbie got up to get everyone more coffee and the room was silent.

"OK," said Jeff. "In two days they either act like professionals or they can pursue their petty agendas at their own peril. Mom's going to Washington and so am I. How about you, Hal? Are you planning to go?"

"Absolutely," smiled the youngest son. "I wouldn't miss all of this for anything."

Bobbie interrupted with several questions. "How are we getting there? Do we have reservations yet? Where are we are staying?"

Jeff answered the last question, "Yes, we have reservations at the Ritz Carlton again, but I made them in the corporate name of Harold's company so that all the gremlins in Washington wouldn't call or come to the hotel when we got there."

Charles had calmed down and was sipping his coffee. "One more thing. The subpoena tells me to show up at the Senate Office Building, but it doesn't tell me where to report. I think I may have a little surprise for the snooty Senator Mitchell when I get there the day after tomorrow." Charles then detailed his plan.

After a short pause, Charles started again. "I'm not usually this irritable, but I'm really irked at those birds. I'm the guy that does the research to show that we are all being killed by the electromagnetic rays, and this Mitchell character acts like I'm carrying the black plague. OK,

I've gotten it all out of my system. Anyone want to get skunked in a game of scrabble?"

<u>The White House</u>

The President was meeting with Surgeon General Ralph Gardner and Federal Communications Commission Chairman Kevin Stoneman.

"From what I've heard, Mr. President," remarked Dr. Gardner, "Senator Mitchell has gone out of his way to antagonize Dr. Hancock. He's now even sent him a subpoena requiring him to testify. I don't understand why there should be such discord there. Charles Hancock is an easy man to get along with and very cooperative in everything we've asked of him."

The President was frowning. "Unfortunately, Trevor Mitchell is the problem. He's so heavily in debt to the broadcasting industry and the unions that he has little objectivity in these hearings. I don't think he's really looking for the truth. He's managed to delay the hearing past the Christmas holidays, but his time has now run out. He's looking hard to find a way to allow the networks and radio stations to stay on the air. His treatment of Charles Hancock seems to point to that conclusion. Incidentally, have any of you heard from him recently?"

Heads shook sideways and finally the Surgeon General answered, "The word is that he's so upset with Mitchell that he refers all inquiries to his attorney and no phone calls are returned. There's even some speculation that he will ignore the subpoena and not show up for the hearing."

"Well, that could be very interesting," remarked the President. "I've found Charles Hancock to be a very solid citizen and guys like him aren't grandstanders. Charles will show up and be ready to stand his ground. You saw what he did to Barry Burlington when he was a guest on that talk show. Burlington is still sore from the drubbing he got. Mitchell will be a little better prepared, but he better watch himself. A lot of Americans will be watching, and they're all interested in their health. If Mitchell tries to cuff around one of the guys in the white hats, he may get more than a taste of his own medicine. I don't know about you guys, but I plan to watch as much of the hearings as possible. I assume they're being televised. Do we know who else Mitchell has lined up to testify?"

The Surgeon General was a little uncomfortable with his answer. "Actually, I don't know very much about who he plans to call. There are few reputable professionals who are willing to risk their reputation on this one. The evidence is convincing and anyone who sees a different side of this issue better have something that hasn't been discovered yet. I know, but can't prove, that the Council of Broadcasters has been working with Mitchell, but I don't think they've been much help. The American Medical Association's also a player in all this. But they have to be very careful. They don't want to come across to the American people and the Congress as being in favor of illness and cancer. However, a cure for cancer will cause a lot of patients to have no need to see their doctors. After dorking up the initial article by not publishing it, they're trying not to lose any more ground. So, it's going to be an interesting show in the Congress in a couple of days, and everyone will be tuned in."

When the President got to his feet, it was the signal for the others to rise and be prepared to leave.

"OK," said the President as he shuffled toward the door of the Oval Office. "Thanks for coming by, and we'll see what happens in the next week. It will be interesting." The four men shook hands, and the President headed for the living quarters to call his daughter in Georgia.

CHAPTER TWENTY

Wednesday, January 4

Washington, D.C.

The trip from Ohio to Washington was largely uneventful. The van that Bobbie had insisted on renting had proven its worth during the trip with a comfortable ride and lots of luggage room. After pulling up at the Ritz Carlton, Charles helped Bobbie out and then helped the boys get the luggage out and transfer it to the bellboys. When the luggage had been moved, Charles turned over the keys to the valet who drove off to park the van. Charles led the way inside and Bobbie and Charles checked into the suite. Jeff and Hal each had his own room. An hour later they met for dinner and enjoyed the Ritz's cuisine and service. It was wonderful. Charles, feeling somewhat paranoid, insisted on a corner table, and they discussed their plans for the next day. When they finished dinner, Charles was smiling, as was everyone. They were all looking forward to the big day with Congress.

Havana, Cuba

Dr. Raul Gonzales was the best internist in Cuba. He had been trained in Cuba with follow-on training in London, Paris and Moscow. As the director of El Cimeq, he had a generous budget, by Cuban Government standards, the best medical equipment and best-trained staff in the country. His assistant for the past nine years was Dr. Manual Rodriguez, who was generally acknowledged as the second best internist in Cuba. They were the one-two punch in the most prestigious medical facility in Cuba. The El Cimeq was known throughout Cuba as the facility where Fidel Castro and his family, friends, and high-ranking guests received medical care. It was not a surprise that it was first class. While it had the best facilities in Cuba, Dr. Gonzales knew that it wasn't comparable to the top-of-the-line medical facilities in other parts of the world. The equipment was clean and shiny and the staff looked like the best available. It was illusionary. A medical professional would know that much of the equipment was out-of-date and inadequate for treating the leader of Cuba. Of course, the doctors had asked repeatedly for upgraded equipment, but their requests had always been turned down. The Budget Director needed to make ends meet and some of the extravagant medical prices made the equipment simply too expensive. What information had been given to Castro was unknown and never brought up for discussion.

The only patient to the clinic today would be Pablo Palance, the most secretive and reportedly the cruelest assistant to Castro. His name is whispered when spoken and it strikes fear in the country. He was at Castro's side from the beginning and had been a faithful and reliable advisor over the years. He reportedly did all the dirty work that even Castro didn't want to be associated with. He could be extremely charming when necessary and very diabolical and merciless when necessary. Some of the whispers were that even Castro was afraid of him. If true, it wouldn't be a surprise. Everyone else was afraid of Pablo Palance.

There was a standard procedure for every patient that was treated at the clinic. Dr. Gonzales would personally call Castro and advise him of the medical problem and the treatment. Pablo Palance was the only exception to that standard procedure. He advised Dr. Gonzales after the first visit that "he would inform Fidel" personally and Dr. Gonzales had complied with that instruction.

Once, when Castro was at the clinic, he commented that he knew that Pablo had also been treated at the clinic, but he never asked why he had not been called. Dr. Gonzales assumed that Castro was satisfied with the arrangement.

After a thorough medical work-up and lab tests, Dr. .Gonzales conferred with his associate, Dr. Rodriguez and made his diagnosis. The tests showed that Pablo had a fast growing cancer in his prostate gland. While the symptoms were clear, the treatment was not. The equipment in the facility was not sophisticated enough to fully identify the full scope of the cancer. Dr. Gonzales and Dr. Rodriguez agonized over their plight. They obviously had to tell Pablo that he was very sick and needed serious medical treatments. Confessing to him that their equipment was inferior and that they were not up to date on the latest medical advances would be very difficult. They would have to explain why, and the consequences could be very difficult depending on how Fidel saw the situation. Fidel was not a man to accept "oops," as an excuse or an explanation. Cuba was a country that dealt with issues like this in a very drastic manner.

Gonzales and Rodriguez talked at length before today's appointment with Pablo. When the time was set, they appeared together.

Pablo was there as well as his assistant, Felipe Gorgas, who waited outside. Gorgas was the chief of the secret police and responsible for all internal and external espionage. The meeting was tense and the stakes were high, but Dr. Gonzales put on a masterful show.

"Good morning, Senor Palance, how do you feel today?"

Pablo knew he was sick but he was polite. "I'm fine doctor; I hope you're here to tell me everything's proper and I can go home!"

Dr. Gonzalez kept a straight face and began. "Senor Palance, as we mature in life and enjoy the sweet memories of our younger days, and the love of our families and grandchildren, we sadly must face some of the very hard facts of life. Most among those facts of life is that our bodies are not the same as they were many years ago. Time wears on our bodies and sometimes even the very best care is not enough. But, all problems are not fatal. In most cases there is treatment that can be provided to remedy the problem and make us well."

The doctor's remarks were some stilted, and Pablo overlooked the flowery introduction. He remained very interested and serious.

"Our tests indicate," continued Dr. Gonzales, "that you have a cancer. In your case, a serious problem has developed in your prostate gland. As you probably know, the prostate is a gland in the lower part of your body. It's about the size of a very small lemon or walnut, and it produces the semen that is necessary for sexual reproduction. Unfortunately, in later life, men have a problem with this gland."

There was a pause while Dr. Gonzales gathered his strength and wind for the final words.

"In your case, sir, the prostate gland has been infected with a cancer. Untreated, that cancer will be fatal. Fortunately, prostate cancer can be treated if diagnosed properly, and if it hasn't matured."

Pablo interrupted, "Well, if it can be treated and cured, let's do it!"

A still very somber Dr. Gonzales continued, "Mr. Palance, there are some problems. We have good equipment here in El Cimeq, and we have well-trained physicians and nurses. We can provide the care you need. However, we believe there's better equipment and better-trained physicians elsewhere that specialize in all aspects of this disease. They can treat you better."

Senor Palance looked puzzled. "We don't have the best here?"

Dr. Gonzales showed a smidgen of sweat on his forehead before he started his answer. "Senor, we have excellent equipment here and an excellent staff. But in medicine, there are so many parts of the body that can be affected and advances in medicine are so fast, that it's impossible

127

to have all of the latest equipment for every possible disease. When I was in the Soviet Union for training, none of the hospitals had all of the equipment for every medical problem. In America, there are specialists, and in some cases entire hospitals dedicated to only one disease. It takes extensive training and very expensive equipment to take care of every possible disease. It's impossible to keep a staff current on every aspect of medicine and it's very, very expensive to keep all of the medical equipment. Some pieces of equipment cost over a million dollars. No hospital in the world has all of the most up-to-date equipment for every disease. The cost is too much."

Pablo looked somewhat surprised. "I understand what you've said," he replied, "but I guess I thought we had a very complete facility here. I'm surprised that it isn't as I believed it to be."

After a pause to think he continued, "But I guess I understand that we can't have the best of everything all the time. What can be done?"

Dr. Gonzales began a detailed list of possible treatments which included surgery, radiation, chemo-therapy and what he could expect from all the treatments, which was followed by the comment, "no guarantees." Pablo asked many questions over the next twenty-five minutes and was quite satisfied that the two doctors were thorough in their diagnosis and available courses of action.

After they answered his last question, he thought for a few moments and said, "Have you ever met this American Doctor, Charles Hancock, the cancer specialist?"

Dr. Gonzales was surprised that Pablo even knew about Dr. Hancock. "No, Senor Palance, I only know of Dr. Hancock and his work, but I don't know him personally."

After a long pause, Pablo said, "I would like for him to review my situation. I'll have our Office of External Affairs make contact and let you know. Thank you."

Pablo stood up and left the room without another word.

As they walked down the hall, Dr. Gonzales remarked prophetically, "He acted like he knew Dr. Hancock." Dr. Rodriguez nodded agreement.

CHAPTER TWENTY-ONE

Thursday, January 5

Washington, D.C.

Over breakfast, the Hancocks discussed the upcoming testimony and remarked how amazing it was that the person who discovers a significant cause of cancer is subpoenaed to testify before the Congress. Charles had reviewed the anonymous data that had been left at the front desk by a messenger. There was a note on paper without letterhead that simply told him that Congressman Trevor Mitchell had one intention in mind with the hearings. That intention was to protect the broadcasting industry that had so generously financed his campaigns over the years. Protecting them meant whatever it would take, including destroying Charles Hancock. Also included were copies of speeches Mitchell had made favorable to the broadcasting industry and summaries of legislation he had introduced on behalf of the industry. There was also a summary of who had contributed to Mitchell's last campaign for the Senate. Charles was mildly apprehensive about his testimony, but at the same time, looking forward to meeting this Congressional bully. Bobbie was not as competitive and saw more of the bad side of what could happen. At one point, she actually thought about not attending the testimony, but she was both talked into going and assured by Charles that it would be OK, and maybe even fun.

After breakfast they decided that they would take two cabs to the Capitol. The cab that Charles and Bobbie got was dirty and noisy. The driver spoke so little English that Charles finally told him to follow the other cab that his two sons were in. When they arrived at the Capitol, they proceeded to the first entrance. Once inside, they asked directions to the hearing room reserved for the cancer testimony. The guard provided directions and Charles, Bobbie, Harold and Jeff headed off in the direction provided. It was a short walk and, although they were thirty minutes early, the room was almost full and people were still entering. At Charles' urging, they all sat near the back of the room and didn't announce their arrival to anyone. Surprisingly, nobody recognized them.

At fifteen minutes to the hour and the start time of the hearing, some of the Congressmen were arriving with their staff and preparing for the hearing. It was obvious that there was some concern by the frenzy of the committee staff. They didn't have their star witness and without the witness, they would look foolish. Senator Mitchell was irked. He recognized the dilemma he was in. First he had been talked into issuing the subpoena, which he had done against his better judgment. He knew it would look bad, but for some reason, had relented and ordered Charles to appear at the hearing. What would he do if the doctor that discovered a cause of cancer didn't comply with the subpoena? Would he have Hancock issued a contempt order or have him arrested? Mitchell constantly badgered the staff to find Dr. Hancock and ranted because nobody even knew if he was in Washington. Mitchell was having premonitions that this wasn't going to work out as planned. He could not have been more prophetic.

At five minutes to the hour, the staff in desperation finally came to the hearing room and asked if Dr. Hancock was present. Their relief was comical when a hand came up from the back of the room and a voice said, "I'm Dr. Hancock."

The astonished and thankful staffers quickly rushed to the back of the room and invited Dr. Hancock to the front of the room where they had reserved ten seats for him and his party. Having never seen Charles in person, Senator Mitchell couldn't resist taking a peek through the curtain at his first and only witness for the day.

After more administrative shuffling, the members of Congress finally got settled with their staff members sitting behind them, and Senator Mitchell called the room to order.

"Good morning," he began. "This is the official opening of the Special Congressional Committee designated to review the impact of electromagnetic rays on the human body. We know there has been research that purports to prove that exposure to the electromagnetic rays generated by TVs, radios, satellites, and other transmitting devices, can cause cancer. The intent of this Committee is to look into these findings and reach an evaluation of just how much danger America is in as a result of this exposure. We all agree that there are electromagnetic rays in the air and that those rays are hitting our bodies. What we are looking into are the effects of that exposure. I've allowed each member of the Committee a total of five minutes for an opening statement and we'll start with the gentleman from Kentucky." Each of the committee members had to be given time to talk; after all, they were all politicians.

The comments were substantially the same. Each expressed interest in protecting their constituents and all Americans. The statements were dreary and wasteful. Charles and his family paid attention simply to be polite, but Charles was thinking to himself, "what a bunch of windbags!"

After the last Senator finished, Senator Mitchell spoke again. "Most of us know the tragedy of cancer. We've either experienced it personally or have a loved one that was afflicted. There's now the possibility that a cause of cancer has been identified. The media has comprehensively reported this, and the President has charged the Surgeon General to designate a Blue Ribbon Committee to review all the medical information. It's an important task and will take considerable time and resources to reach a definitive opinion. In tandem with the President's research, the Congress has decided to hold hearings to determine the depth and extent of opinion and fact on this subject. We're honored to have with us today the author of the medical article that first identified this possible cause of cancer. He's Dr. Charles Hancock, and he's the author of 'Radical Cancer Prevention.'"

The crowd in the room cheered loudly and heartily to the point that Senator Mitchell had to bang his gavel to quiet everyone down.

It was the second time that Senator Mitchell felt uneasy.

"Dr. Hancock, if you would like to sit at the witness table, we can start the hearing. Of course, anyone who is with you is welcome to join you."

Charles, Bobbie, Jeff, and Harold rose and went to the witness table together. Charles stayed standing while the others took their chairs. Jeff sat to his right and Bobbie to the left. The clerk asked Charles to raise his right hand and Charles swore to tell the truth. Senator Mitchell got another gnawing in his stomach.

"Let me begin our day by welcoming Dr. Hancock and his guests, and thank them for coming to talk to us about the scourge of cancer. Let me also ask Dr. Hancock if he has any comments he would like to make."

"Yes, I do have a few comments," replied Charles.

Senator Mitchell had expected Charles to have something to say before his testimony began. Most witnesses used the time to put the best explanation to any information they might provide that could be unfavorable to them later in the testimony.

"You may proceed, Dr. Hancock."

"Thank you."

In the two instances that Charles spoke to Senator Mitchell, he omitted any reference of respect such as calling him "Senator Mitchell." This lack of a more respectful greeting and deference usually shown to members of Congress was intended. Charles didn't know if anyone noticed, but he intended it. After the treatment he had received already from Mitchell and his staff, he wasn't going to pander to them in public.

After opening the book to the pages of big type, capital letters, he began. "Before I begin my statement, I'd like to ask if this hearing is being televised by any news organization or by C-SPAN?"

Senator Mitchell had yet another gnawing in his stomach and looked around the room. The cameras were there, but he couldn't tell if they were turned on. He looked at some of the staffers who didn't seem to know either.

The senator lied. "I'm not sure if they are, Dr. Hancock, but it doesn't really matter; what's important here will be reported by all the members of the press in attendance."

A stern-faced Charles looked directly at Senator Mitchell and replied, "It matters to me. I would very much like this hearing to be televised. I was assured by a member of the Committee staff that live television coverage would be part of my testimony."

Senator Mitchell was caught off guard, as were Bobbie, Jeff and Harold.

"May I ask why, Dr. Hancock?"

"Certainly," said Charles and ignored his notes. "Since I wrote the article 'Radical Cancer Prevention,' I have been shunned by both the radio and TV news organizations. My work has been given comprehensive coverage by the printed media, but the broadcast media has ignored me. This is an opportunity for the citizens of America to get the same first-hand information that their government is getting in regard to the cause of many types of cancer. I think they deserve to hear and see for themselves what I've found."

Senator Mitchell knew well that the cameras were turned off. He hadn't directly ordered that the hearing not be telecast, but his office never replied to the request to televise the hearing. The commercial broadcast stations had no interest in airing testimony that they were killing people and C-SPAN never televised anything without approval of the hearing chairman. Of course, Mitchell hadn't expected Charles to bring up the subject either.

132

"Well, let's take a short recess and I'll try to determine if the hearing is being telecast."

Jeff covered his microphone and whispered to his father, "Score one for Dr. Hancock."

After twenty minutes the Committee returned and Senator Mitchell nervously moved his microphone, "I've checked into the televising of the hearing and found that the hearing is not being televised live. It seems that there was a miscommunication between my office and the C-SPAN office. As a result, the scheduling office didn't include this hearing for telecast. Other programs are being aired, and there's no way to televise these hearings at this time. However, I'd like to point out that there are ample journalists here to record what's being said. I think we should start the hearing. Are you prepared to make your opening statement, Dr. Hancock?"

Charles looked directly at Senator Mitchell again. "It's amazing, isn't it? Cancer's a disease that directly affects almost forty percent of all Americans and indirectly affects almost a hundred percent of all Americans when family and friends are stricken. We spend billions of government and private dollars yearly on research, prevention, and treatment of this terrible illness. The Congress is holding a hearing on a significant cause of much of the cancer, and not one major TV station in America covers the hearing. What are those commercial stations showing that's of more interest to the American people? Not only that, the Congressional television station has more important programming to air? What program could the Congressional station be showing that could be more important? I'd like to know the answer to those questions and who made those decisions. I'll bet the American people would also like to know."

From the crowd in attendance there arose a roar of applause that made Senator Mitchell bang his gavel again and shout for "order in the room." The cheers didn't stop until finally Dr. Hancock put up his hand.

There was a pause and Charles continued. "My desire is not to testify before this committee until the proceedings can be televised. However, since the committee sent me a subpoena, I don't suppose I have the option. Is that correct?"

A gasp went up from the audience when Charles mentioned that he was under subpoena. Senator Mitchell was clearly embarrassed and irate about what had just happened, but he could really do little. He couldn't give in and postpone the hearing so the proceedings could be televised.

Witnesses had been arranged for and members of Congress had schedules that had to be kept.

"I'm sorry that there's no television coverage, but we have a very tight schedule. This information is important to the Congress. Please proceed, Dr. Hancock."

Charles paused and stared at Senator Mitchell. He then opened the binder that he had brought with him and began. "As I said before, if I were not under subpoena, I would leave and provide this testimony when all Americans could judge for themselves what's being said. Regretfully, I don't have that luxury, and I don't suppose the Chairman will release me from my subpoena."

Senator Mitchell sat stone-faced and didn't reply.

Charles continued, "As a backdrop to my statement, I want it to be a matter for the record that not televising this hearing is a disservice to the American people, and it's very simply wrong. Whoever decided there was something more important for the American people to see should be held accountable for that decision and made to explain why it was done that way."

Every reporter in the room took that note, and Senator Mitchell shivered.

"What I'm going to testify to affects every single American to some degree." Charles paused, "With the possible exception of tax legislation, there is little legislation debated in this Congress that affects so many American citizens. I'm not talking about tobacco subsidies or highway beautification projects. I'm talking about something that personally affects each and every American."

Senator Mitchell had been boxed into a corner, cuffed around, and he knew it. Worse than that, they were only at the "touch gloves" part of the boxing match. Round one hadn't even started yet!

Charles looked back at his book and began. "My name is Charles Hancock and I live in Columbus, Ohio. I've been studying, researching or practicing medicine for almost twenty-five years and have specialized in the prevention and treatment of cancer. My career has been dedicated to treating victims of cancer and doing research at the College of Medicine at Ohio State University. In my research I found that electromagnetic rays in the atmosphere are captured in the body and cause cancer."

Dr. Hancock paused as Jeff reached into the case he had brought with him and took out a small battery powered radio. Charles turned on the radio, and classical music began to play. Charles looked at the Congressmen. "When I turn on this radio, you can all hear the music

134

playing." Charles then turned the music off. "When I turn the music off, there's no further sound. However, the same electromagnetic wave that brought you that music is still in the air and still hitting your body. That's happening for every radio station, television station, police and military transmission, cell phones, and an unknown number of satellites that are beaming down signals with everything from TV programs to spy photos. When you make a call to someone's cell phone, the telephone company sends the signal to cell tower near you. Right now, every call on a cell phone near you is hitting your body. Now, you might say that the extremely low power used by these signals would not hurt your body. I agree with that. However, when you drastically increase the number of contacts, it increases the exposure to your body and affects your vital organs.

With the explosion of technology today, the atmosphere is literally jammed with electromagnetic rays. Those waves are hitting our bodies and doing significant damage to primarily the denser body organs. I have done experiments with animals living in hemispheres with and without electromagnetic rays. The results are clear, unequivocal and can be easily replicated. The organs of those animals are gray and unhealthy looking, while the animals living in a shielded environment have healthy organs. We've seen the same result when doing autopsies on human beings who have lived in similar environments. We also see significantly higher cancer rates in those animals and humans exposed to EM rays." Charles turned the page in his notebook.

"I'm not alone in this research. I've asked leading researchers in other countries to duplicate my research, and they've exactly replicated the results I'm describing. There's no question as to the validity of my data, or the data of others who have examined these EM rays and their effects on the human body.

"It's also been reported in the press that the Blue Ribbon Committee appointed by the President has tentatively advised him that a preliminary review of all the research indicates that my findings are solid science. EM rays are responsible for many of the cancer incidents. I'm not surprised. There's no difference between my work and what the Blue Ribbon Committee found. They basically reviewed our records and findings along with the records of other researchers in the world. They also did examinations at autopsies and actual testing when possible. According to the newspapers, the committee fully agrees with me and my colleague researchers." Charles paused again.

"What I've summarized are some very grim findings. Electromagnetic rays are helping to kill everyone in this room, and everyone in America. At this point, I can go into significantly more detail regarding the actual research if this committee would like. Or, I can respond to questions that the committee may have. This concludes my opening remarks."

The room was as silent as a funeral home, and no one broke the silence for several minutes. Charles stared at Senator Mitchell who seemed frozen and unable to respond.

Finally the Senator spoke, "That's a very dire report, Dr. Hancock, and one that needs a complete review. The Congress is prepared to take whatever action is indicated, and we're here to sort out the exact parameters of the problem and try to find a solution."

After another pause Senator Mitchell spoke again, "Dr. Hancock, before we get to the subject of your research, would you mind telling America about yourself. You've made considerable contributions to the health of the citizens of Ohio, and you've completed your research into a horrible disease. But most Americans don't know who you are. Could you share with everyone a little bit about yourself?"

Charles looked at the Senator. "Of course. Most of my life has been detailed in the newspapers of this country, and these reporters here know well my background and life history. I'm not interested in any personal recognition for what I've done. I've had a very enjoyable life and a fulfilling career.

"Practicing medicine is the perfect occupation for me and I've enjoyed every minute of it. I'm not interested in being on the cover of any national magazine or any personal enhancements. My life has been no different than many other Americans.

"I grew up in the heartland of America - Ohio. I'm the only child of parents who were very much in love with each other. I did all the things that young children do and enjoyed my childhood. After high school I entered Ohio State University. I found a very professional and dedicated group of educators who worked hard to see that their students attained the education they went to Ohio State to earn.

"While an undergraduate at Ohio State I met my wife, Bobbie, and we've been married ever since. She's a wonderful person and the ideal partner for me. After being accepted into medical school, I found that my life's work would be medicine. The opportunity to practice medicine and do research to advance the state of medicine was a marriage made in heaven, just like my marriage to Bobbie. I've worked hard to make a contribution to the general welfare of mankind and have helped many people who were afflicted with some dreaded form of cancer."

Charles paused and took a sip of water. "Unfortunately, I was unable to help them all, but I did everything humanly possible and applied every known medical protocol."

"Did you serve in the military?" asked one of the committee members.

"No, I didn't," replied Charles. "I now wish that I had. When I was getting out of high school there was a draft by lottery. My number for induction was very high and I was not drafted. The following year I entered college and received draft deferments the remainder of my education period. When I graduated from medical school, I was offered a position with the University. By then Bobbie and I had two young children, and I accepted the offer from Ohio State University; I've been there ever since.

"While I haven't served in the military, I have only the highest respect for the military and have provided assistance when I could. I've served in numerous volunteer capacities with various government agencies trying to provide a better life for those less fortunate. I have thousands of hours of volunteer time with a number of social agencies providing medical care to those in need. I also provide the health care for the ROTC units at Ohio State without charge."

Senator Mitchell wanted to ask about the "Miami-year," as the Council of Broadcasters was calling it, but it didn't seem to even closely fit into the conversation. He resumed the questioning.

"Dr. Hancock, let me start by asking you a hard question, but one that I only ask because I want to set the stage for all Americans. Some people don't accept your conclusions and believe that your findings are simply not true. How would you respond to that?"

Charles again looked the Senator directly in the eye. "Unfortunately, there are people that don't want to believe things. For those people we can only explain what the facts are and hope they accept what is irrefutable. There are still people who don't believe that the earth is round. There's nothing I can do about that.

"This is America, and you can believe whatever you want. If someone expects to fall off the earth when they reach the edge, they will be disappointed. That disappointment will be nothing compared to learning that you, or your loved ones, will discover you have cancer that could have been prevented. Anyone who can read and understand will come to no other conclusion than I have if they read my paper 'Radical Cancer Prevention.' You have it, don't you?"

Senator Mitchell didn't answer immediately and then said, "Actually, I haven't read the entire paper. I read an executive summary and then discussed it at length with several staff members who had been trained more extensively than me in medicine."

Charles looked at the Congressman with disdain. "You're chairing a panel to determine what action to take as a result of the research and you haven't read the paper???"

Senator Mitchell got a little defiant. "Yes, that's correct Dr. Hancock. It's not as important that I read the entire report as it is that I have a good understanding of what it says. I have that understanding."

Charles looked at him again. "Do you agree with the conclusions?"

Senator Mitchell once again had been trapped and felt yet another gnawing in his stomach. "The research seems very sound, very comprehensive and very complete. On the surface, it makes an excellent case. My interests are to get all the details and questions answered so that we can craft a comprehensive response to this danger to our citizens if the research is validated."

Senator Mitchell then inexplicably blurted, "In summary, yes, I believe the report. I just want a full understanding of all the aspects of the report."

The principal aide to Senator Mitchell shuddered and thought to herself, 'If there is another election in the future for Senator Mitchell, he'll need to raise considerable more money than last time. The Broadcasting Industry won't be available to pay many of his bills after that comment. Maybe I should start looking for another job.'

The Congressman from South Carolina then took the first turn at questions. "Let me ask you, Dr. Hancock, about the conditions of the bodies you examined that had not been exposed to the EM rays."

"Gladly," replied Charles. "In fact, I have with me enlarged copies of pictures that we took during some of the autopsies."

Harold handed a pile of large pictures to a clerk who handed them to the Chairman. The pictures showed the internal parts of bodies, and the organs were noticeably pink and healthy looking.

"The picture that my son Harold just gave you is that of a fifty-five year old woman who lived in South America in an area with very few EM rays. She was killed when she was hit in the head with a stone while working near a quarry. You can see that the body looks healthy, and I can assure you that those organs show little damage."

Harold then gave another pile of pictures to the clerk to give to the chairman.

"This picture is that of a forty-two-year-old woman who was hit and killed by a taxicab in New York City. You can see that the organs look gray, dried out and generally unhealthy. Those organs should not look like that. They didn't look like that when she was born."

Charles waited while the pictures were passed around and examined by the committee members. Then he continued, "My assessment is that that EM rays did damage by attacking her body over her lifetime. We also found small cancers on her pancreas. This is not the body of a healthy human being.

"Regretfully, this is the kind of thing we usually find. At the many autopsies in New York City, the only instances when the cadavers didn't look like this were those times when the person had not been in the city for a long time. Most often it was immigrants from small countries or villages that had recently moved to New York City. I'd speculate that the cadavers that are examined here in the District of Columbia morgue look exactly like these."

Silence again filled the room. The Congressman from South Carolina finished his questioning, and the Senator from North Dakota asked detailed questions regarding the research. He started with questions concerning how the metal boxes were constructed to screen out the EM and keep the animals free from exposure. After about three more hours of testimony, it seemed like everyone had asked their questions.

Senator Mitchell finally started to close the hearing. "We thank you, Dr. Hancock, for your patience and time to help us in this endeavor. I know you're interested in getting back to your research and your patients. We wish you a safe trip back to Ohio. Our hearings are going to continue, and I'm sure you'll be interested in the outcome. This brings me to my last question for you personally. Other scientists will be coming before this panel and testifying in disagreement with your findings. Can you tell us what you think about that?"

Charles thought for a second. "Actually, I'm very doubtful that what you said is true. There are no experts who will come here and disagree with my findings. True experts value their professional reputation too much. You'll probably get a handful of people who will have little or no experience and who have certainly not replicated the experiments themselves. They'll tell you they have questions and concerns and generally raise a lot of doubts. None of them will say what I've done is flawed. They won't say that because the research is solid and factual. They'll not have any hard facts. They'll have theories and questions and possibly some anecdotal stories. However, they won't refute the findings." Charles paused and it was the silence in the room was overwhelming. Nobody wanted to miss any words that Dr. Charles Hancock had to say.

"My work is based on fact, and there is no distortion of those facts. I've replicated them often, and my professional colleagues have also replicated these findings. To test your own beliefs, do this when you get home tonight. If you've concluded that the EM rays don't cause cancer, say that aloud in the presence of your family, and assure them that everything's OK. If you can't do that, then you know the answer and you know the lethal danger to all Americans."

Once again the crowd in the hearing room broke into applause. When the cheering ended, Charles and his family stood up and left.

After getting back to the hotel, Charles asked everyone for opinions on the day's events.

Hal started. "The way it looked to me was that we had support from everyone in the room and eventually even from Mitchell."

Bobbie chimed in. "I still can't believe that nitwit admitted to not having read your report." She then stood up and said she was going to the lobby for a paper to see what the newspapers had to say. "I'm interested to see what the Washington crowd thinks of the hicks from Ohio."

The conversation continued for the 15 minutes that Bobbie was gone from the room until she returned all excited. "You won't believe this, Charles. Your picture is on the front page of the Washington Post."

"I'm not really surprised," replied Charles, "considering all the reporters that were at the hearing today." Bobbie had a huge smile on her face looking at Charles' picture.

While Charles was looking at the paper, Bobbie was looking in her handbag for a letter. "I also got this letter from the desk; and it's addressed to you."

Charles was looking at his picture in the paper. "Go ahead and read the letter, Bobbie."

Bobbie looked at the letter that was on State Department stationery and signed by someone with the title of Assistant Secretary of State. "This is interesting, Charles. It seems that the government of Cuba has asked that you be allowed to treat an aide to Fidel Castro. Apparently, this person has cancer and the Cuban government has asked our government if you can provide treatment."

Charles was still smiling at his picture in the paper while Bobbie continued. "The name of the patient is Pablo Palance. The State Department wants to know if you're agreeable to treat him before they respond. That's kinda' exciting, isn't it?"

The smile left Charles' face and he stood up to read the letter. Charles' reaction was stoic and not the kind of response expected with such news. "Yeah, that's exciting," he said, but not with any gusto.

"You don't seem very excited, Charles," remarked Bobbie. "After all, the President of another country wants you to treat one of his aides! What's the matter?"

Charles clearly lacked the spirit that Bobbie expected. "Of course I'm excited, but it's really nothing more than another patient. I'm not that excited because if I have to go to Cuba, it'll take away from the patients in Columbus that need me now. This will be the second distraction and postponement of work that needs to be done."

Bobbie sat down and said little more the remainder of the evening. She had never see Charles like this before.

The White House

"Well, I guess we score another win for Dr. Charles Hancock," mused a very happy President. "It seems like that guy knows his way around pretty well. You can't help but like him. He's like the all-American boy. He's lived an exemplary life and is in a profession that helps others. And, he doesn't back down to anyone. He has a velvet glove of professionalism and calmness. Yet, there's an iron fist in that glove and he's not afraid to use it when he has to. He's a tough character and you'll find out if you test him. He made Mitchell look like a fool today starting with the comments about televising the hearing. It's a good thing we had tapes there. Undoubtedly, Mitchell had some agenda that was orchestrated by the Council of Broadcasters and it flunked miserably. After his comments about the effects of the EM rays, I doubt if Mitchell will see a penny in his next election campaign, and his opponent will be well financed."

Secretary of Defense Grey nodded in agreement and was almost giggling. "It was quite a show! When he first showed up and sat in the back of the room, it was a hoot. The staffers were running all around and Mitchell was screaming at everyone. When they finally found Hancock, Mitchell was still tight as a drum, but got back into character to hopefully undermine everything. It was a disaster. When Hancock asked if he had read the paper and Mitchell had to say he hadn't, I could see the hatred in Mitchell's eyes. It was a terrible look."

The President sipped his glass of white wine. "You're right, Sam, it was quite a show. But that's been Hancock's reputation. He's on the money with his research, and he isn't letting anyone get him off target. I admire him for what he's done and what he's doing to defend his work. It's a damn serious problem, and we need to get something done about it soon. I'm sure the broadcasting industry has a few more cards up their sleeves, but in the end they'll fail. We know that there is a level of support in America for every conceivable cause, but I can't see a very large constituency willing to allow themselves to be given cancer."

CHAPTER TWENTY-TWO

Friday, January 6

<u>Columbus, Ohio</u>

When Charles and Bobbie returned to Columbus, there were headlines in the Columbus Dispatch about his testimony, and further demands for the government to do something about the EM rays. Five more transmission towers had been destroyed during the week, and one person was killed when the tower fell the wrong way and landed on his truck. Reporters were massed in front of the house when Charles and Bobbie returned home. Charles didn't really add anything to what he had said at the Congressional hearing. He handled the questions in a very low-key manner and gave credit to the University for developing the world-class medical school where the most advanced techniques were available to help cancer patients. He indicated that he looked forward to getting back to work and providing care for his patients.

<u>Washington D.C.</u>

The situation with the Council of Broadcasters was desperate. Their plan to discredit the work that Charles had done by discrediting him had failed miserably so far. The door-to-door survey in the south Miami area was producing no results. If there was anyone there who knew anything, the years had taken them away and left no real leads. Their hopes that Mitchell could get Charles to talk about the Miami year or how he funded his education failed wretchedly. How to get at that information was becoming more and more difficult. Their efforts to develop a campaign to cast doubt on the work were likewise falling on bad times.

Charles was accurate in his testimony to the Congress. No reputable researcher or physician would come forward and refute the findings. Professional reputations are difficult to build and very fragile. Nobody of any stature is going to go before a national audience and trade fifteen minutes of fame for a remaining career of chuckling embarrassment.

There were unknown names that would refute the findings, but their status was such that their comments would aid Charles instead of detracting from his research. The only real hope left for the Council of Broadcasters was the appeal to the court alleging that any cancellation of broadcast licenses would be unconstitutional. After all, freedom of speech was a sacrosanct right of all Americans and it must be defended. The lawyers were putting a legal brief together that was a work of art. They even hired a man who called himself a 'quotationist.' His expertise was in supplying quotes on any subject from historical and respected figures to bolster any argument being made. He actually turned out to be very helpful and supplied a number of quotes that reinforced the point being made in the brief.

However, once you got past the window dressing, the case became very fundamental. The First Amendment was actually a restrictive clause prohibiting the government from abridging the right of free speech. There's a formidable argument that the government is not required to provide the vehicle for free speech; it must just not inhibit it. The government only regulates the airwaves to keep order, much like it regulates the airline routes. That doesn't mean you can fly an unsafe airplane and endanger people on the ground. Also, there is ample room for free speech other than on-air broadcasting. After all, anyone can start a newspaper, write pamphlets, put a sign in their yard or stand on a public corner and talk.

The second and more serious concern was the safety issue. The classic ruling by the Supreme Court about yelling fire in the theater is very compelling and simple for the ordinary people and Supreme Court Justices to understand. Does free speech in this case permit cancer to be transmitted to citizens? In the filing with the court, the Council's lawyers would have to decide if they should allege that the EM rays were not harmful, and therefore permitted.

This argument would be difficult to support since the evidence was that the rays were harmful. A more direct appeal that the right to free speech is only limited by extreme danger would also be difficult to support – what could be a more extreme than cancer?

Ultimately, the lawyers settled on a plea that basically said that the minimal nature of the exposure is such that it's not harmful enough to cause the findings that Dr. Hancock alleges. The EM rays could possibly be part of the problem, but there were undoubtedly other parts that also contribute. Of course, the lawyers knew that if there were other causes, they should identify them. They also knew that they couldn't.

So, in the end, the plea that was prepared for submission to the Supreme Court was a hodge-podge of arguments that basically said here's the reason, but if you don't like this one, how about this reason, and if you don't like that one, how about this one? It was a scholarly document, well put together, and it would need a lot of creative interpretations by a judge to succeed.

On the other hand, the government had a very simple defense. They first argued that they were not violating the constitution. Each of the broadcasters had an absolute right to free speech. They could say anything they wish to say, and the government wasn't advocating any restrictions. The government had no obligation to provide anyone with the means to exercise their free speech, much the same as the government wasn't required to provide newspapers with printing presses and paper.

While this was a credible argument for the government, it wasn't their best. The most compelling defense for the government was that the transmission of EM rays through the atmosphere was inherently dangerous and harmful to all Americans. Essentially, you can't transmit EM rays and cause cancer. The government was very confident of their case.

The White House
President Harrison Jenkins had gathered the principal players to the meeting in the Basement Operations Center for one last discussion. Around the table were Dr. Ralph Gardner, Surgeon General; Ken Croby, Attorney General; Sam Gray, Secretary of Defense; and Kevin Stoneman, Chairman of the Federal Communications Commission. The President had also invited a number of his White House staff advisors to the meeting.

After everyone had gotten coffee and been seated, the President began, "I've been thinking about this situation regarding the electromagnetic rays causing cancer. I've read every paper that you've sent me, and I've discussed much of this with each of you and with others whose opinions I value. There's no question in my mind. EMs are killing American citizens. There has not been one scrap of reliable evidence that I've seen that refutes the findings of Dr. Hancock and the other researchers that have looked into this situation. You've all commented that one way to solve this problem would be to pull FCC permits to broadcasters, and you each offered your thoughts on the consequences of doing that. Some have been more detailed and catastrophic than others, but I think that you all agree that it would have a major impact on businesses, society and the legal system. I believe from the mail I've been receiving and the mail that members of Congress have been getting, that the American people are afraid of the EM transmissions and afraid that they're causing cancer. The continued and increasing destruction of transmission towers is more than a series of individual acts of vandalism. Adults are dynamiting very expensive towers because they're afraid. They're afraid those towers are killing them and their families. I've decided that I'm going to direct that the maximum number of broadcast certificates be pulled. There will be exceptions, of course, but for the most part, we're going to have to clear the airwaves. I've asked FCC Chairman Stoneman and Attorney General Croby to put the final touches on a plan they've worked up and have it ready for a press conference early next week."

The President paused, but nobody spoke.

He continued, "Basically, what that plan says is that all but the most necessary broadcast frequencies are no longer available for use by private citizens. Emergency channels, essential services and broadcasts of that nature will be permitted. However, the frequencies that carry the programs that most of our citizens have watched or listened to, will no longer be available.

"Local TV, satellite TV, radio, wireless telephones, and similar devices will no longer be permitted. I expect a firestorm of reaction from industry, and their complaints will be valid to some degree. We've had broadcasting for so long that we probably don't even build a car without a radio. Those car radios will be useless unless they have CDs or tape players. The era of free TV will end in a month. Radio and television will have to be enjoyed on cable now.

"I'm not sure of the answer on cordless telephones. Since the base station and the phones are both in the personal area of the owner, they may have to be permitted, but maybe not. If they are in a multiple-use building, they may be transmitting and hitting other people. My guess is they will no longer be permitted, but the Department of Justice is looking into that. Here's how I'd like to handle this." The President paused and thought briefly.

"First, I'll call in key Congressional leaders and explain what I'm doing and why. I'm also going to invite Dr. Hancock to sit in on that session with me. He makes a very compelling case for his work, and we all agree with it. Ken, I'd like you and your folks at Justice to work with the Commerce Department. Call in the major industry leaders and explain what we're doing, why and when. I'd like to hear what measures they think are necessary to minimize the impact of this and if any legislation

146

might be appropriate to help them. I'll want that plan in a week and I want a lot of specifics. Call any other cabinet members for help if you need it and refer any reluctance by anyone to me personally.

"Second, we have to deal with the Department of Defense. Your people will have a lot of problems with this, Sam. I'd like a top-to-bottom scrub of the Defense Department to see where more cuts can be made. I don't want to decrease readiness, but that's a very subjective determination. Every colonel with a cell phone or a walkie-talkie thinks he needs it for readiness. You need to verify what the need truly is.

"Third, we have legal problems." The President turned towards the Attorney General. "Ken, in the pizza business, more business is good. Too bad you're not in the pizza business. You're going to get a lot of work out of this, and I expect everyone who is harmed by this decision to sue us. I know your teams have been working on the expected immediate appeal to the Supreme Court. That's just one of many cases the Justice Department can expect in the very near future. I plan to have a press conference next week, and I'll explain it to the American people. The amount of work we have to do and the people we are going to talk to will make my talk anti-climatic, but it's the right thing and has to be done. Any questions?"

After about fifteen minutes of discussion the meeting broke up. After they left the cabinet room, President Jenkins went to the Oval Office and instructed his secretary to call Dr. Hancock at Ohio State University.

Charles had a patient miss her appointment, and he was catching up on his paperwork when the President called. The Secretary was obviously excited when she called Charles on the intercom. "Dr. Hancock, the President of the United States is on line one!"

Charles picked up the phone, "Good morning, Mr. President."

"Good morning, Charles," came the reply.

Charles smiled, "I hope this is not a professional call, Mr. President. You looked very healthy the last time I saw you."

The President chuckled. "I hope you're right, Doctor. As much as I admire your skills, I would prefer not to experience them first-hand. Now, to be clear, I'm not calling to talk about Buckeyes' football. I'm calling to give you some advance information. I just met with the cabinet and we discussed the government's plan regarding the problem with electromagnetic rays. What we have decided to do is to cancel all FCC broadcasting permits. It'll cause problems for a lot of people and companies, but the health of our citizens is at stake, and we need to act decisively. I'd like you to keep that information under your hat until it becomes public. I also want you to know how much your work has meant to this country and our citizens. What has to be done will benefit all Americans, and you're responsible for the improvement in the lives of all our citizens. The next year will be painful, but it'll be well worth it considering the health of all Americans."

"Mr. President," Charles replied, "your actions, in my opinion, are absolutely correct. I applaud you for taking such direct and firm action. I'm not sure every political leader would do the same thing."

A more serious President responded, "It had to be done, Charles, and it will be done. But there are a couple of other things. First, I wanted to comment on your performance at the Mitchell Committee. You handled that worthless Senator superbly!"

"Thank you, Mr. President. I really didn't intend to do anything but testify, but it didn't exactly work out that way."

The President continued, "Charles, I'm going to be briefing some Congressional leaders and addressing the American people in a few days, and I'd like to invite you to attend. It's not the normal way of doing things but you're such an integral part of all of this; I think it would help if you attended."

"That's a compliment, Mr. President. I'll be there."

"Thanks, Charles. By the way, the First Lady asks that you bring Bobbie along with you. You can plan to stay here the night before the meeting and we'll all have dinner."

"It's a deal, Mr. President. Let me know when you want us, and Bobbie and I will both be there. Thanks again."

Charles hung up the phone and for a brief moment thought of the dichotomy of talking to the President of the United States one minute and writing in a medical folder the results of a blood test the next minute. Charles finished his notes and called Bobbie to alert her to their upcoming trip and overnight stay in the White House.

He finished his conversation with Bobbie by saying, "You've come a long way, baby!"

"A long way is right," chuckled Bobbie. "Overnight at the White House isn't bad for a farm girl from Ohio."

Los Angeles, California

The loss was too great. Linda held up for a short time and her parents went back to Washington, but then she fell apart.

After she missed her rent payment on the apartment and refused to answer the door, the landlord called the police. A wretched and very sick

148

woman was lying in a soiled bed when the police forced their way into the apartment. It looked as though she had not been out of the bed for days, and the rancorous aroma of human waste was sickening. With the help of medical technicians, Linda was taken from the apartment and admitted to the city's mental hospital. The landlord provided information from her rental application which listed who to call in case of an emergency. The police easily located her father and called him.

The phone number went to a private direct line that was answered by Steve Parson's secretary. The police secretary was momentarily stunned and said, "Oh, that Parson!"

She quickly regained her composure and continued. "Good afternoon, my name is Susan Jackson with the Los Angeles Police. I'm trying to locate Steve Parson. This call is in regard to his daughter, Linda, who lives in the Los Angeles area. Is it possible to talk to him?"

"One minute, please," replied the secretary.

After a minute a deep male voice tersely spoke. "This is Steve Parson."

"Good afternoon, Mr. Parson. I'm Susan Jackson with the Los Angeles Police Department. We believe that you may be the father of Linda Parson who lives in this area. Is that correct, sir?"

"I have a daughter named Linda living in the Los Angeles area. Something must be wrong if the police are calling. What is it?"

Susan Jackson followed her training and attempted to ease any problems common with notifications over the phone. After confirming the address where Linda lived, she continued, "Mr. Parson, your daughter is alive and is physically safe; unfortunately she seems to be very mentally disoriented. We found her in her apartment this morning. She was confused and incoherent. She wasn't physically harmed or injured in any way, but she seemed very distraught and in need of professional help. We took her to a city facility in Los Angeles that handles these sorts of situations, but we need a family member to help us. Can you help?"

"Of course, I can help. I'll leave for California immediately. Please tell me where she is now?"

The monotone voice continued, "She's at the Los Angeles Central Hospital in the psychiatric ward and it's located at…"

Steve Parson interrupted, "I know where it is; I'll be there as quickly as possible. Please don't let her be discharged until I arrive!"

"Mr. Parson, at this point, she won't be discharged until she is released to a family member or a judge orders her released."

"Thank you for calling, Miss Jackson, I'll be there in the next couple of hours."

"You're welcome, sir!"

Within 30 minutes Steve Parson had left his office after advising the staff that he would be gone for several days on an emergency. He called his wife to meet him at Washington National Airport where he parked in his usual reserved parking place. Within seven hours after the call, the Parsons were in the Los Angeles Mental hospital looking at a pathetic woman with glazed eyes with no idea where she was. She simply looked straight ahead. There was no life in her face and her depression seemed hopeless.

After a discussion with doctors, Steve was more optimistic. He was told that this condition isn't rare and that people with high ideals or expectations often react this way when they fail. Linda was more or less a classic case. She would recover, but the time of that recovery was not known.

Steve made arrangements from the hospital to have Linda flown back to Washington and entered into a private hospital that had a reputation for the very best care. Three days later everything was taken care of and the entire Parson family was within twenty-five miles of each other. Steve had met the director of the hospital at several charity functions and was able to have Linda admitted under the name of Linda Parks. There was no need for any publicity that served no purpose other than to spotlight a tragic situation. After Linda recovered she could go public with her story if she cared to, but Steve left that decision to her. He also didn't see any reason to notify her ex-husband. Given his lack of response when Joey died, he certainly wouldn't respond to Linda being in the hospital. No notification was attempted.

The belongings in her apartment including the precious pictures of Joey, had been moved to a storage area, and the furniture that the hospital thought would be helpful had been moved to her room. There were no pictures of Joey in her room. They would be introduced back into her life as her treatments showed some results.

Rickenbacker Air National Guard Base, Ohio

During the 50s and 60s Rickenbacker Air Force Base was a Strategic Air Command base and the home to nuclear-armed B-52 bombers ready to go to the Soviet Union. Over the years and the realignment of the military, the base was drastically reduced in size and turned over to the Ohio Air National Guard. They still had a number of air-to-air refueling tankers, and it was a weekend drill base for reservists. Located just a little south of Columbus, Ohio the base served as an ideal landing site for VIP or aircraft with a high security need. It would provide the privacy from demonstrations by members of the Cuban-American groups should they learn of the arrival of Pablo Palance. This would have been a prime opportunity for such demonstrations. Anyone who knew anything about Cuba knew of Mr. Palance.

While the State Department, and the President, agreed to the treatments of Mr. Palance, his arrival was kept private.

It was on the same day that Steve Parson's daughter was being admitted to the hospital in Washington that a Russian Tupelov 22 landed at the Ohio base after a flight from Havana, Cuba, with a short stop at Boca Chica Naval Air Station in Key West, Florida. On board was the principal advisor to Fidel Castro, Pablo Palance, a small security detail, a translator, Dr. Gonzalez, a chef and several aides and assistants.

On hand to greet the Cuban party was a representative of the State Department several levels below the rank of Ambassador. Also meeting the aircraft were military police from the Air Force Base near Dayton, Dr. Charles Hancock, and several employees from the University.

After descending the steps of the aircraft and being met by the official greeter from the State Department, Pablo Palance shook hands with Charles and said in a low, but audible voice, "Charles, it's good to see you again!"

Charles had a weak, but polite smile on his face as the men greeted each other. Charles introduced Mr. Palance to Bobbie, and they all got into the van that had been provided by the university. There was no further mention of the comment indicating that the two men had met before, and only the flight from Cuba and the weather were discussed.

Once at the university hospital, patient number 123-456-7898 was admitted to one of the surgical suites normally reserved for high-ranking OSU officials, other doctors and state officials. Pablo Parlance's aide was the curious type and asked about the number of the patient. He was told that the accounting system for patients used social security numbers. Since Mr. Palance didn't have a social security number, they used a standard number and the significance of the number was that he was the ninth person admitted to the hospital that we didn't have a social security number for.

Three guards were posted for protection. One Cuban guard stayed outside the bedroom in the living room area. An Air Force guard was posted outside the door with a University policeman stationed at the nurse's station to prevent any entry into the wing where Mr. Palance was housed.

After getting settled in, Mr. Palance was escorted on a tour of the University including the football stadium. When he saw the street sign marked Woody Hayes Drive, he asked, "Who's Woody Hayes?"

Charles smiled and tried to explain that American football has the same amount of interest in America as soccer has in Cuba, and that Woody Hayes was once a coach at the University. Pablo seemed to understand but didn't seem to know a soccer coach anywhere who had a street named after him.

The evening concluded at the famous Germantown district of Columbus and everyone had a hearty meal of wiener schnitzel and potatoes to the accompaniment of authentic German music.

Charles assured Pablo that he would see him and Dr. Gonzales first thing in the morning to assess his medical condition and work out a course of treatment.

On the way home Bobbie asked about the comment that Mr. Palance had made that it was good to see Charles again.

Charles was in an unusually testy mood. "I don't know what he meant. When I lived in Miami I met many Cubans and maybe he was one of them. I'm not sure."

A woman can't be married to a man for over 25 years and not know the difference between what he says and what he means. She knew there was more to this than Charles indicated, but she said nothing more. When they arrived home, Charles professed fatigue and said he wanted to go to bed immediately.

Once in bed, Charles wondered what the odds were of Pablo Palance re-appearing in his life at this time. The odds of this happening had to be longer than winning the lottery and he certainly didn't like it. He thought of the various ways that it might play out. Pablo might just remain silent and complete his cancer treatments and return to Cuba. Or he could start to talk. He hadn't worried about the investigation by the Council of Broadcasters since they were amateurs on a cold trail, that didn't have access to the proper people. But, the government was a different matter. With the proper information from people like Mr. Palance, it could be a lot different.

After returning to his hotel room, the State Department representative filed a report immediately with the political section of the State Department with a copy to the Intelligence Section. The report highlighted the comment Mr. Palance had made about being glad to see

Charles again. The comment was the first thing the Secretary of State noticed in the morning, and he immediately reported it to the President. A surprised President sent a copy of the report to the CIA and asked them for an opinion of the comment.

The President also sent a note back to the State Department asking for a daily briefing on the visit of Mr. Palance. The Secretary of State asked that the representative in Columbus be extra vigilant and alert to any other comments made by Mr. Palance. The State Department representative would read those instructions and sneered aloud, "What do they think I'm doing here, anyway? How can I be more vigilant?"

CHAPTER TWENTY-THREE

Monday, January 9

Columbus, Ohio

Dr. Gonzales had advised Charles that money wasn't a consideration when deciding on the medical treatment for Pablo Palance. Consequently, the resultant medical tests were as extensive and as thorough as a physical could be. Mr. Palance spoke excellent English which it helped immensely when Charles talked to him about the tests and the nature of the examination. A surprise to Charles was Pablo's agreeability to translate for Dr. Gonzales if he thought that the official translator had missed a point or didn't understand some medical terminology. In this case the possibility of an erroneous translation was very unusual since the translator was also a physician and had been trained in London. Charles didn't know what to expect from Dr. Gonzales. He knew that he was the director of the premier medical clinic in Cuba and that he was responsible for treatment of Fidel and his family plus other local and visiting dignitaries. However, nothing was known about his training or experience. Charles was very pleasantly surprised when he saw the degree of knowledge Dr. Gonzalez had about cancer treatments. It was obvious that he worked hard to keep himself as current as possible on medical developments. Also, from some of his questions, it was obvious that his clinic didn't have the most up-to-date equipment available. Nevertheless, Dr. Gonzales knew of recent developments and surgical techniques. His only need was the technical experience to perform the procedures.

By the end of the first day, Charles had reviewed the records that the Cubans brought with them and the results of the tests that had been performed. He had worked out a very preliminary course of treatment. There was some lab work still incomplete, but he felt that he would be ready the following day to provide his patient with a comprehensive picture.

Charles had heard of Pablo's reputation as a tough and ruthless man. Having had some dealing with him many years ago, Charles didn't doubt the reputation was accurate. Charles also knew that a person who was facing a serious medical problem and possibly death had a predictable reaction.

Priests and preachers were always the easiest to deal with. Charles believed that they had always expected death and looked forward to meeting the maker they had spent a lifetime praising. They rarely got upset, and to see them leave the office, one would think they had received good news.

Royalty and the rich were the most difficult. They believed that they were indispensable and it was necessary for them to live. More importantly, they also believed that their money should be able to buy a cure. They were the saddest and most pathetic to deal with. It wasn't uncommon for them to break down and cry in the office.

Paupers and common people were the most heartbreaking. They went through life with so little that they never really valued good health that much. Their focus was on the loved ones being left behind. They knew that they had nothing to leave them, and they suffered disappointment at their failure to provide a better life for their families.

Criminals were the most interesting. They placed little value on life, except their own. They had a persona of toughness, and they couldn't let that mask be taken away, even when facing death. They rarely asked questions and took the news of their impending death with the same outward emotion as hearing the score of a football game. Inwardly, they were shattered and often cried at the first opportunity when alone.

Of course, nobody fits the pattern exactly. Charles thought that if he had to tell Pablo that he was dying, his reaction would be that of a criminal.

Pablo had gone from a very sociable glad-hander at the airport to a pleasant, but very serious patient. He tried hard not to show his concern, but he was clearly worried about what news he would get at the consultation. Charles thought how ironic it was that he was now experiencing the same emotion that he had caused in hundreds of other people throughout his life.

It was late afternoon and Charles invited Pablo to his office and offered him a seat. As the Cuban was sitting down, Charles suggested that perhaps he might like to hear the news by himself. Pablo agreed and snarled something in Spanish to Dr. Gonzales and the translator who quickly left and closed the door.

"It's been a long time, Charles. You've done well for yourself," said Pablo as he crossed his legs and got comfortable in the chair.

Charles was still looking at some forms and didn't look up immediately. Then he spoke. "It has been a long time, Pablo. And I think you did all right for yourself, also. We've gotten a lot older and meet under much different circumstances than the first time. You helped me once and I haven't forgotten it. I can assure you that you'll get the very best medical care that I and this hospital can provide."

Charles took a seat behind his desk facing his patient.

Pablo responded, "I know that, Charles. When I saw the publicity about your research, I recognized you immediately. I knew that I had a problem and thought that there can't be anyone better at curing cancer than you. So here I am." A big grin crossed the Cuban's face.

Charles smiled back "Now, we have work to do, don't we, Pablo?" The smile disappeared and Pablo steadied himself for the report.

Charles started, "I rarely provide information this soon to a patient. We simply don't have enough tests complete to provide a comprehensive assessment. Since you insist on a daily report I'm going to do that. But I must stress that the information is preliminary, and could change depending on the test results that we don't have yet."

Pablo nodded his head and said nothing.

"Pablo, overall you seem to be in remarkably good health. Your vital signs are strong, and the tests we've completed so far show that your vital organs are healthy. Problems that affect most men your age and what most American men worry about are absent. You've taken good care of your body over the years and it shows. You'll probably live another active and healthy thirty years before you succumb to the ailments of an old man. If all of my patients took such good care of themselves, many of my colleagues in the medical profession would be driving trucks."

Pablo laughed heartily. Both he and Charles knew that Mr. Palance had started his working life as a truck driver!

Charles continued, "The only problem I've found so far is in your prostate."

Pablo nodded his head again.

"The diagnosis that was made in Cuba is correct. We have more sophisticated equipment here than is available to Dr. Gonzales, and we can more comprehensively determine the problem. My diagnosis confirms the initial diagnosis. You have a cancerous condition in your prostate."

Charles stopped and looked at his patient. "You're aware of where the prostate is and what it does?"

Pablo nodded his head again indicating that he understood.

Charles went on. "The total extent of the destruction of the prostate won't be known until we operate and visually inspect the gland. I don't know if the cancer has spread, but we'll know more tomorrow when we get additional lab results. My guess right now is that it hasn't spread. I believe we'll be able to remove the cancerous tissue successfully. But, I need to stress again strongly that these are preliminary results and the blood tests may modify what I'm saying. I'm happy to report that we've made a lot of advances in prostate surgery in the past few years. Until recently, prostate surgery always left the patient impotent. Those days are now over for most prostate surgeries. We can now operate on most cancers and leave the nerve system attached to the prostate gland intact, thus preventing impotence."

"Good news on two counts," smiled Pablo.

"Yes, it is good news," continued Charles. "The patients where we've diagnosed the cancer before too much damage has been done survive nicely and enjoy a normal life. Now, my initial assessment is that you'll have to have surgery and then a series of chemotherapy treatments that will last for approximately four months. I'll do the surgery. Subject to your approval, I've invited Dr. Gonzales to assist me.

"He has studied the procedure, and he can get some firsthand exposure on how it's done. We have other similar operations scheduled for the next couple of days, and he's going to attend those procedures also. So, you'll get your treatment and free training for Dr. Gonzales while you're here. The follow-up therapy can be done here or in Cuba. Dr. Gonzales is very knowledgeable and experienced in those procedures. Of course, it will be your decision."

"When do we operate?"

Looking at his chart again, Charles answered, "Assuming all of the lab work comes back tomorrow and confirms my initial diagnosis, I think we can operate in three days. I have to leave for Washington tomorrow night and will be back the following day. We'll do the surgery the following morning. You'll be required to stay in the hospital for two additional days. After that, you can be discharged. You can stay here for the follow-up treatments or return to Cuba."

Pablo looked like he was playing poker. "In my business, Charles, being away from the job is a real bad idea. I will return to Cuba as quickly as possible. In fact, if there's a way that I don't have to stay in the hospital for two additional days, I would prefer to leave immediately after the surgery."

"Pablo, a patient can always check himself out of the hospital at any time. That's your decision. My strong recommendation would be that you stay for both recovery days. We have to be careful of your health and complications. If something unforeseen develops, we need all the medical expertise that's in this hospital to be available to us."

Pablo didn't speak for what seemed several minutes. "OK, what's next, Charles?"

"There's no more today, Pablo. You can return to your room or whatever the State Department and your security people permit. I have no further medical work to do."

"Good. Thanks, Charles. I appreciate your help." Pablo rose from his chair. "You know, all of this is very ironic. After our dealings so long ago, I never thought I'd see you again. In fact, we keep track of a lot of people, but you were never one of them. We didn't know of you until the recent publicity regarding the electromagnetic wave experiments. As I said, your name rang a bell and so we looked into our very old files and there you were. Our relationship so many years ago was obviously very beneficial to you. I think it's fair to say you wouldn't be here had it not been for help from me. Do you remember Ray Echeveria?"

Charles thought for a minute. "Of course, I remember Ray. How is he?"

Pablo looked stern. "Ray is still living in Miami close to the Ocean Ranch Hotel. But don't worry about any problems with him."

Charles didn't know exactly what Pablo meant, but it didn't sound good. "I'm not exactly sure what that means, but I appreciate not having to be concerned about what he might say. You helped me, Pablo, at a time when I needed some help. I'm where I am partially because of you. We both know that you could undo that help you provided in 1971. I hope that's not in your plans. Now, I have a chance to help you and I'm going to do my best."

Pablo Palance didn't reply.

Charles extended his hand. "Well, that's about all I have for now. I'll see you tomorrow with more test results and we can discuss more fully your treatment."

Pablo stood up and extended his hand. "Thank you, Charles. I'll see you tomorrow morning."

On the drive home Charles' mind was reliving events from 1971. His first thought was that Pablo didn't seem a lot different than when they had met so many years ago. He was an affable and pleasant young man who had grown into a very secretive and cruel older man. He could still

158

be pleasant and even charming if he wanted to be. He could also cause Charles a lot of trouble. Charles would like to hear from Pablo that he was only here for medical treatment, and that Charles could forget any possibility that the past would be mentioned. But why would a man like Pablo Palance give such an assurance? It was better for him to have Charles worried about it until the airplane left for Cuba. On the other hand, it would also seem prudent to have a surgeon only thinking about one's good health when an operation is scheduled.

Amid the concern about Mr. Palance, Charles remembered that he and Bobbie were leaving tomorrow afternoon to join the President and First Lady for dinner. After dinner it would be back to the Oval Office and the President's announcement about withdrawing all the broadcasting licenses. He understood that the Surgeon General and his wife would join them in the family quarters of the White House after the announcement.

Charles childishly hoped he and Bobbie would be in the Lincoln Bedroom. He had heard so much about it.

Washington, D.C.

The Council of Broadcasters had put the finishing touches on their legal brief to the Supreme Court. They asked for an immediate Temporary Restraining Order to prevent the President from withdrawing the FCC broadcasting permits a number of legal reasons. The primary reason that would involve the Supreme Court was that the President's action would violate article I of the Bill of Rights. The Temporary Restraining Order, or TRO as the lawyers call it, would keep the Federal Communication Commission from acting until a federal court heard the lawsuit. If the TRO were issued it would effectively delay any action for years unless there was some speedup of the hearings or the case would be heard at the Supreme Court – a very unusual action. All that was needed to start the proceedings was the official announcement by the President tomorrow night.

This was really the last hope for the broadcasters. Even if they were successful with the Supreme Court, they still had the problems of towers being toppled. On the average there was one tower going down every day somewhere in the United States and two a week throughout Europe. If the situation wasn't resolved, only the largest broadcasters would still be in business in a couple of months because they would be the only ones that could protect their towers. Even that might be a hollow victory. If businesses were pressured not to advertise on the airwaves, there might not be any customers for the broadcasts. The broadcasters were banking on the American people disregarding the danger of EMs, much like they disregard the danger of smoking.

Mr. Mahoney likened his situation to a comment he once heard about a new play that opened in New York. The critic had said it was, "a bad play with a worse ending."

Fort Valley, Georgia

Vonda had learned that the President would be on television again tomorrow night and that Charles had been invited to attend. She made sure that she didn't schedule anything for the evening so she could see Charles. She was still steadfastly resisting comments from her sister that she get involved in his life.

Vonda had hired a couple more employees to be around the house 24 hours a day since she thought she was being followed. She hadn't seen any evidence of anyone following her recently and thought that maybe it was all over. It seemed like the announcement tomorrow night would shift all of the attention from Charles and his research to the President and his expected restrictions on broadcasters.

CHAPTER TWENTY-FOUR

Tuesday, January 10

<u>Columbus, Ohio</u>

Charles was in the office early to check the results of Pablo's lab tests and found no surprises. The Cuban's health was excellent except for the prostate gland.

At 9:00 a.m. he had another meeting with Pablo in the hospital suite the nurses had started calling "the fortress." After the meeting, Charles would have a few hours to take care of some other paperwork that was piling up before heading to Port Columbus Airport for the short flight to Washington.

Charles knocked and entered when the Cuban guard opened the door. Inside, Pablo was eating a hearty American breakfast with Dr. Gonzalez.

"Hey, great breakfast!" yelled Pablo. "I always liked American breakfasts. Can I have grits again tomorrow?"

Charles smiled his doctor smile. "Of course, I'll make arrangements with the kitchen to be sure you have grits with your next breakfast."

Charles took a seat in the remaining empty chair and opened his chart. "I won't have to take a lot of your time, Pablo. Everything looks very good. The lab work was all within normal limits. So, you have a date with me in the surgery suite the day after tomorrow."

"OK," said an unusually cheerful patient. "I've talked to Dr. Gonzales and he attended one surgery yesterday and will assist you with my surgery. Fidel also wants my security guard to attend. Will that be a problem?"

Charles furrowed his eyebrows, "A security guard in the operating room?" A suddenly more serious Pablo finished nibbling his omelet. "Well, it seems that the security people in Cuba get very nervous when someone like me is made unconscious. They think somebody might inject other drugs into us and question us, or we'll say something we shouldn't say. It's just a precaution."

Charles pondered a minute. "I don't suppose I have any problems with that, but the guard will have to be in sterile surgical garb and he won't be able to carry a weapon."

Pablo looked up surprised. "What good is a guard without a gun?"

Charles pondered for a minute. "Well, if someone with a very sharp knife was cutting my prostate, I'd want that person thinking every minute about what he was doing. I wouldn't want his mind to wander and think about somebody behind him with a gun in his pocket."

Pablo roared with laughter. "I didn't think of it that way. OK, OK. The guard will have no gun, just ears!!"

Charles stood up to leave, and Pablo raised his hand as a gesture to stay. He then looked at the guard and Dr. Gonzales. Both rose immediately and left the room.

"Before you leave, Charles, I want to talk a minute. I know that you're going to Washington today to meet with the President. That's a big honor and you deserve it. I also understand you'll be staying overnight at the White House."

Charles nodded his agreement.

"So, you'll get to speak to the President often. I have a message I would like you to give to the President."

Charles didn't respond.

"Before the revolution our countries were the best of friends. Fidel changed that and many Cubans have suffered for years. After Fidel goes, our countries can be good friends once again. Fidel has very little time left. I don't mean to suggest some overthrow or anything like that. Fidel has an organization that is very strong and they're very good at their job. Fidel and I know every dissident in the country, and they are taken care of when they get too active.

"We're not quite as brutal as in the old days, but we are thorough. Fidel is an old man now and his time is limited. Everyone, including me, who has any possibility to succeed Fidel disagrees with his policies and will change them immediately. Cuba will actively seek reconciliation with the United States. With the loss of support from the Soviet Union, we suffer even more than before; our economy continued to decline.

"Fidel will only do the minimum to help the Cuban people. He will never renounce his personal goals or the goals of the revolution. He simply can't find the strength to repudiate his communist policies. The situation is desperate and worsening every day. And, as I said, Fidel is an

162

old man and not in the best of health. He's suffering from many maladies of old age and it won't be long before he can't fulfill his duties.

"At some point he'll appoint a successor, and retire to his villa as an elder statesman. His successor will be kind to him and show him the respect of a man who saved Cuba from the dictator Batista. Fortunately, he will not continue his policies. All change will be slow, and hidden under the umbrella of helping the poor people.

"Fidel will know it's a change but he won't do anything about it. He'll rationalize the actions, as keeping up with a modern society and the early changes will be helpful. The first changes will be things like increased medical care, better transportation, and better housing. Then efforts will be made to increase tourism to supplement our treasury, and eventually democracy. I know that will happen. I'm sure because I know every possible successor."

Charles listened and still offered no response.

Pablo didn't expect or want a reply. "Now, my message for President Jenkins. Please ask him to reconsider your policies toward Cuba. When there is any chance for a peace offering, it should be done. The people of Cuba need help now. We do not need further hardening of feelings between the countries. When Fidel leaves, we'll need the help of our old American friends desperately. That's all I ask you to say. Thank you."

Charles rose from his chair. "I'll mention what you've told me to the President, and I'll see you in two days. And, I'll be sure to have grits sent up with your breakfast in the morning." Both men smiled.

As Charles headed for the door, he stopped and turned. "One more thing, sometime before you leave, I'd like to hear how you handled the moncy." Pablo smiled the biggest smile Charles had seen and nodded his head.

Charles and Bobbie arrived at the Washington airport at 3:30 and were met by a black limo that took them to the White House. The President and First Lady were at an event downtown and weren't available to greet them when they arrived. After going through security, the protocol staff escorted them to the hoped-for Lincoln Bedroom so they could freshen up. The bowl of fruit on the nightstand had a note from the President welcoming them to the White House and apologizing for not being there when they arrived. A schedule was in another envelope, and it indicated that they would be called for dinner at six. At 7:30 they would go to the Oval Office in preparation for the 9:00 address to the nation. Charles remembered that he had thought an hour and a half was a long time to get ready, but recalled how they just about made it the last time he was in the Oval Office for a telecast.

At 6:00 there was a light knock on the door and a member of the protocol staff escorted them to dinner in the residential section of the White House. It was the first time Charles and Bobbie had met Marcia Jenkins, the First Lady. She had abundant southern charm and was as enchanting in person as she appeared to be on television. Dinner conversation was led by the President who talked about his days at Ohio State and the fond memories he had of his college years. He chided the First Lady for attending that 'trade' school in Georgia, and said he would never forgive her for sending their daughter there. The First Lady defended herself and her school very respectably and everyone had a good laugh.

The conversation got serious for a short period of time when the President asked about Charles' patient from Cuba. He indicated that his diagnosis was nothing special and that Pablo would be operated on in two days and Charles didn't expect any complications.

Charles then added, "There is one interesting thing, Mr. President. Before I left today, I had a meeting with Mr. Palance to go over his course of treatment. After that he said he knew I was going to be here tonight and he asked me to give you a message."

The President put down his fork and paid full attention to Charles.

"He reminded me that Cuba and the United States were very good friends and good neighbors before Fidel. He said that nobody who could succeed Fidel agreed with his current policies. He added that since they lost the support of the Soviet Union things have been very desperate in Cuba. He asked that you be told that when Fidel is gone, once again Cuba and the United States can be good neighbors and good friends. He added that he would like you to keep all that in mind when formulating your policies and actions toward Cuba."

The President seemed pensive for a few moments. "That's interesting. We were scheduled to have coffee after the address tonight and I had invited the Secretary of State to join us. Unfortunately, he had to cancel due to an injury to one of his children. I'd like to invite someone else from the State Department to join us tonight. I'll get someone who's a specialist on Cuban matters. Any objections?"

Charles was a little surprised at the President asking if there was any objection to someone being invited to the White House. "That's fine with me, Mr. President. But, I don't know any more than I've already told you."

164

The President had started picking at his chocolate cake. "I realize that. But the State Department people have information that you might be interested in and, more importantly, they might want to send a message back with you."

Charles agreed. Minutes later the door opened and a protocol assistant appeared to remind the President that it was time to go to the Oval Office and prepare for the speech.

It was Bobbie's second visit to the Oval Office and she was again surprised at how small it was. When they crammed in the TV cameras and assorted support equipment, there was very little room for the President.

Charles and the Surgeon General would again sit next to the President but off camera. Sometime during the talk, a camera would pan to both of them, and their attendance would show their support for the President. At ten minutes to nine everyone, including the President, was in place. Lighting, sound levels, colors and clarity had been checked and double-checked. The maid was re-dusting and other housekeeping staffers were double-checking everything behind the President. All was in readiness when the final countdown started. One minute and thirty seconds later the President began his talk.

"Good evening, my fellow Americans. I've asked for broadcast time this evening so I can report to you a very important decision that I've made on behalf of all Americans. President Truman had a sign on his desk that said 'The Buck Stops Here.' President Truman was right. The most difficult decisions that affect all of us are made here. For the past several months there has been considerable discussion regarding a research paper that was authored by Dr. Charles Hancock regarding the effects of electromagnetic rays on each of our bodies. The conclusions that Dr. Hancock reached were that the cumulative effects of the rays are very harmful and, in fact, produce cancer. Dr. Hancock is with me tonight along with Dr. Gardner, the Surgeon General of the United States."

The TV cameras focused on the two physicians for about ten seconds and then back to the President.

"The work by Dr. Hancock has been reviewed by Surgeon General Gardner and a blue-ribbon panel of scientists and physicians appointed by him. The findings of Dr. Hancock have been validated. The electromagnetic emissions generated by radio station, television stations, mobile phones, and satellites are lethal. The radio and television stations in your town are emitting electromagnetic rays, and those rays are hitting your body twenty-four hours a day. They are like the proverbial straw that broke the camel's back. One straw or one electromagnetic ray emission is harmless, but when many are added together, they damage your bodies and cause cancer. No one is immune including our children. After a careful and detailed study, I've decided that for the benefit of all citizens, as many of these electromagnetic emissions that can be eliminated, must be.

"I've directed Federal Communication Administrator, Kevin Stoneman, to deny any future requests for the use of the airwaves for commercial purposes. I have also directed that most current broadcast certificates be revoked within the next thirty days. Our airwaves will no longer be available for use by such things as cellular phones, satellites, TV, radio, or any use that's not essential to our society. Approval will still be given for emergency use. The FAA will still be permitted to use the airways for air traffic control; the military, police, and organizations of that nature will continue to have use of the airways for communication. Guidelines will be issued in the Federal Register as required by law, and those guidelines will be published as quickly as possible.

"These restrictions will be a sacrifice for many of our citizens. But considering the damage that these rays are doing to our citizens, they must be terminated.

"I've also directed that attention be paid to the rate structures for the remaining forms of communications to ensure that there's no price gouging or excessive profit. This is a time of national need and I won't permit profiteering.

"There will be some who claim the actions I'm announcing tonight are violations of their First Amendment right which guarantees that the government will not interfere with their right to free speech. I disagree with those comments. There are legitimate limits on free speech that government can require. For example, someone cannot put large bullhorns on their cars and cruise your neighborhood at 3 a.m. making speeches and waking everyone up. This is the same thing. If exercise of some portion of your free speech is causing citizens to be less healthy and contract cancer, it must be regulated. Again, I regret the inconvenience that this will have on many citizens, but the steps I've taken are necessary to protect us all. Thank you, good night and God bless you."

All the cameras were immediately switched off, and the local stations switched back to their commentators. The President looked relieved and waved his hand for Charles, Bobbie and Dr. Gardner to follow him and the First Lady out of the Oval Office. The five of them went back to the residence section where Assistant Secretary of State

Mary Perkins met them. Secretary Perkins and the President had served in the Coast Guard together and had been friends for many years. After being elected to the Presidency, Harrison Jenkins had persuaded his old friend to leave her teaching post at the University of Miami and join his administration. Mary was excited about the new job and was particularly happy about being responsible for South America and Cuba in particular. She had many Cuban friends in the South Miami area, and the subject of Cuban relations was a personal interest of hers.

After introductions and everyone had ordered drinks, the President asked, "Well, what do you think?"

All heads nodded up and down, and Secretary Perkins answered first. "It was a very difficult decision, Mr. President, but it was the right decision. I'm sure the TV stations will be very critical, but it had to be done."

The President reached over and picked up the TV channel changer and turned on the Barry Burlington Show. "Charles, I'm sure you watch this show every evening," chuckled the President.

"Yeah," chortled Charles, "my very favorite show." They watched the show for about five minutes and listened to Barry Burlington and two doctors and a constitutional lawyer he had as guests.

The criticism of the President's speech was bitter and bordered on cruel. The doctors alleged that there were insufficient data to prove that electromagnetic rays were harmful, and the lawyer contended that it was a clear abridgement of the free speech clause of the Bill of Rights. Barry Burlington was the most vicious and kept alleging that there was a sinister plot afoot by the government. None of the four men ever produced a shred of proof for any of their comments.

At one point, it seemed that Barry Burlington was going to break down and cry when he said that in a month he might be off the air. He suggested that losing his show would be like closing a window where the American people can clearly see what's really going on in America and Washington. Barry made it sound like there was a lot of lying and trickery going on in Washington, and that he, and only he, was the protector of the American people from the devious Washington crowd.

After a few minutes the President clicked off the TV. "I guess that's how it's going to go for the next month. As they say, 'the dogs bark, but the caravan moves on.' Now let's get to a little business regarding one Mr. Pablo Palance. Mary?"

"Yes, Mr. President. We reviewed the comments that Mr. Palance made to Dr. Hancock and, frankly, we weren't surprised. We know Pablo

Palance very well. If you have any doubts about him, I can assure you that he's Fidel's hit man. He's also very bright and something of a thinker. The intelligence we've been getting from our sources confirms significant dissatisfaction by just about every citizen in Cuba. They know that the other communist governments have failed, and they have always known about the prosperity of the United States. They want to enjoy the same prosperity and they also want Fidel out. However, Fidel long ago found out how to keep the military and the police loyal. There's little chance of any action until he's gone.

"There's speculation about who will replace him, but the odds-on-favorite is the General who is the Army Chief of Staff. He's been loyal to Castro for many years, and is much younger than Fidel. He also likes to be seen whenever the army provides any support to the people during hurricanes, floods, and things like that.

"He's always been absent when there've been abuses by the army and has never been on television except under favorable circumstances. People like him. He also has the respect of the field commanders and the police. Should the General be the next Cuban leader, Mr. Palance will definitely be out of work, and more likely dead or in prison.

"It depends on what kind of backlash there is to Fidel and the desires of the new leader. There could be something like the truth commission that was formed when South Africa changed governments. If that happens, Mr. Palance will be in deep trouble. Of course, he could also succeed Fidel; we, and the CIA, think that's very unlikely.

"We have to assume that Mr. Palance will ask you if you passed on his comments to the President. My recommendation is that you tell him you did talk to the President about it and that the American government is acting very much like Mr. Palance has suggested. We're looking for ways to help establish democracy in Cuba. We look forward to the day when it will once again be a good friend and a good neighbor.

"You can also suggest to Mr. Palance that if he can be of help to us in any way, we would be most appreciative. He now has reason to contact the United States, and any information he would like to provide could be provided through you, Dr. Hancock. I'm not suggesting that you become a spy. If Mr. Palance has information of interest to the government he could get it easily to you and you can pass it on to us. Also, if Mr. Palance would like a contact in Cuba to get information to us, we could provide him one."

Bobbie looked at Charles for a reaction, but saw none.

"I don't have any objection to being a conduit for information," said Charles. "Of course, I have no experience whatsoever in any kind of espionage."

The President guffawed. "Hey, I like that. Dr. Charles Hancock, physician and researcher famous for discovering a cause of cancer, unmasked as a working spy! It's a great headline for the next edition of the 'Real News' and the Barry Burlington Show."

Everyone laughed, but Charles felt a little shudder inside. He changed the subject

"Mr. President, if you will excuse me for just a minute, I have something for you."

The President nodded while Charles stood and went to the Lincoln Bedroom and returned with a parcel wrapped in a scarlet and gray.

"Since you're an Ohio State Alum, I was asked by the University President to give this to you as a small remembrance of Ohio State and your days there."

The President accepted the box, opened it, and smiled a broad grin.

"Well, I'll be - A football from the last Rose Bowl win signed by Archie Griffin. Archie's still the only player to win the Heisman Trophy twice. What can I say? I know – 'Beat Michigan'."

Everyone had a hearty laugh and made small talk for the next 20 minutes before the President said he had a big day tomorrow and that it was time for him to go to bed.

Charles reminded the President that he and Bobbie were leaving early in the morning and wouldn't see him before they left. He thanked the President and First Lady and cordially invited them to return to Columbus to visit the University. Charles was looking forward to his night in the Lincoln Bedroom.

Peach County, Georgia

Vonda watched the television show and was delighted to see Charles. It brought back memories of the old days and how much fun they had had in Miami. She wondered for the last time what his little secret was there, but then made a decision to erase that year and Charles Hancock from her mind. She concluded that it had been a great time, a lot of fun, and that it was over a long time ago. She vowed never to talk or think about it again – and she never did.

<u>Washington, D.C.</u>

The Council of Broadcasters had watched the President's address and weren't surprised. John Mahoney and his assistants would be knocking on the door of the Chief Justice of the Supreme Court of America as quickly as they could get there after the President's speech to the nation. In their briefcases would be a voluminous request for a Temporary Restraining Order against the President of the United States.

<u>Columbus, Ohio</u>

Harold and Jeff were watching the President's speech and were very impressed, and proud, when the camera showed their father in the Oval Office next to the President. They also turned on the Barry Burlington Show to see his reaction and were disgusted at the effort.

Pablo also watched and wondered if Charles had passed his message to the President.

CHAPTER TWENTY-FIVE

Wednesday, January 11

Columbus, Ohio

The day started at 7:00 a.m. for Charles and Bobbie with a light breakfast served in their room by the White House domestic staff. They had packed only two suitcases, and the staff whisked them off when breakfast was served. By 7:45 they were back in the White House limo being delivered to Washington National Airport for the flight to Ohio.

The flight was routine and Charles easily found the car in the short-term parking lot at Port Columbus Airport. Charles hadn't planned to work that day but did stop by the hospital to visit with Pablo before he and Bobbie went home for the remainder of the day.

The visit was short. Charles reviewed the medical chart to be sure there were no changes since he had seen Pablo the last time. During the visit Pablo indicated that he had seen Charles on TV with the President and said he was very impressed. He added that he knew how important it could be to be seen with the President of the country. Before Charles left, he expected Pablo to bring up the subject of the message he had sent to the President. Since Pablo did not mention it, Charles decided he would discuss it. He gave Pablo a report of the conversation and basically said that the American Government agreed and that the U.S. Foreign policy was consistent with the request.

The only comment from the Cuban was, "Thanks, Charles, I'd like to discuss it once more before I leave."

Charles nodded his head.

Washington, D.C.

John Mahoney and three of his assistants were in the limo and heading for the imposing edifice of the Supreme Court of the United States. They were dropped off and given a small card with the number of the limo so they could call and the car would reappear from wherever the driver could find a parking space near the Court. The four men walked up the steps, which were already populated with some tourists who wanted to see if there was a session today. Earlier in the day, Mahoney had tipped off the press, and a large number of reporters were also on hand to greet him. He stopped briefly to answer some questions from them and reiterated his position on the unconstitutionality of the President's decision.

The request for a Temporary Restraining Order that was in the two boxes being pulled behind one of the assistants was the product of hundreds, and possibly thousands, of hours of research and writing. It outlined the entire case that they would be pleading when they got to court, and the request for the Temporary Restraining Order outlined why the President's decision should not be implemented immediately. They all had prearranged for entry badges and were passed through security very quickly. They headed to the area in the building where the justices had their chambers and passed through security again. This time, the guard rang the security officer inside the locked doors who verified that the Chief Justice was expecting Mr. Mahoney and his assistants. Once all the checks had been done, Mr. Mahoney was escorted to the outer office of the Chief Justice of the Supreme Court. It was all very impressive. Justices very rarely personally accept anything for the court. There are procedures that are followed and for the Chief Justice to personally get involved so early was unheard of. Mr. Mahoney wondered why.

When they arrived there were also representatives from the Justice Department. The attorneys shook hands but said little. The spokesman for the government remarked on how the government had not finished writing a brief and they were very surprised to be summoned to the chambers of the Chief Justice.

As expected, the outer office was done in dark wood paneling and rich thick carpet with portraits of all past Chief Justices on the walls. The furniture was a rich red/brown collection of sofas and chairs with a table and lamp next to each one. On the wall, an antique railroad clock ticked and reminded everyone of the importance of being on time. After waiting almost twenty minutes, they were ushered into the Chief Justice's conference room. The room was next to the office of the Chief Justice, and he had his own entrance into the room.

A prize assignment for a recent law school graduate is a chance to perform law clerk duties at the Supreme Court. Only the top students are even considered for the prestigious assignments. Attending hearings and doing research for the justices was a very satisfying job for any clerk and also a stepping-stone to a lucrative attorney's position in the future. One of the side benefits was the actual witnessing of history that sometimes happens. Those clerks who were involved in the impeachment trial of President Clinton got very enriching experience at the time. Today was another one of those days. Requests for temporary restraining orders are relatively common in courthouses across America and are often granted. A request directly to the Chief Justice asking to restrain the President of the United States was rare and truly history making. Having the Chief Justice personally accept the request was unprecedented.

There were over ten law clerks sitting around the conference room to witness the event.

A young woman who appeared to be one of the law clerks was standing when Mr. Mahoney and the other lawyers were ushered into the room. She identified herself as a clerk to the Chief Justice and assured everyone that the Chief Justice would be there shortly. Everyone took seats at the table where the young woman indicated they should sit.

John Mahoney was uncharacteristically bewildered by all the action. First the Chief Justice is accepting the request, and the government attorneys were invited. Nevertheless, an air of confidence surrounded Mr. Mahoney and his party as they anticipated their discussion with the Chief Justice. They were not clear exactly what to expect but had high expectations that their request for a Temporary Restraining Order would be granted.

Their research into obtaining TRO's was that they were granted very often to prevent harm to organizations that could be caused by implementation of judges' orders or, in this case, the President's. In this case, there were billions of dollars and thousands of jobs at risk. The impact of the government's action was massive, and mandated that a TRO be granted until all the details could be assessed by a judge in a federal courtroom. Also, it was a serious matter of constitutional interpretation, and the Supreme Court liked to take its time on matters of this nature.

None of the clerks talked to Mr. Mahoney or anyone else while they waited for the Chief Justice. It was a silent five minutes that seemed like five hours. After the tense wait, the door at the head of the table started to open, and a young man appeared and spoke in a loud voice. "Ladies and Gentlemen, the Chief Justice of the Supreme Court of the United States of America, the Honorable Steve Parson. Please rise."

Everyone rose as the somewhat haggard looking Chief Justice entered the room and sat at the head of the table. "Please be seated."

Since it was basically a request that was being delivered, there were no rules of court to apply. John Mahoney spoke from his seat.

"Thank you, Mr. Chief Justice, for agreeing to hear our request for a temporary restraining order. I know your time is valuable and I'll try to keep my comments as brief as possible."

The sunken eyes of the Chief Justice showed no reaction to Mahoney's comments, but his head nodded.

"Sir, last night the President of the United States made a speech to the American people. In that speech he announced that he was withdrawing broadcast permits for all radio and television stations plus most other forms of broadcasting. There were exceptions for some defense, emergency, police, air traffic control and limited other users.

"His reasons for this withdrawal of permits, and presumably prison for anyone who continues to broadcast, are based on scanty evidence that these broadcasts are a medical danger to the human body and could cause cancer. The President has reached conclusions that are, at best, inaccurate and, at worst, prohibited by the Constitution. Let me first discuss the constitutional question. The First Amendment to the Constitution says that..."

"I know what the constitution says," snapped the Chief Justice.

The comment caught Mahoney off guard. "Of course, you do," replied Mahoney. "I was simply providing a basis to outline our request."

The Chief Justice sat mute. Mahoney wasn't actually prepared to argue a case. He had only come to deliver it. Of course, he knew the subject in depth and looked on the meeting with the Chief Justice as an advantage for his client. He wasn't exactly sure what the Chief Justice wanted, so after a short pause, he resumed.

"The President's actions are a clear violation of the First Amendment to the Constitution of the United States. His order deprives citizens of the guaranteed exercise of their free speech rights. This is not a murky area of free-speech law like flag burning, draft card burning or exotic dancing. The President has clearly prohibited radio and television stations from exercising their free speech. This is a right that they have enjoyed from the early part of this century. It's government censorship, pure and simple."

Mr. Mahoney referenced various cases where the court found numerous forms of expression to be protected. In a monotone voice, he methodically ticked off the reasons why the constitution was not being observed and the President was wrong in his interpretations. As the monologue reached the forty-five minute point, everyone was amazed that the Chief Justice asked no questions nor made any other comments. He seemed to have an expression of disinterest and a mind that didn't seem to be in the same room as everyone else. The normally active and inquisitive Justice was impassive and almost in pain with the arguments of Mr. Mahoney.

After concluding his comments on the constitutional questions, Mr. Mahoney went to the argument of harm. "The second point, Mr. Chief Justice is that the basis of the President's decision is simply unproven and will cause irreparable damage to a large segment of business. This harm will be in the form of thousands of lost jobs and billions of dollars that were invested in the infrastructure of the corporations. The President claims that a panel that he appointed has replicated the research of one scientist. Based on that evidence, he decided to take these draconian steps. We've not seen any of this validation, but we've been told it will be provided sometime in the future."

Mr. Mahoney spent considerable time discussing the research and analysis that had been used in the past when large actions had taken place. He mentioned the thalidomide scare of the fifties, automobile recalls for safety defects, and the recall of food products when harmful products were manufactured.

"In each case, Mr. Chief Justice, there was considerably more research and much less economic impact than what the President has based his decision on."

Mr. Mahoney went on with details of medical assertions that contradicted the findings of Dr. Hancock and cited numerous cancer studies and other studies of high-voltage energy where there was no conclusive proof that the emissions contributed to cancer. He thought to himself that he was proud of his memory. He hadn't expected to go into this detail but he seemed to remember everything that was in the brief.

"In summary, Mr. Chief Justice, we ask for a temporary restraining order for two reasons.

"First, allowing the President to take the actions he has indicated will trample the Constitution and the Bill of Rights. His decision violates the sacred principles that have guided this great land for so long and provided our citizens with the information they need to be an informed and learned society.

"Secondly, the broadcast industry employs thousands of employees who would be immediately unemployed. Billions of dollars of investments would be lost, and negotiated contracts would be broken and cause bankruptcies that could not be recovered."

After a short pause, Mr. Mahoney completed his plea. "Mr. Chief Justice, contained in the official request I've brought with me are the details and citations that I believe fully support our request and we urge that you grant a temporary restraining order and let the courts determine the validity of everything under review."

After an hour and fifteen minutes, Mr. Mahoney completed his presentation.

The Chief Justice had sat stone-faced and stoic throughout the entire presentation. The only exception was when he snapped that he didn't have to be briefed on the Constitution.

Chief Justice Steve Parson looked at the lawyers from the Department of Justice. "Does the government have any comments pertaining to this request for a TRO?"

The government lawyers were unprepared and one of the Assistant Attorney Generals replied. "Mr. Chief Justice, the government is not prepared at this time to reply formally. We believe that the President has acted properly and will be prepared to defend his actions at the proper time. However, we were only notified today to be at this meeting, and we have not been served a copy of the request nor read it. It's impossible for us to reply. We request adequate time to review the request and referenced materials."

To everyone's surprise, the Chief Justice said, "Let's take a fifteen-minute break," and he stood up and left through the same door he had entered the room. Some of the clerks left the room by the main door. The law clerk who had greeted everyone advised that there was coffee in the back of the room and the restrooms were in the hall. Mr. Mahoney and his assistants gathered in the hall for a quick post-mortem of the presentation and unanimously agreed that Mahoney had made an excellent presentation. The government lawyers stayed in the room.

After exactly fifteen minutes, the Chief Justice returned to the room and everyone stood again in respect.

"Mr. Mahoney, you made a very good presentation of your concerns in this case. You're undoubtedly a very good attorney, or you wouldn't have been chosen for your present position."

The Chief Justice looked at the government lawyers. "I understand that the government is not prepared at this time to make comments. You'll have your chance."

Turning back to Mr. Mahoney, the Chief Justice spoke again. "I have a few questions to ask of you Mr. Mahoney."

The room was quiet as a tomb waiting for the Chief Justice to ask his questions.

"First, the President, in his speech last night, reminded the nation on the limitations of free speech. One example was the decision by this court that recognized that there are legitimate restrictions on the free-speech clause. One example of those restrictions prohibits someone from yelling 'fire' in a crowded theater. Do you agree with that?"

"Yes, sir," replied Mr. Mahoney.

"Second, the President also gave the example that a citizen could not put loud speakers on his car and cruise through a residential neighborhood in the middle of the night making a speech and disturbing the residents. Do you agree with that?"

Mr. Mahoney paused. The answer for anyone who lives in a residential area was obvious. But Mr. Mahoney knew there were no cases specifically on this point. After the President's speech last night, Mahoney had one of his assistants look for a case of that nature.

"Mr. Chief Justice, I don't believe there are any cases of this nature decided by the Supreme Court. However, on the surface I agree that prohibiting such an action is a permissible restriction of free speech."

"Thank you, Mr. Mahoney," resumed the Chief Justice, "I agree with your answers on those two issues and believe that is the proper application of the First Amendment."

"Now, I have a third question. It seems to me that a loudspeaker truck would affect a relatively small number of people, as would the situation with the patrons in a theater. We both agree that these instances of restricted free speech are appropriate. So, if restriction of speech in these small populations is appropriate, can you explain why a similar restriction on free speech doesn't apply when it's a safety issue for every single person in America?"

Mr. Mahoney had been trapped and he knew it. He also knew that this was the gaping hole in their case.

"Mr. Chief Justice, as we've said there is no proof that the electromagnetic rays cause cancer. So we don't acknowledge there is a safety question as there is with the theater example. There is also no nuisance question in this case, as there is with the car and a loudspeaker."

"Excuse me, Mr. Mahoney," intoned the Chief Justice. "We're not talking about the validity of the cancer-causing transmissions, we are only talking about the propriety of restricting free speech. I'd like you to answer assuming that the emissions are cancer-causing."

The line of questioning did not surprise Mr. Mahoney. He had expected and dreaded having to reply to these kinds of questions.

"Mr. Chief Justice, if it could be shown beyond a shadow of doubt that the emissions caused cancer, I would agree that terminating the broadcasts would be a permissible restriction of free speech."

The Chief Justice resumed in what seemed a very weary voice. "I'm glad we agree that if there's a danger, the President could take the action he's announced and it would be in harmony with the First Amendment."

Mr. Mahoney disliked it when someone re-phased the obvious but did it in such a way that everyone had to agree. "Now, Mr. Mahoney, you say that there is no proof, presumably acceptable to you, that the electromagnetic rays caused by the broadcasts are harmful. I've read the study and just about every piece of literature that's been published on this subject.

"First, we have Dr. Charles Hancock, a cancer researcher with many years of experience, who has conducted these studies for a number of years. His analysis is that the electromagnetic rays cause cancer. That same researcher solicited other experts in the field to replicate his work. They did the work in areas of both high-EM and low-EM emissions, and unanimously reached the same conclusion as Dr. Hancock.

"Ohio State University, one of the finest universities in America, and one with a renowned medical college, also reviewed the work. That University agrees and fully supports the conclusions of Dr. Hancock. The Surgeon General of the United States appoints a panel of distinguished physicians, physicists and researchers to review the study, and that group reports that they also agree.

"I've watched numerous talk shows and seen countless interviews with physicians who validate the conditions of human bodies that Dr. Hancock describes in his study. Dr. Hancock went on the only show that invited him and described his findings for all Americans to hear. We have numerous comments and interviews with physicians across the country that raise questions, but not one single person has said Dr. Hancock is wrong.

"And lastly, the President of the United States is the one person in the world with the most resources available to him on any subject. He's undoubtedly consulted with other people besides the ones I've just mentioned. The President of the United States believes that the electromagnetic rays transmitted across this country are causing cancer in many Americans." The Chief Justice stopped and looked directly at Mr. Mahoney.

"Given this amount of evidence, Mr. Mahoney, can you tell me what evidence must be produced to convince you, and your clients, that electromagnetic rays cause cancer?"

Mr. Mahoney had the sinking feeling that the case no longer had any possibility of being won. In fact, he worried not only about the case, but also about himself and his professional reputation.

The government attorneys had a look of shock on their faces and sat mute.

Mahoney replied, "Mr. Chief Justice, I'm not sure that I know exactly what kind of proof is necessary before everyone accepts the research of Dr. Hancock as factual. The kind of proof my client is expecting is the kind of full disclosure that is presented in a court of law and subject to examination and cross-examination by numerous professionals knowledgeable in the field.

"This is a major decision that will impact millions of people directly and millions more indirectly. Before we risk all of that, we must have a full and complete examination of all the facts and all the opinions that are not in harmony with Dr. Hancock. I don't know what level that is, but it's clearly more than has been presented to date."

The Chief Justice looked deceptively like he was about to fall asleep, but the law clerks and anyone who ever saw him in action knew he was evaluating what was being said and weighing it in terms of truthfulness and logic.

"Mr. Mahoney," said the Chief Justice, "when the weather service in Kansas says there may be tornados, people take cover and protect themselves. Why? Well, they believe the weatherman even if it costs store owners lost sales or hospital and police forces increased overtime costs. How does this differ?"

Mr. Mahoney had been trapped again and he hadn't really prepared for this exact question.

"In my opinion, sir," replied Mahoney, "there are several differences. The first is cost. We're not talking about a few hours of overtime or a couple hours of lost sales in a grocery store. We're talking billions of dollars and countless jobs that will be lost. We're talking about the livelihoods of thousands of employees and their families in the broadcasting industry alone."

Mahoney continued, "A second difference is that that the weatherman has a history record of being right on a regular basis. It's not speculation by a handful of people. There is a large and extensive network of weather data and equipment that make these predictions. We don't have that in this case.

"Lastly, the people involved in the situation you mentioned can recover quickly. The shopkeeper who loses sales can make them up the next day. If we dismantle the broadcast industry, as the President's decision does, it can't be rebuilt. It's more permanent and much more difficult to recover from if the President is wrong."

The Chief Justice pondered and spoke again. "One last question, Mr. Mahoney. The President remarked about the small children and the newborns that will be affected. What is your view as to what we owe our children? Do you believe that if there's a possibility of danger we should disregard their bodies and their health in favor of the profits of the broadcast industry?"

"Mr. Chief Justice," replied Mr. Mahoney, "I'm the father of two children. The health and protection of these children is one of my most awesome responsibilities and one of my greatest concerns. The profits of any industry are distantly behind my concern for those children and the other children in our great land. If the broadcast industry believed there was any danger to those children, we wouldn't be here."

The Chief Justice remained passive and paused for almost a minute before speaking. His voice was very deliberate, and he talked noticeably slower than normal. "Mr. Mahoney, I presume you have brought a comprehensive package with you to persuade me that a temporary restraining order is appropriate to protect your clients' interests and the interests of the people of the United States."

The woman who had announced the arrival of the Chief Justice could feel her stomach tighten. She had been around the Chief Justice long enough to know when something significant was going to happen. He had a tough side that was rarely seen outside of his chambers, but it was there and it bordered on cruel. One sign of that part of Chief Justice Parson was the tone and speed of voice. He was in the mood now and she was becoming concerned. She also knew he had been under considerable stress with the loss of Joey and the hospitalization of his daughter just days ago. As his trusted assistant she had unlimited access to his office and once walked in while he was crying. In respect she had said nothing, but she knew he had talked to his daughter about little Joey in California. The other clerks had only heard the stories about the Chief Justice, but they too were beginning to be apprehensive and uncomfortable.

The Chief Justice looked directly at Mahoney and started to talk very slowly and very precisely. "Mr. Mahoney, I appreciate the concern you have for your clients and for the people of the United States. Although I haven't read your brief yet, and I haven't seen the government's reply, I intend to read both very, very carefully. I hope your brief has information significantly in excess of what you've provided here today. I expect detailed proof. I don't want opinions that EMs aren't harmful to the families and children of this country.

"I also want clear proof that this is a constitutional question and from what you said today, I have serious doubts of that being true. You have already told me that there are legitimate restrictions on freedom of speech and the examples are drops of water in the ocean compared to the size of this case. Your request has a very heavy burden to convince me that there is merit to your accusations. At this point I haven't seen support for your argument that the President's actions are unconstitutional or that the EMs are harmless.

"You should know that, based on what I've heard here and what I already know, I'm under no inclination to grant the Temporary Restraining Order." With a voice rising slightly he continued, "In fact, the more I hear about your clients' positions, the more I find it to be almost reprehensible in this matter. I can only see one reason for their position since their interpretation is at variance with virtually everyone who has looked at the facts. Their only reason for a different interpretation is profits, and only profits. To risk the health of the citizens and the defenseless children in this country for profits is absolutely appalling!"

The Chief Justice's voice had risen and he was almost yelling at the four lawyers.

"Maybe you have never experienced a child dying of cancer. Maybe you need to get out of your posh corporate offices and see what goes on in America. Maybe you should experience the heartbreak of losing a young family member. I'll bet you wouldn't be here asserting that we couldn't be absolutely sure the electromagnetic rays are harmful, so we want to go on exposing everyone to them."

The Chief Justice was clearly swept up in his anger.

"Unlawful as it is, Mr. Mahoney, I respect the citizens of this country who are destroying your transmission towers. They don't have a lot of so-called experts running around telling them everything's OK. They know it's not OK, and they're doing something about it. They're today's Minutemen who truly care for their children. They can read English and understand facts that jump off a page and hit them square between the eyes. They're not running around hiring overpaid lawyers to draw up laughable court documents to say that white is really black and black is really white!"

The room was very still and every eye was on the Chief Justice, wondering what was coming next.

"I noticed, Mr. Mahoney, that when you discussed the applicability of restricting free speech if it's causing cancer, you answered that your clients believe their actions were safe. You know what, Mr. Mahoney? I'll bet that if your clients get their way and this TRO is approved, they'll be getting metal linings around their homes and offices to keep out the EM rays they consider so benign!"

The Chief Justice was almost spitting out the venomous words and was starting to shake.

"Mr. Mahoney, in this action I find the broadcast industry to be cowardly, hypocritical, self-serving and more interested in profits than the health of their fellow citizens."

The clerks lining the wall were almost in shock. They had never seen a judge act in such a manner, and certainly not the Chief Justice of the Supreme Court of the Unites States. Nobody had seen him even remotely show any disrespect toward anyone before the court.

"Now, Mr. Mahoney, I wish you would leave this building and report back to your clients that you've made the most persuasive presentation possible for an unconscionable, disgraceful and reprehensible request; one that shows contempt for our Constitution and for the health of the people of this great land."

With that Chief Justice Parson got up, went back to his office and took off his robe, sat down and wrote a note to his assistant. '**I believe this request for TRO is best assigned to another Justice. Please see that it's transferred to the next Justice on the list to hear this type of request.**'

He then left through his private entrance to go visit his daughter.

The clerks quickly left the room, as did the government lawyers. A stunned and traumatized John Mahoney and three other lawyers were left with the young woman who had initially greeted them. No one said anything for a few minutes. Mahoney was speechless. He had never been treated in a manner like this by a judge in all the years he had practiced law. Now, to be abused by the Chief Justice of the United States was unbelievable. He knew the pleading had some problems, but he had never suspected the Chief Justice would see the inadequacies of their work so clearly and react so fervently. Finally, Mr. Mahoney got to his feet and looked at the young woman.

"I suppose I can leave this file with you for the Chief Justice to review?"

"Yes, I'll see that he gets it."

"Thank you," said a departing and dispirited Mahoney. "Given the comments by the Chief Justice, I guess I can expect a quick reply."

"I don't know how long he will take," replied the woman.

The Chief Justice stewed all the way to the hospital. His stomach growled and he was unconsciously grinding his teeth. He had never acted like that before and never anything like that in front of the clerks. He didn't know Mr. Mahoney, but he could only assume him to be an honorable man. Of course, there were decency limits that lawyers have to respect. It may be that criminal defendants have to have legal representation, and some lawyer has to do it. Billion dollar corporations don't enjoy the same protection as citizens accused of crimes. There are disgraceful cases that respectable lawyers have to turn down for professional, ethical and moral reasons. Lawyers who accept fees from clients of that ilk deserve what they get. After all, they're well paid for their services.

When Steve Parson got to the hospital, he was heartened when he saw Linda. In the short period of time she had been in the hospital, he could see improvement. The doctors had moved a picture of Joey into her room, and she recognized it and looked at it for hours. The doctors assured him that Linda was making good, steady progress. The recovery would still take considerable time because of the trauma of losing a son.

So far, their observations were that she was physically healthy and had a good attitude. The doctors thought that recovery was simply a matter of time with continued treatment. They estimated that, within the next six months, she might be able to be released from the hospital. Steve Parson was relieved to hear such heartening reports and was looking forward to passing on the good news to his wife. After a forty-five minute visit with Linda, he got into his car and headed home in a much better mood than when he had arrived at the hospital.

CHAPTER TWENTY-SIX

Thursday, January 12

Washington D.C.

The President was finishing his morning grapefruit and coffee while reading the Columbus Dispatch. He believed the Columbus newspaper was much more reflective of real America than the Washington newspapers. There were some critical letters to the editor, but for the most part the public had accepted the need to cancel TV and radio transmissions. Since the President's announcement, there had not been any more tower bombings.

Polls showed the public's opinion of the Supreme Court soared when Associate Supreme Justice Laurie Brown wrote a caustic refusal to grant a temporary restraining order to the Council of Broadcasters. Judge Brown was considered somewhat more conservative than the other justices and usually voted pro-business. For her to issue such a harsh ruling on the TRO request was an extremely bad sign for Mahoney.

A related action to the legal opinion was the unexpected resignation of John Mahoney. He submitted his immediate resignation to the Council of Broadcasters indicating his desire to pursue other interests. Two lawyers from the legal office also resigned.

The government sent revocation notices to all Broadcasters advising them that licenses were withdrawn thirty days from the date of the letter.

The President had a joint call from the truckers' association and their unions, regarding the loss of their CBs and cell phones. The President personally knew both of the officials who called him and very politely explained the reasons for his decision. He reminded the truckers that the trucks had delivered goods for many years without CBs, links and cell phones. He indicated that he would permit emergency phones in the trucks for breakdowns or for assisting law enforcement.

The stocks of the major communication companies dropped significantly while cable industry stocks rose dramatically. The President called the cable executives and told them in blunt terms that if they even tried to increase their prices, they would get more federal scrutiny and oversight than they could ever deal with. The President thought of the famous "jawboning" that Lyndon Johnson had used on industry when he was President.

Morton Bruken was being replaced as editor of the Journal of American Medicine magazine.

Columbus, Ohio

The early morning visit before the surgery by Charles to Pablo Palance was very interesting. Pablo was clearly agitated, and Charles learned later that he had received a call from Cuba the night before. He was quite honest with Charles and said he had done some very bad things in his life and when Fidel was replaced there would be no place for him in Cuba. He even said that he might not be able to return to Cuba.

He confided that Fidel lost trust in his senior officials if they ever left Cuba. He warned Charles not to be surprised if something happened to him. He also confided that he had followed the example of Fidel and put a considerable amount of money in Caribbean banks. He planned to go into exile when the time came, if he could get out of Cuba in time and avoid prison.

He finally commented on the remarks from the State Department. He wasn't interested in being a spy for the United States, but he would contact Dr. Hancock when he had something that might be helpful in rebuilding the American-Cuban friendship.

He suddenly and unexpectedly started talking about the 'arrangement' they had in 1971. He assured Charles that it was all in the past and a secret shared by only two people. Pablo recounted how he had personally handled all the details and even Fidel wasn't aware of who Pablo's contact was. The only other person who knew was Ray Echeveria. Pablo smiled when he said, "we don't have to worry about Ray any longer." Pablo even volunteered that there were no records in Cuba.

He then went on to explain that the almost $200,000 dollars had been kept in one place for about two years. "I knew that someday we would have a use for that money, so I just kept it until that opportunity came forward. In 1973 the opportunity presented itself. A jet from Atlanta was hi-jacked and flown to Cuba. When we examined the cargo of the airline we found several electronic devices. We didn't know what they were, but the passenger who owned them was very nervous.

"We learned that they were experimental devices that had been built for your space program. Loss or damage to the devices would have delayed the schedule of your space program. Our Russian friends would have encouraged us to keep the machines since they were embarrassed with your moon landings. It was an opportunity for me.

"I sent word through our representative in the Swiss Embassy that we had the money we bought from you. Since we had the electronic equipment from the hijacked airplane, we thought we could turn a profit on your money. We offered to exchange it for a half a million in clean dollars. In return we could guarantee that one of our cargo handlers wouldn't drop your precious machines and we would never discuss the money again.

"If agreement couldn't be reached, we might start spending the money in our embassies around the world. Your government saw a way to avoid further ridicule about your actions and accepted. So, we exchanged aircraft, machines and money.

"They almost quit the deal when we only had $194,200 dollars and not $200,000. They thought we were keeping some of the money for future use against them, but we assured them it was all we had. I guess they finally decided it was a deal they had to take. When the remaining $5,800 was found in 1980 they knew we were telling the truth. And that's always been a question I've had for a long time. What happened to the $5,800, Charles?"

Charles had a bemused smile. "Some people thought I threw it away to confuse the issue. I can assure you I didn't. I noticed a hole in my backpack and can only assume it fell out before I patched the hole. I didn't realize I didn't have it until I got to Miami."

Then Charles laughed. It was the first time he had felt any assurance that the actions of 1971 would stay a secret. "After all this time, it's amusing to look back on it. Everything worked out well for everyone except whoever provided the $200,000. There was some ridicule of law enforcement in America, but there would have been a lot more if that money had started surfacing and they still couldn't find me. A lot of people had fun talking about me, and they still do. I used to be amused when I was in college and saw my fellow students wearing t-shirts about me."

Pablo changed the subject to the surgery and again expressed complete confidence in Charles and said he looked forward to getting the surgery complete.

Before leaving, Charles expressed his belief that it would work out and told Pablo that he would do his best.

CHAPTER TWENTY-SEVEN

Friday, January 13 (Morning)

Columbus, Ohio

The surgery had been more complicated than Charles anticipated. There was more cancer than he expected, and he had to remove more tissue than he expected. As a result, Pablo would need a longer recovery period and he would have to discuss that with Pablo.

In the morning Charles stopped by the room to see how Pablo was doing. He was surprised that the hospital security officer at the Nurse's station was gone. The Air Force guard was likewise missing from the door to Pablo's room. When Charles found the empty room, he inquired at the nurse's station and found that Mr. Palance had checked himself out before dawn. Charles had clearly told him that he was not fit to travel for at least two days after the operation, but it seemed that Pablo decided otherwise.

While trying to figure out why a sick man would do that, Charles could hear the special reports that were coming over the television in the waiting area. The reports were confusing. The news alerts were reporting that an airplane had been shot down over the Cuban coast. The newscasters couldn't confirm who owned the aircraft. American government officials were assuring Americans that it was not an American plane. Other reports attributed to a Cuban official were that the plane was traveling from Madrid to Havana and had crashed.

Air traffic control knew that a special diplomatic plane had arrived early from Ohio in the morning at the Boca Chica naval station near Key West, Florida. The aircraft departed immediately for Cuba. It was shortly after takeoff that aircraft launched from Cuba met the plane and the passenger jet disappeared from radar. American authorities believed the Cubans had shot down their own aircraft, but no public announcement was made. The official State Department position was that the crash was in

Cuban waters and was a Cuban matter. If Cuba needed any search and rescue assistance from the U.S., we would be available to help. No request was received or reported.

Charles froze. When he finally returned to his office, he had a call from the State Department representative who was still in Columbus. The representative said that the government believed that the Cuban Air Force had shot down the aircraft that was taking Pablo Palance back to Cuba. He provided the details and time of the aircraft leaving Columbus and making the stop-over at Boca Chica. He had no idea why the Cuban government would do something like that.

Charles was immensely relieved that the secret that he shared with Pablo would now never be told. But, even knowing how ruthless Pablo was, he was saddened by his death. In some of their conversations, they had shared stories about their families and Pablo's grandchildren. Charles had seen a side of Pablo that only his immediate family ever saw. As he got to know him better, Charles had actually started to like him.

Charles had planned to work on some research he was doing and didn't have any patients scheduled for the rest of the day. He decided to take the day off and stopped at the first liquor store on High Street to buy a big bottle of rum.

CHAPTER TWENTY-EIGHT

Friday, January 13 (Afternoon)

<u>Columbus, Ohio</u>

For the time of the year, it was surprisingly pleasant outside, and Charles poured himself a large glass of rum over ice and threw in a slice of lemon. It wasn't a classic drink, but it had been his favorite when he lived in Miami. Sitting in his overstuffed chair, he decided that he had about three hours before Bobbie came home and found him drunk. She had seldom seen him drunk, and it would be a surprise. It was a big day for Charles Hancock; a worry that he had for 33 years had come to an end.

After his third rum he started to remember 1971.

His initial parachute training at Wilmington Airport was fun, and it provided the extra spark for what became one of the greatest unsolved mysteries of the century. His father applauded his spirit of adventure and courage. Mom and Dad both worried about his jumping, but he obviously loved it and they were proud after every successful jump.

Then high school ended and he told his very surprised parents that he was going to Miami, Florida, for a few weeks. They objected, but he insisted and assured them he would be fine. In 1971 you could still hitchhike safely, and Charles took the $2,000 he had in the bank and headed for Florida. He enjoyed the first bit of phenomenal luck that would be part of everything he did in 1971.

Once in Miami he checked into the YMCA for the least expensive room and looked for a job. He found one at the Ocean Ranch Hotel that included a room in the old hotel building where the rooms didn't have a private bath. He also received meals in the restaurant. He worked in the hotel as night auditor and did whatever he could during the day for the guests. He was always there and always helpful. Guests were very thankful and didn't forget tips. Charles worked like a sled dog from June until he briefly left in November, and he was saving almost all the money he was earning.

In his free time he was in the local library learning about actor's makeup, maps of the Northwest and airplane schedules. The makeup was relatively easy, and he could buy some cheap cosmetics to practice with. He was actually getting quite good at aging himself. The airline schedules were a little more work, but he kept at it. He also had minor problems with the maps since there wasn't much demand in Miami for detailed maps of Washington and Oregon.

He also made a few friends, including a Cuban named Pablo Palance. They met through Ray Echeveria, a mutual friend and co-worker at the hotel. Charles learned from Ray that Pablo might have some contacts in the Cuban community. He eventually had a private meeting with Pablo and talked about a deal that would develop later in the year. Pablo was interested and thought they could do business.

Everything was going well until September of 1971 when he met Vonda, his first real "southern belle." She was a guest at the hotel, and it was relatively unusual for a single woman to stay at the Ocean Ranch; she had some distant relatives in Miami and was planning to visit them. Charles learned that she also was just getting away after completing high school and a summer of beauty queen appearances. They hit it off immediately and began dating. Charles persuaded her to stay beyond her scheduled two weeks.

She couldn't afford to keep the room in the new building, but Charles convinced the manager she could be helpful around the hotel and would be glad to stay for room and board in the old building. The hotel manager agreed and she also got a job at the hotel.

It was late November when Charles told Vonda that he would be leaving for about a week. He lied and said he had to go home because of an illness in the family, but he promised to be back as soon as possible. Vonda said she understood even though she didn't. For some reason she was suspicious of the sick relative story.

Vonda had a car and gave Charles a ride to the airport on November 21. She wanted to go in to see him off, but Charles insisted that she just drop him at the entrance to the airport. The earlier worry she had about him leaving was re-kindled, but she complied.

Once inside the airport, Charles boarded an airplane that would take him to Chicago for a plane change and then to Seattle, Washington. Once there, he purchased a three-year-old VW Beetle and a very well used motor scooter and headed for the forest. With his maps and calculations complete, he found the area he was interested in and left the Volkswagen, clothing and survival gear hidden in the woods. He rode the scooter back to Seattle and got an airplane to Portland, Oregon. In Portland he visited the local Goodwill store and bought clothing suitable for an older man and stayed in a cheap motel near the airport. Shortly after noon on November 24, he took a cloth bag and a briefcase and left for the airport. The baseball cap he wore covered the hair that he had sprinkled some gray into the night before. Once in the airport he changed to his Goodwill clothes, put on his dark glasses, and threw the other clothes and the makeup in the trash. He then went to the Northwest Airlines counter and bought a one-way ticket to Seattle, Washington, in the name of Dan Cooper.

After boarding the Boeing 727, he went to row 18 and was the only passenger in that row. Before the 4:35 takeoff, he handed a note to Stewardess Flo Schaffner saying he had a bomb and wanted $200,000 in unmarked bills and four parachutes. Stewardess Schaffner thought it was some kind of love note and didn't bother to read it until the plane was airborne.

After she read the note she immediately talked to the captain who asked her to see passenger Cooper and verify what he had said in the note. She sat next to him while he opened the briefcase and showed her wires and what appeared to be dynamite sticks inside.

The Seattle airport was alerted and, eventually the FBI provided the $200,000 in unmarked bills and four parachutes. The aircraft landed, and passenger Cooper allowed the passengers and all but the pilot, co-pilot and one flight attendant to leave. The luck of 1971 was in full force. It seems that the pilot and co-pilot could actually have escaped but were unable to get the attention of the remaining stewardess to leave with them.

After the passengers were gone and the money and parachutes were on-board, passenger Cooper ordered the aircraft back into the air and directed the pilot to circle Seattle and prepare for a flight to Mexico. The crew objected because they didn't have sufficient fuel. Dan Cooper had anticipated the fuel problem and expected the crew to balk. He considered it a check to see if they were lying to him. He then directed a flight to Reno to gas up. He instructed the pilot to stop circling Seattle and head to Reno at 10,000 feet and no faster than 170 miles an hour…almost stall speed for the aircraft.

At 7:44 passenger Cooper ordered the flight attendant to lower the stairs in the tail of the aircraft and go to the first class section and close the curtain. At 8:11 there were bumps that investigators believe were from passenger Cooper jumping off the staircase and the stairs bouncing back; but after a full investigation, it turned out that nobody is sure when passenger Cooper jumped out of the aircraft. The night was cold and rainy, and the Air Force chase planes never saw anyone jump. As a precaution, the FBI searched the aircraft when it landed in Reno to be sure passenger Cooper was actually gone.

Charles' calculations were relatively good, and his incredibly good luck held. He landed within two miles of the Volkswagen and was able to find it in the early morning light. He quickly removed his makeup and old clothes and put on the college student clothes that were in the car. The police were looking for a middle-aged man. A college student in a VW Beetle wouldn't attract suspicion. Somehow, before he got to the Beetle, $5,800 in twenty-dollar bills fell out of his bag, but he didn't know about it until he got to Florida. When the bills were found in 1980, Charles finally understood what had happened to the missing money.

But Charles still had almost $194,000 and was driving back to Miami and Vonda! He thought briefly and estimated that in current money values, $194,000 would be worth somewhere around $800,000 adjusted for inflation.

Once back in Miami he and Vonda resigned their positions in the hotel and moved into a much larger room in the new building and stayed there until the next summer. He contacted Pablo Palance and cut a two-for-one deal. For every two marked twenty-dollar bills that Charles provided, Pablo would exchange them for a clean $20. Charles was still happy. $100,000 in 1971 would easily pay for the rest of the year, college and medical School…and it did.

Charles was always amused that the hijacker was always referred to him as 'D. B. Cooper.' He later found out that a man named Daniel B. Cooper in Washington was being investigated and somehow the press assigned the name of 'D. B. Cooper' to the hijacker. The legend of D.B. Copper has never died. The FBI still considers it an open case and has no plans to close it. Since there is no statute of limitation on skyjacking, Charles would always be in some danger, but it was extremely minimal. He still chuckles when he sees the occasional tee shirt on campus commenting on 'D. B. Cooper.'

It was the only secret he had from Bobbie. He felt a little bad about it, but it had to be!

CHARACTERS

DR. CHARLES P. HANCOCK
Oncologist and Professor of Medicine at Ohio State Medical School

ROBERTA "BOBBIE" HANCOCK
Wife of Robert Hancock and Manager of a Dress Boutique

DR. SHEILA GORDON
Dean of the Ohio State Medical College

DR. RANDALL BROOKMAN
President - The Ohio State University

DR. JEROME 'JERRY' WILSON
Physician and friend of Dr. Hancock

MS. MITCHELL
Ohio State President's Secretary

Mr. ROBERT PILLARS
Chief Legal Counsel for OSU

DR. MORTON P. BRUKEN
Physician and Editor-in-Chief, Journal of American Medical Association
JAMA

JOHN MAHONEY
Executive Director

HARRISON JENKINS
President of the USA, OSU Graduate and Coast Guard Hero

LAURIE JENKINS
Daughter of the President and Student at University of Georgia

RALPH GARDNER
Physician, Surgeon General of the USA and cancer survivor

194

RICHARD "STEVE" PARSON
Supreme Court Chief Justice

JEFF HANCOCK
Son - attorney

HAROLD HANCOCK
Son, President of a personal security business

VONDA FLUELLEN
Peach Farm owner and former girlfriend of Charles Hancock

JACKY JONES
Resident of Miramar, Florida and Miami Beach, Chef

BARRY BURLINGTON
Talk show host

DR. LAMONT TURKS
Professor and colleague of Dr. Hancock

DR. CHESTER KIDD
Doctor, Oncologist from Chicago, Ill

SAM FORBET
Special Agent, FBI

CHARLIE MCDERMOTT
Investigator hired by The Council of Broadcasters

KENNEITH 'KEN' CROBY
Attorney General

SOLOMON LEE
Vice-President.

SAMUEL ULLYSES GRAY
Secretary of Defense

TREVOR MITCHELL
Senator from Rhode Island and Chairman of select committee to investigate effects of EM waves

SOMEBODY
Editor of the GLOBE

DR. GONZALES
Physician in Castro's hospital in Cuba

PABLO PALANCE
Primary advisor to Fidel Castro

FELIPE GEORGA
Aide to Pablo Palance

LAURIE BROWN
Supreme Court Justice

KEVIN STONEMAN
FCC Administrator

LINDA
Joey's mother

SUSAN JACKSON
Police Secretary

WILLIAM 'BILL' HUGHES
CIA Director and Chief of Central Intelligence